Tainted

Tainted, Volume 1

Toby Spencer

Published by Toby Spencer, 2025.

TAINTED

First edition. September 29, 2025.

Copyright © 2025 Toby Spencer.

ISBN: 979-8999474810

Written by Toby Spencer.

Dedicated to my lovely wife Amy. I could not have published this book without her.

Prologue

October 14, 2006

The ringing of the phone interrupted the quiet and stillness of the night. Tony and Miranda Roberts were both sleeping quietly after a long day when the early morning ringing of the phone pierced the silence. It took multiple rings until eventually Tony awoke with enough clarity to answer.

"Hello" Tony mumbled into the receiver.

"Yes, it is."

"Uh huh?"

"Okay, don't send them yet. I'll go down and check things out."

He placed the phone down and sat up in the bed. His wife stirred from her sleep enough to become curious. "Who was that?" She asked in a quiet tone, barely audible.

"Someone pulled the fire alarm at the school. I'm going to go check it out." He said with a hint of agitation in his voice.

"Do you have to go, Tony?" She asked as she yawned.

"I'm not waking up the entire fire department for some stupid prank. It's bad enough I have to go in." He said as he stood up.

"I wish you would just stay."

"I already had to give up my Friday night for that stupid dance; now these kids have to screw around!" he grumbled as he walked towards the bathroom.

"What if it's not just kids?" Miranda mumbled.

"This is Anderson. I'll be fine." Tony said while walking back to kiss her on her forehead.

Miranda drifted back to sleep as he got ready. Though he tried to be quiet, his anger caused him to slam some items down on the counter in the bathroom. He was angry; it had been a long week. Tony was the principal of Lake County High School, and this week ended with the school's biggest dance, The Fall Ball. It had long been a tradition, and the week leading up to it included games and dress-up days.

Events like this always disrupted the relative calmness of the school. Tony was busy dealing with pranks and other minor issues that had added up at the end of the week. The week leading up to the Fall Ball always seemed to bring out the worst in the students as they tested the boundaries of the dress code for spirit week, held senior pranks, and other hijinks. Now, at the end of all of this, some kid had pulled the fire alarm. After he got ready and made himself presentable, he walked over to Miranda, who was now fast asleep. He gave her another gentle kiss on her forehead. She stirred just enough to mumble, "Love you," before she rolled back on her side.

Tony then left and quietly walked down the stairs. He was a tall man and well built. He played college football for Tennessee and later coached most of his career as a high school teacher. This was his second year as principal of Lake County High School. He appreciated the advancement in his career, but he missed the football field. He did not like being constrained to the office and dealing with the menial things that often make up a principal's day.

Once Tony got into his car and backed out of the driveway, he looked up at his house. He looked longingly up at the second floor, where his bedroom was located. He was tired, annoyed, and wanted to join his wife back in bed. However, he had to deal with this issue, so he took a deep breath and turned out of his driveway.

Calmness once again overtook the house as Tony left for the high school. His wife slept soundly in her husband's absence. The only sound emanating from the house was the quiet drip in the bathroom sink. As she slept, a gentle breeze, much like the one outside, cast over her body. This breeze, though, had a coldness to it, and it caused her to adjust in her covers as it hit her body. It did not cause her to wake, but as coldness filled the room, she quickly swaddled herself in the blanket.

The temperature in the room decreased more and more as each moment passed. However, she still slept unphased by the changes in the temperature. Silence still dominated the house, but out of the silence a soft creak arose. The creak of the springs of the bed sounded like a loud moan as something unseen appeared to make depressions in the mattress. She felt these movements, but remained mostly unconcerned. Feeling someone lay beside her in the bed, she stirred slightly.

She turned over to Tony's side of the bed and slightly opened her eyes, expecting to see Tony back from the school. However, he was not there. This caused her to jolt awake. In her mind, she felt as though someone had crawled into bed with her, but there was no one there. She then turned to look at the alarm clock. Tony had been gone nearly an hour. The school was only about five minutes from the house. *He should've been back by now.* She thought to herself. Sitting up calmly in the bed, she realized how cold the room had become. A shudder came out as more of her body emerged from its cloth cocoon. Staring at the alarm clock again, she worried. She looked over at her phone, which was charging, and there were no missed calls. Picking up the phone, she dialed her husband to check on him. However, the call immediately went to voicemail. She tried two more times before she sat up in bed.

Hoping that he had arrived home and maybe just settled downstairs, she decided to check. Downstairs was quiet, and there was no sign of her husband. Checking the garage, she saw his car was still gone. Anxiety filled her mind as she thought about the worst.

She quickly got dressed and decided to drive by the school herself to check on him.

When she arrived at the school, she noticed Tony's car parked in the fire lane near the main entrance. Before getting out of the car, she looked around the parking lot and saw no other vehicles. She tried once again to call him on his phone, but it again went straight to voicemail. She was now growing concerned. Tony always answered his phone, but now after over fifteen minutes, the calls were still going straight to voicemail.

She pulled directly behind Tony's red sedan and shut her car off. Removing her seatbelt and shutting off the car, she slowly exited and walked towards the front doors. Someone had turned off the fire alarm, and everything around her seemed silent. As she walked closer to the front doors, she scanned the inside looking for signs of her husband. As she got closer to the doors, she felt a cold chill run down her spine. Her body sensed danger, but her heart encouraged her to continue forward.

As she reached for the handle of the door, she noticed her arm was covered in goosebumps. It was cool this morning as the sun had still not risen, but she felt it odd that she had so quickly felt a much cooler chill in the air. Nonetheless, she continued forward, reaching for the front door. Giving it a quick tug, the door gave only slightly, but the lock held it in place. She then tried the adjacent doors, but each was locked. Growing fearful for her husband and with the uneasy feeling that now dominated her body, she pounded on the door. She pounded loudly, hoping to get her husband's attention. After pounding several times, she stopped and listened.

There were no sounds; it was quiet. Everything seemed quiet. Almost like an eerie silence that she had never heard. The absence of all sound, the absence of all life. Peering closely into the window, she looked for any signs of movement. Taking advantage of the silence, she listened intently for any response to her pounding on the door. There remained nothing, just an unearthly silence.

The worry for her husband overtook her thoughts as she panicked. *He should have heard me,* she thought to herself. She was becoming more desperate than ever to get his attention. She needed to know that he was safe inside the building. Lifting her fist to the door once again, she began pounding away furiously so that the sounds could be heard regardless of where he was in the building. After releasing the latest volley with her fist, she paused and waited. There were no sounds, just again silence.

Peering once again into the window, she looked and prayed for a sign of life. Then, out of the void, a face abruptly popped up in the window. She was caught off guard and screamed at the sight, falling backwards and nearly to the ground. Once she had regained her composure, she tried to focus on the face, hoping to see Tony. To her disappointment, it was a short and skinny teenage boy with blood on his face and a disoriented look on his face. For a moment, they made eye contact, then he pounded on the glass. He then stared back into her eyes. "1-5-8 Peter, 1-5-8 Peter, 1-5-8 Peter!" he shouted through the glass, with his voice rising each time that he repeated the phrase. He then broke his gaze with her and took off running down the hallway and disappeared from sight, leaving a smudge of blood on the glass from where he had pressed his face.

SHE WEPT. THE SUN WAS rising, and she still had no answers. Once the police and fire department arrived, they forced her to go back to her car and wait. Each time that the number progressed on the digital clock on her car radio served as a painful reminder of how long she had been awaiting answers. Time had a powerful sting, each and every moment that it moved forward. Her thoughts remained on Tony. *Where is he? What happened? Is he alive?*

It had been so long since anyone had even spoken to her. They left her in the dark, though the answers lay just feet in front of her. She had cried, and she had prayed, but neither of which seemed to bring her any release or comfort in the situation. She knew she must look a mess, so she decided she should try to clean herself up while she sat and waited. *Perhaps this would make the time go faster,* she thought to herself.

She reached into her purse to grab some of her emergency makeup. After fumbling for some time, she finally collected everything that she needed. She adjusted her rearview mirror to use. As she lined the mirror up with her face, something caught her eye. At first, it was just a shadow, but as she looked closer, it was a person staring back at her from the rear of the car.

Her mind struggled to process the image behind her. It startled her and filled her with fear. She froze in that moment, unable to move or make a sound. As she sat staring at the image before her, she trembled while otherwise in some sort of paralysis. When her eyes finally could focus on the figure behind her, she realized that the familiar figure was Tony. Although at the same time, she realized it was not him. Where his bluish-gray eyes should have been, there were two dark, empty voids staring back at her.

Finally able to break free from her frozen state, she screamed. She screamed so loudly that the heavy-set police officer, who stood nearly twenty feet away, heard her and rushed over to the car. The officer came quickly over to the car and looked in at the now hysterically crying woman.

"Are you okay?" he asked with a sense of urgency.

At first, she could not speak, though she stared directly at the officer. She glanced once more in her mirror to find an empty backseat.

"Mrs. Roberts! Mrs. Roberts! Are you okay?" The officer continued shouting through the car window.

Eventually, she regained her composure just enough to roll down her window. Still shaking, she finally responded, "I'm sorry, I thought I saw something in my mirror."

"What? What did you see?" the officer inquired.

"It was nothing. I'm just tired, and my eyes were playing tricks on me, I guess." She said in an embarrassed tone.

Another, older officer approached. "Miranda, I really think you need to go home and get some rest." He said in a gentle tone.

"No, I'm not leaving until I know about my husband."

"Miranda, there is nothing you can do here. I have your number. I will call you or come by the house as soon as I know something." The older officer responded.

"David, I can't leave him. I just can't leave without knowing."

"We are about to have more officers arriving. I know your heart is in the right place, but I really need you to leave so they can have their space to find the answers. I promise you, as soon as I know something about Tony, I will let you know." The officer continued in a gentle tone.

A third officer approached and called out to David. "Captain, the Dodge County Canines are on their way."

David turned to Miranda once more. "Please let us do our job. You need to go get some rest."

"Do you promise to call me or let me know?"

"I promise as soon as I know something," David responded.

Miranda felt defeated. She knew she couldn't stay sitting in the car. She knew she had exhausted herself from being in the parking lot for hours, even to the point of seeing things that weren't there. Reluctantly, she agreed and pulled out of the parking lot.

She drove back home, glancing once more back at the school. Throughout the entire brief trip, she avoided looking in her rearview mirror. When she arrived home, she didn't bother parking in the garage. She just left the car parked outside and left it. She was heartbroken as she walked up the steps of the front porch. When she entered the house, it felt unusually cold. It was not just cold, but it felt empty and hollow. The house that once held so many wonderful memories now felt more like a tomb. She walked up the stairs slowly toward their bedroom. The silence of the house was almost unbearable. Each step that she took made an eerie creak.

As she finally made it to her bedroom, she looked at the bed. *Just hours ago, he was here with me. I shouldn't have let him leave.* She thought to herself as she glanced down at his side of the bed. She felt uneasy and restless. In deciding what to do, she decided to take a hot shower. She went into the bathroom and started running hot water in the shower. As she stood there waiting for the shower to heat, she felt as though her mind was in a fog, much like the rising steam. She couldn't think straight. Things just did not feel real in the moment.

Eventually, she shook herself back to reality enough to step into the waiting shower. The warmth of the hot water brought relief from the cold confines of the house. For a few moments, she just stood under the shower. She just could not bring herself to do much of anything, much less even bathe. So, she just stood and allowed the hot water to cascade down her body.

Everything was silent except for the sound of the hot water splashing against her and the floor of the shower. A loud clash coming from her bedroom suddenly interrupted the silence. This caused her to jump with a jolt. Already unstable and in a fog, her sudden movement caused her to lose her footing and slip in the shower.

She lay there for a few moments with the hot water falling on her. She was in pain and in shock over the sudden fall. As her mind once again focused, she thought about the noise. She slowly attempted to stand, and once she was fully up and could steady her feet, she turned off the water and listened. To her horror, she thought she heard footsteps running in the hallway. Her blood ran cold, and she felt an overwhelming sense of terror.

She knew she had locked the door behind her, and suddenly the sense of terror gave way to a feeling of hope. *Tony!* She thought to herself as she grabbed the towel off the rack beside the shower. As she turned, she glanced down at the floor of the shower and noticed a small pool of blood where she had hit her head. She raised her free hand up to her head, and it was tender to the touch. When she glanced back at her hand, she saw the crimson color that now covered her normally white hand.

She once again heard footsteps running. The sound once again startled her, but she allowed hope to overcome any negative feelings. As she walked cautiously out of the bathroom, she glanced over towards the bed and noticed that the sound had come from a picture that had fallen from the wall. She walked over to it and realized that it was her and Tony's wedding portrait. The picture looked unharmed, but the glass of the frame had shattered, sending shards of glass in multiple directions.

As she stepped back away from the picture, she felt a sudden sense of pain in her right foot. She gasped as it sent a wave of pain up her leg. She looked down and saw a piece of glass now sticking out of her big toe. The sound of footsteps once again came from the hall. She jerked around quickly, causing her to feel dizzy as she tried to catch a glimpse down the hallway. As she turned, her foot once again sent a wave of pain.

She leaned down, looking at her toe, and gave the piece of glass a quick tug. This caused a sudden surge of pain and relief as she removed it from her toe. Removing the object made more blood come out of her wound. She slowly stood up, feeling dizzy, and she carefully took a few steps, placing no weight on her toe.

She once again heard creaking on the floor. "Tony?" She called out, but there was no answer. She slowly stepped out into the hallway. As she did, she noticed that the coldness of the house seemed to hit her like opening a freezer door. "Tony?" She called out once again. But there was no answer.

She thought she saw a shadow in the corner of her eye toward the guest bedroom, but when she turned, there was nothing. She stood still for a moment, listening. As each second passed, the hall seemed to become colder, until she thought she would be able to see her breath soon. Walking towards the stairs, she continued to listen for any more sounds. She glanced down the stairs at the front door to ensure that it was closed and locked. Then she heard something directly behind her. It was just a gentle creak on the floor. At the same time, she got the feeling that someone was now there with her.

Her blood once again ran cold, matching the temperature of the hallway. She took a deep breath and slowly turned around. As she turned slowly, she began making out a masculine figure. Her heart was beating so fast that it felt like it would burst. Yet, she continued turning slowly until the figure came into focus.

"Tony?" she whispered.

He stood there looking down towards the floor, not moving, nor saying a word.

"Tony?" she whispered again.

He slowly moved his head upward and looked at her. She screamed as she looked at his face and saw the same black empty eyes that had stared back at her from the mirror. She took one small step backwards to distance herself from this imposter of her husband. The next thing she felt was a sudden shift in her body as she lost her footing on the top step of the staircase. Panic set in as she felt her body falling backwards. The last thing that she saw before all went black was those black eyes and the figure before her smiling.

Chapter 1

An Unheeded Warning

The dogwoods and Bradford pears dotted the horizon like freshly fallen snow. Winter had finally surrendered its hold on the south. The sun filled the sky with barely a cloud in sight as Terrance traveled along roads where a wall of trees lined either side. The two-lane road wound through the countryside, passing farms, pecan orchards, and tall, stoic pines. It was a stark contrast to the vast concrete structures and traffic that he was leaving behind in Atlanta. It had been many years since he had been this far south. Terrance had nearly forgotten what rural Georgia looked like.

The slight hills and uneven terrain of Georgia's Piedmont Region gave way to the continuous flat land of Georgia's Coastal Plains as he worked his way further south. Terrance had not been to his hometown since he graduated from high school. He had hoped to leave those memories forever behind, but the death of his mother brought him back to the sleepy South of the Peach State.

After driving for what seemed to be an endless amount of time, he came upon the intersection of two roads. This intersection was not very different from many intersections that Terrance had crossed during his journey. However, at this intersection, Terrance took pause and battled an internal conflict. Turning right would lead him back to his childhood town in about an hour. There he would see relatives and people he had not seen in years, and many he never wanted to see again. Turning left, though, presented something very different. There seemed to be a sense of adventure in turning left and going into the unknown. Though this left turn would delay his trip back to his family, the short drive would open doors to maybe his greatest story yet.

Terrance was a freelance writer and independent investigative reporter. He had made quite a name for himself on the local Atlanta news and had just published a successful article, which had increased his local celebrity status. His keen ability to uncover corruption in government had made him the bane of existence for many state and local Atlanta politicians. Now, as timing and luck presented themselves, he had an opportunity to investigate a new story.

Now, he had a choice to make; he could wait on the story and head home to be with his family, or he could head to Anderson and perhaps begin an investigation that could lead him beyond just local fame but propel him further towards that national stage that he so desperately desired. Internal conflict worked through him. *It was his mother's funeral. Business could wait versus his mother would want him to be successful.* They once had a strong relationship that had been damaged by time. Back and forth, his thoughts battled as he sat at the intersection debating his next course of action.

Fortunately, the traffic was nearly nonexistent, and there were no cars behind him as he pondered his options. If he went left, he could still arrive on time for his mother's funeral next Wednesday. This would give him less time to deal with family struggles, which he had already dreaded. *After all, his family had dealt with his absence for nearly a decade. One more day would not make that much of a difference.* While he continued to ponder, a small silver sedan with dark tinted windows pulled up behind him. The arrival of the sedan went unnoticed as Terrance sat deliberating on his next move. It was not until the sedan blew its horn to encourage Terrance to move in either direction that Terrance even noticed its presence.

Terrance jumped with a jolt when the deep honk of the sedan's horn sounded behind him. The sound was even louder as it broke through the peaceful silence of the countryside. Time was up, and

Terrance had to make a choice. So, after weighing his options and thinking about the morals of his decision, he made his choice, perhaps hastened by the sound of the horn. In a split second, Terrance decided and acted. He abruptly turned to the left without a second thought or glance and began his five-mile drive to Anderson.

The sun glowed through the canopy of magnolias and oaks that lined the main street in the small downtown that made up Anderson's city center. It was a warm, calm day, and a chorus of birds added to the symphony of sounds that made up Anderson's soundtrack. In what would appear to be a picture from a magazine cover, the perfection of the moment was interrupted by the nervousness of a middle-aged man.

Along the buildings that dotted the street, a small cafe sat at the corner of Main Street and Georgia Ave. The cafe, with its own appearance, resembled something from a staged movie set in its perfection. Underneath one of the bright blue umbrellas at a small circular table, there sat an overweight man wearing worn jeans and a t-shirt that barely covered his bulky stomach as it hung above his belt. The appearance of this man seemed to contradict his perfect surroundings. He appeared out of place and dirty in an otherwise perfect setting.

The man's face looked like worn leather, and his hair was unkempt, with stray hairs emerging in either direction from the bald spot on the top of his head. He had a five o'clock shadow that neared eight. Salt and pepper graced both his hair and stubble. He appeared dirty and sad. The smell of old bourbon and tobacco permeated his pores, despite his attempt to mask with cheap cologne.

This man sat alone as he nervously took drags from his cigarette. His hand shook each time he placed the cigarette to his lips. In the ashtray stood a pile of spent butts that showed this was not his first cigarette of the day. His foot tapped nervously as he waited anxiously for his rendezvous. He looked around nervously in every corner, as though he feared being seen. He thought to himself about how things had come to this point in his life. A decade ago, he had reached his dream of becoming a detective and was at the peak of his career. He was a stark contrast to the man who now sat under the bright blue umbrella surrounded by puffs of gray smoke.

As a child, he religiously watched all the detective and crime shows that made up the syndicated evening lineup of local television. He dreamed of wearing flashy clothes and a chain with a badge dangling from his chest, just like the fancy New York detectives that appeared on the screen in the living room. He had dreamed of being a hero, a crime solver, but now he looked nothing like his childhood image of perfection. His badge had long been retired. The woman who once thought of him as a hero had long become an absent feature in his life. Now, he was a pathetic man, barely surviving on the brink of his own self-induced destruction.

He never would have imagined the toll that his work would take on his life. Not in this small town, not in Anderson. He was not a detective in some big city fighting drug lords and mob bosses, and yet this town and his former job had nearly destroyed him. He was now left to rot, as all the others had long left or had become more successful. Now, this was his last chance to make things right. Get the money from this big-city writer and leave this godforsaken town forever. He felt trapped and on the border of hopelessness. Yet here he set about betraying the very job that nearly ended him, hoping to escape the world that he so intently hated.

Terrance Greene was in stark contrast to the withered man who awaited him. Having made his money and fame from investigating and exposing corruption, he was clean-cut and well put together. Though he didn't travel outside of Atlanta often, Terrance was fond of towns like Anderson. Though these towns presented themselves as if they should appear on a magazine cover, he knew that under every perfectly picturesque town, there was something that lurked in the shadows. Terrance had spent much of his time in the wealthy suburbs of Atlanta, where kickbacks from developers had become his specialty.

Terrance's hard work had made him enough money to afford his Mercedes Coupe and a two-bedroom condo that overlooked the Atlanta skyline from a Midtown high-rise. He had made his success by destroying others, especially local government officials. He justified himself as a modern-day Robin Hood, a man of the people who would expose the corrupt system and bring justice across the land. It didn't hurt that each time he finished a story, his own capital grew. As he awaited his first payment from his latest article, his mind drifted to the Maserati that awaited him at the Buckhead dealership north of Atlanta.

Terrance's light brown skin, neatly trimmed black hair, and lean build made him look as though he had walked right out of the pages of a magazine. He wore designer jeans and a high-priced burgundy shirt. Terrance was confident and scheming. He could negotiate like a highly paid corporate lawyer and always seemed to get his way. He was a confident man. In Atlanta, he was well liked by the ladies, never keeping relationships so that he could sample the buffet of women that Atlanta offered. He often covered his arrogance with an act of sympathy, but in the end, he and meeting his goals were all that mattered. The surrounding people were simply tools to achieve goals.

Coming back to this small town gave him a haughty feeling. He considered these small-town people to be simple, and he considered them easy tools to be manipulated at his whim. As he drove deeper into the countryside, only about a mile from his rendezvous, he looked at the farms and houses and thought to himself, *how ignorant these people must be.* He knew this was going to be one of his best stories yet, and he cared not about the disruption he would cause. After all, the end would justify the means. To Terrance, the means were anything necessary to get what he wanted.

As Terrance drove closer to the town, the farms gave way to houses. Humble houses, which slowly transitioned from the brick ranches to rows of small shotgun houses. Terrance's drive took him further into the town of Anderson and further into the neighborhoods that surrounded the downtown. The assortment of houses slowly gave way to a dark brick structure. One that appeared to be lost to time. He cautiously pulled off the roadway as far as he could before a chain-link fence blocked his approach. He wanted to get a look himself before he met with the man at the cafe. Once he pulled in, he shut his car off and stepped out to catch a glimpse.

There, covered in overgrowth, and unmanaged privet, was the site that brought him here. It was an old school that time had forgotten. As he walked up to the fence-line he became caught in the moment. Everything was so tranquil. It was a stark contrast to the city he had come from. But it was almost too quiet for his own comfort. There were almost no sounds at all, except for an occasional passing car. It almost had an eerie presence in the silence. There were no birds chirping, and silence reigned. The world around seemed muted. In the silence stood the imposing shadow of a school that once housed the local high school. Now that it was devoid of life and sound, it was a dead and lifeless building.

This carcass of a building had beckoned Terrance's arrival to this town. He had received word of the school and community's demise that dated back ten years. Then, the school housed over eight hundred students from Anderson and the surrounding area. Seemingly just another small-town high school filled with jocks, nerds, and those who were just trying to find their way in life. Terrance thought of his own high school experience. He attended a small-town school just like this in rural South Georgia.

Momentarily, he remembered the jocks and others who had once tormented him. Instead of bringing back memories of sadness and trauma, the thought caused Terrance to smirk. He thought of all those who had wronged him and where they stood now. The girls who refused to date him because he did not have a pickup truck or did not play on the football team. Now, all of them are trapped by kids and marriages to blue-collar farmers or factory workers. His success allowed him to have whatever he wanted, while they remained trapped in their decaying small town, living in a self-imposed purgatory.

These memories, located deep in Terrance's mind, serve as his motivation. Merciless bullies targeted him, and one day the local police chief's son beat him and left him in a ditch because he was tutoring a girl the son liked. He had no justice, no protection in his youth. Instead, those essentials were absent from his life, leaving him vulnerable and living in fear. From that moment, he had committed his life to no longer living in fear, but causing those like that chief to fear him. He had destroyed his share of local officials, and in his mind; he was not nearly finished with his lifelong mission.

Terrance's thoughts ventured back to the present as he stood staring at the school. This school was the trophy that awaited him. It had the potential to be the capstone of his hard work and mission. Ten years ago, this very school was the site of something that somehow escaped the attention of the national media. In one night, nine students and one adult vanished without a trace. Only small deposits of blood remained, staining various locations with frightening precision. At least physically, one teen survived, but a mental institution now holds him. Though never formally charged, this teen, a young man that reminded Terrance of himself as a nerd. *Maybe he actually got justice,* Terrance thought to himself.

When Terrance first learned about this place, its having escaped attention perplexed him. Though now thankful that he could have all the glory. He wondered, *How could someone lock away a young man without trial or charges?* This all gave Terrance the drive to set this town boldly on fire.

As he walked back from the fence, he noticed a black Ford Crown Victoria parked across the street. It had not been there when Terrance first pulled off the roadway. He always took notice of those things. As he walked back to his car, he exchanged glances with the uniformed police officer, who was staring him down through the dark sunglasses that hid his eyes. Terrance knew now that he was already being noticed, and it was a little early in the process for his liking. As he confidently and boldly walked to his car in defiance of the young officer who was staring at him, he thought to himself, *Let the games begin.*

Terrance got back into his dark-colored Mercedes and cranked it up. The sound of the engine interrupted the silence of the surroundings. Almost immediately after he drove off, the police car turned around and began following him down the tree-lined Georgia Avenue. Most people would look back in their rearview mirror in nervousness, but Terrance was confident and almost feeling a sense of joy. He counted slowly in his head: *1....2....3...* and then, like clockwork, the lights on the top of the police car illuminated and the chirp of the siren sounded. Terrance thought to himself, *these idiots are so predictable.*

Terrance complied with the request of the police officer to pull over and found a turn lane on the right to pull his car over and shut off the engine of his car. While the officer talked on his radio and got his stuff together to prepare for their encounter, Terrance reached into his center console and pulled out his tape recorder. He slowly placed the recorder into his front pocket and activated it. This was not Terrance's first encounter with local law enforcement, whom he often viewed as corrupt and his adversaries. So, Terrance prepared himself. He had a digital recorder that connected to his phone and recorded everything to a file in his cloud storage. If anything ever went south in these encounters, he had his insurance policy that even in the direst of interactions, the truth would echo from his freshly dug grave.

The officer slowly exited his vehicle and tugged at his belt. He centered his hat and nudged his knockoff Aviators so that you could not see into his eyes, but only a reflection. He then strutted up to Terrance's car with a sense of pride or, in Terrance's mind, arrogance. Terrance had already rolled down his window and had the appropriate documents waiting in his hand.

Without the normal pleasantries of such exchanges, the cop gruffly stated to Terrance, "This is private property with clear no trespassing signs."

Terrance did not waver in his conviction. "I never entered the property, but remained on the public right of way of the road, sir."

Terrance's tone and confidence instantly seemed to irritate the cop, who responded, "I need you to step out of the car."

Terrance complied without objection and followed the officer's instructions to follow him to the rear of his vehicle.

Once there, Terrance asked in a sarcastic tone, "Am I being detained?"

The officer, even now more irritated, stumbled for an answer, and responded, "Yes, for suspicion of criminal trespass."

Terrance responded. "You were looking right at me. I parked on the public right of way and never entered the fence line that showed the property line. I remained on public property the entire time."

The cop, now agitated, responded, "I need to check you for weapons. Place your hands on the trunk of your car."

Terrance complied, but as the officer began patting him down, he asked, "Sir, may I ask why you are searching me? Terry v. Ohio clearly states that you can only search me if you have a reasonable suspicion that I am armed and dangerous. Have I given you that idea?"

The officer, now trading agitation for anger more forcefully, began his search and kicked Terrance's feet apart. "You were in an area known for illegal activity, and you have Fulton County tags on your vehicle, which shows you are a long way from home."

Terrance grunted as the officer kicked his legs apart. However, his confidence never broke. Instead he responded, "Is it a crime to be from Atlanta and driving a Mercedes?"

The officer grabbed Terrance and spun him around, and glared at him through his sunglasses. "Let me tell you, boy, this ain't Atlanta, and your smart mouth is going to get you straight into the county lockup."

Terrance smirked. "Boy?"

"I'm going to give you one last warning, boy. You need to shut your mouth." The officer said with anger, almost turning to hate.

"You come in here driving a Mercedes and think you're something. I wonder just how someone like you got a car like that. Now you're parking near a well-known drug area. Run your mouth one more time." The cop said through gritted teeth.

"You mean someone who is black?" Terrance responded.

As the encounter escalated and added fuel to Terrance's mission, another police car joined behind the first police car. This car was different. It was unmarked, and instead of a uniformed officer exiting; it was a heavy-set man. The man was wearing blue jeans and a light-blue button-up shirt. His belly protruded over his waistline by at least five inches. The man wore a gun on his side and a badge on his belt. With the arrival of this new officer, the overzealous officer harassing Terrance seemed to pause.

As the new officer approached, he asked, "What seems to be the trouble here?"

The officer, who now changed his demeanor to one of calmness, responded, "This guy here was parked by the old school and has Fulton County plates, Chief."

The chief approached and calmly asked Terrance if he had any identification. Terrance complied and handed over his driver's license. The chief intently studied the license, then glanced over Terrance as though he were studying every feature.

The chief handed back the license to Terrance and extended his hand. "Mr. Greene, my name is Chief David Pierce, and I am the chief of the Anderson Police Department. I want to apologize for Officer Hartley's being overzealous. I would assume, since you are here, that you know what happened back at that school."

Terrance returned the handshake with the chief and calmly responded, "I do."

The chief released the handshake and continued, "I know who you are, Mr. Greene, but know this; Anderson is a small town, a peaceful town, but we have deep wounds. You will find some of those wounds on our local street signs that are named for those we lost. It may have been ten years ago, but those wounds still fester. You see Officer Hartley here? He lost his older sister there. Many people in this town lost loved ones."

Terrance looked at Officer Hartley and responded with fake sympathy, "I'm sorry for your loss."

Officer Hartley looked away, as though to avoid the sentiment.

"I read the Atlanta papers. I've read some of your work and seen you on TV. This isn't one of those fancy suburbs. We had a tragic event that caused a lot of pain, and we moved on." The chief said as he looked around, then stared back at Terrance. "You will not find corruption here, but a lot of good old people just trying to get on with life. Hardworking people, whom I want to protect. I'm asking you with the utmost respect, please leave this one alone."

Terrance nodded, then said, "I only come to places for the truth, to bring closure and not harm anyone."

"The truth is out, Mr. Greene, and recovery has taken years. Some people still haven't. I'm asking you to please leave this one alone."

"Thank you for your advice. I'll take it into consideration." Terrance said as he looked up, sniffing the air.

The chief took a deep breath, his patience now wavering. "You know, you city folks are all alike. You come in with your degrees and fancy cars and think we are just a bunch of ignorant folk."

"I do not think of you as ignorant. But when you come and call me 'boy', like Officer Hartley over there, you can bet I'm going to think a certain way."

"Well, I'm sorry that you feel that way. I'll have a talk with Officer Harley when we are done." The chief said, turning a scorching gaze to Officer Hartley, who now turned to avoid the chief's eyes.

Terrance nodded and said, "I appreciate it."

The Chief nodded, then pointed back at the school and said, "You won't have any problems from us if you obey the law."

Terrance rebuffed. "No problem there."

"What happened back then had its own nature. And, people in this town have a nature of their own too, and some of them will not like you poking into those wounds."

Terrance looked at the chief as though he was listening, but had decided long before meeting the chief or the other officer. Nothing anyone said at this point was going to change his mind.

"If you are bent on staying here, you won't have any problems from us as long as you follow the law. But let me tell you this clearly, sir, I'm here to protect the people of this town and now you. If you go trespassing on that property, you and I are going to have problems. Do I make myself clear?" The Chief asked.

"Very," Terrance responded.

"That property is clearly marked, and it is condemned. If you step foot on it past the fence, you will be locked up. Am I clear, Mr. Greene?" The Chief questioned.

"Clear," Terrance replied.

"I will say one more thing, Mr. Greene. I protect all the people in my town, and now this includes you. But you need to understand this. If someone goes kicking the beehive, they just might get stung by the bees. If you go kicking too hard, I just may not keep the bees under control. I'm not saying this as a threat to you, but I'm speaking the truth. There are a lot of emotions here, and I cannot control what happens if you go kicking around." The chief said in a calm voice.

"It's not the first hive I've kicked, sir," Terrance responded.

"Fair enough, but this one just might be different. Mr. Greene, you are free to go. I apologize again for everything that happened earlier." The chief responded, then placed his hand on Terrance's shoulder.

Terrance accepted it and responded with a fake "Thanks."

"Stay safe, Mr. Greene, and please consider what I said," the chief stated with a sense of concern. Then Chief Pierce and Officer Hartley returned to their cars without further interaction. They drove off, leaving Terrance standing behind his car. He then walked back to his car, buckling up his seat belt as he started his engine. Now more intrigued than ever, Terrance continued his journey to meet the gentleman, who still sat nervously smoking his cigarette under the green umbrella.

Chapter 2

The Ghosts of the Past

Terrance slowly entered downtown Anderson. It was not too dissimilar from hundreds of other cities that he had visited or the town that he once called home. Trees lined the city streets, and there was a mix of buildings, few of which were occupied and others that sat as hollowed skeletons that once held striving businesses. Each of these downtowns was all the same, shadows of its former glory, a time when they were the heartbeat of the city. Now they sit as a long-forgotten memory of better days in rural America.

The Baptist church stood in the center of Anderson. It was brick with a tall white steeple that seemed to touch the sky. In contrast with the church steeple, the rest of the landscape remained flat with single-level buildings, reminding Terrance of his childhood home. Anderson had no traffic lights, just a few stop signs that were placed along the busiest streets.

The town that Terrance grew up was not so different. Perhaps his hometown was more alive, but he had not been back in so long that it could have shared the same fate as Anderson. Terrance grew up surrounded by cotton and peanut farms. His own father was a peanut farmer who had a small farm and barely made enough money to support his family or the humble, dilapidating farm house.

Anderson reminded Terrance of the summers he spent on the front porch with his grandmother shelling zipper peas and talking about days past. Though there were some pleasant memories. However, this small town also brought back memories of darker days. Days of suffering as his father's health declined. His father was a hardworking man who had long dedicated his life to working the land. The long days of working the land took their toll on this father's health. The unforgiving Georgia summer sun darkened and cracked his skin. And towards the end, his eyes looked tired. Terrance remembered his father in his last days. The once strong man that he had looked up to in his younger days, reduced to a withered raisin.

Despite the pleas from his family, Terrance had forsaken his father's work and gone to college, leaving the farm and his family behind. In those last days, though, he felt a sense of guilt that he had abandoned his mother and brothers to the scorching field of the peanut farm. After his father's death, Terrance committed himself to distancing from the farm and moving on to greater things.

As Terrance passed the First Baptist Church, his heart filled with anger. He remembered his family's church. It was not as big as the passing church, but a little white country church that sat on a dirt road. It was the church where his grandmother, father, and mother dedicated their lives and money. A church that gave his family false promises of prosperity. As he glanced one more time at the passing church, Terrance thought to himself, *the only prosperity is what men make of it.*

He remembered his father's funeral, with the usual ceremony and Bible verses that were read at nearly every funeral. Despite his grim memories, it was not the funeral or his father's death that filled his heart with anger. It was the aftermath, the events that followed when his mother begged for help to keep the farm. Then, neither the church nor the loudmouth preacher reciprocated all that lifelong support. Though his brothers and mother gave it their all, Terrance was powerless as he endeavored through his college career to save the farm. Eventually, the bank foreclosed and sold the farm on the steps of a courthouse.

Terrance remembered his interaction with the chief only moments before. He thought for a moment about God and his family's church. *How could a God allow his family to lose everything? How could a church that his family dedicated their lives to forsake his family?* He then smugly thought of the pastor's last visit to the farm before he went off to college. "It's just property. God has so much more in store for you. You continue giving to the church, and God will give much more to you," said the Bishop Robert Stout before entering a brand-new Mercedes that rivaled the one that Terrance now owned. *The church could buy that hypocrite two luxury sedans and a sprawling four-bedroom house, but could not even help keep the farm alive for a month after I left.* Terrance hated Stout and others like him. They plagued his community and gave false hope, just to thrive on the money that the poor congregation provided.

Terrance shook himself free from the thoughts of the past and regained his focus on the present. He parked along the treelined street, just down from the church. Taking a deep breath, he stepped out of his car and began his walk to the one cafe, the one restaurant that was alive in the otherwise mostly dead town. As he approached the cafe, there sat one lone figure under a bright blue umbrella at a table on the patio. This disheveled man sat nervously smoking his cigarette.

"Frank?" Terrance asked as he approached the lone figure.

Frank put out his cigarette and stood up. "Yes," he said.

Terrance extended his hand and said, "Nice to meet you."

Frank extended his hand, and the two shook hands. Frank nervously looked around his surroundings as though he felt like he was being watched.

"I have the information for you." Said Frank as he pulled out a large folder containing assorted papers.

"I have a little something for you too," Terrance said as he reached into his wallet and pulled out a check.

Frank grabbed the check and quickly put it into his pocket.

"I got to meet some of your former coworkers on the way into town — some friendly folks." Terrance said sarcastically.

"Who?" Frank asked as his eyes shot open and he almost seemed in a panic.

"Some officer and the chief." Terrance said with some humor in his voice.

"Oh, no!" Frank said. "They know you're here! I shouldn't have met you. Not out here in the open."

Frank jumped up and didn't even push his chair in, and he rushed away, looking over his shoulder the entire time he rushed to his car parked on the square.

Terrance snickered to himself, somewhat in disbelief at how these small-town folks get so worked up. *It's not like this is some mob boss; it was just some ignorant small-town hick that carried a badge and a gun.* Terrance was not concerned as he watched the panic-stricken Frank rush into his car and drive away. Terrance, in fact, just sat and relaxed. He was eager to look at what Frank had given him.

Frank fled in a panic. He was questioning everything. *Why did he agree to this?* He thought to himself. Then, feeling the check in his front pocket — a check for ten thousand dollars. *This was his second chance; this was his freedom from the Godforsaken town and the curse that had haunted his life and destroyed all that he once was and had.* Frank hated Anderson; all over one night that took everything from him, destroyed his dreams. Now this check would serve as the liberator from the bondage that had kept him trapped, unable to leave his dark place, unable to live, unable to thrive. He knew ten thousand dollars wouldn't be enough to cover everything, but combined with what he could earn selling his humble abode, he could still have enough to get out of here.

Frank left the confines of downtown Anderson and traveled along sparsely paved streets until he arrived at his home. His home was a single-wide trailer covered in mold that darkened its once beige exterior. Tall pines and oaks surrounded the trailer that sat back off the road. He hurried up the squeaky steps of his nearly rotten porch and entered his house. Inside, the smell was a combination of mold and old, stale cigarette smoke. Clutter, beer cans, and old food containers spread around the residence as if they were décor. Dishes stood piled past the top of the kitchen sink, and flies and other bugs had free rein of the airspace within Frank's home.

Frank went to his refrigerator and opened it. Instead of the usual food and fresh ingredients, beer cans and boxes of leftover food, much of it moldy, filled Frank's refrigerator. Spills and mess dominated the rest of the space. The smell within was not much better than the aroma of the rest of his house. Frank grabbed a can of beer, breathed a sigh of relief, and went to the one space that was not covered with clutter. His recliner, though weak in its support and creaky when it accepted his weight, this was his safe place. Frank sat and lit another cigarette while leaning back in the creaking chair. As he tried to relax, his thoughts went back to an October night ten years ago.

GEORGIA'S CHANGING seasons brought a brisk night. The heat and stifling humidity had given way to a cooler, more tolerable climate. The heat of the day gives up its claim, and coolness reigned. Fall, like spring, is often a brief season looked forward to by Georgians. It gives a slight reprieve from the hotter temperatures before the cold of winter takes over. Though it is a brief season, it is a favorite season of many in South Georgia.

As the hardwoods drop their leaves, the landscape becomes art as though it were painted by some master artist. Red, orange, yellow, and brown contrast against the evergreens of cedars and pines. It makes for an awe-inspiring view.

Frank was in much better health. He rarely drank, and he gave up the dreaded habit of smoking when he married his wife twelve years ago. His wife, Autumn, was named for this very season, and she was his high school sweetheart. He had a daughter eight years old, who was the apple of his eye. He loved them both dearly. They were his life and his all. Frank had just accepted a promotion to detective in the Anderson Police Department. It was a dream come true, the fulfillment of his childhood dream. All the stars seemed aligned, and all seemed to be aligned.

That one night, though, set in motion a series of events that changed it all. For Frank, the night ended like most. He tucked his daughter in and remained awake for a few moments, watching the rest of a football game on television as his wife went to bed to work her Sunday morning shift at the hospital in a neighboring town. The calmness in the air that night was all set to change to terror as an event would unfold that would touch many lives in this small Georgia town.

Following the annual Fall Ball at Lake County High School, a group of high school students snuck into the high school for reasons unknown. Nine would enter, but in the end, eight would not survive along with the principal, who all seemed to disappear. Frank went to bed that night just as if everything were normal. Though disappointed that his team lost the game, he seemed at peace, knowing that everything was where it needed to be.

The ringing of the phone interrupted the calm quiet of his sleep. Frank was not used to being on call as the only detective in this small town. So, it was not the sound of the phone that awakened him. Rather, it was his wife nudging him awake to tell him that the police department was on the other line.

It took a moment for Frank to wake up from his sleep, but he answered, and it was the patrol captain, David Pierce. He said,

"Frank, something has happened at Lake County High School. We need you to respond."

When he arrived, the scene resembled a television show from his childhood, which motivated him. Ambulances, fire trucks, and what seemed like every police car in the entire department. Crime scene tape sealed off all the school entrances. It was just like a set from a movie. Frank knew this was his time.

Captain Pierce approached. "Frank, here is what we have. Apparently, there was a group of students who entered the high school after the Fall Ball. A fire alarm went off, and Dr. Roberts responded, but canceled the fire department. We got a call from his wife when he never came home. There is blood. We have footage on the cameras that shows the kids walking around, but that's it. There is one kid who made it. Paramedics took him to the hospital. Everyone else is gone, no bodies, nothing. We have the crime scene secure, but need you to see what you can get from the kid."

"Who is the kid?"

"It's Jack's son, Dylan, I think." David responded.

"Alright, Captain, I'll head to the hospital."

"Frank, he's pretty screwed up right now. We couldn't get much out of him. I don't want you to rule him out as a suspect." David said.

"Yes, sir," Frank responded as he began his drive to the hospital in the neighboring town of Cambridge.

Frank's mind raced; *this was it! This was why he became a detective.* This was his moment. His mind went back to all the shows he had watched as a kid. Though he was sympathetic to the plight of the situation, he almost felt a sense of excitement. This was destiny. This is where fate meant him to be!

After Frank arrived at the hospital and identified himself, someone escorted him down a series of corridors in the emergency room to a somewhat isolated room. One of his coworkers stood guard along with hospital security. Through the window in the doorway, Frank could see a skinny, pale teenager lying strapped to a gurney in a padded room. The young man just stared blankly at the ceiling.

Frank exchanged pleasantries with the officer guarding the room and told him he wanted to go in and speak with Dylan. The officer snickered and said, "Good luck; that one has lost his mind." Frank confidently responded, "Thanks, let me see what I can do with him."

Frank entered the room quietly, and there was no immediate response from Dylan. He approached the bedside and tried to speak calmly. "Dylan?" he said.

There was no response from Dylan.

"Dylan, I am Detective Frank Sturgess with the Anderson Police Department. Can you hear me?" Frank said.

There was still no response from Dylan, who continued to stare blankly as though fixated on something on the ceiling.

"Dylan, I really need to talk to you. Can you hear me?" Frank asked in a calm voice.

Dylan just continued to stare.

Frank, growing frustrated, raised his voice slightly to give it more of an authoritative tone. "Dylan, I need to know what happened to everyone."

Dylan's eyes shifted, and his gaze turned to Frank. There were still no words spoken, but at least Dylan was responding to Frank's presence.

"Dylan, I want to help you. In order to help you, I need to know what happened."

With a sudden jolt and incredible strength, Dylan jolted, breaking the restraint on his right wrist. He grabbed the detective's arm firmly with a vise grip. This stunned Frank as he tried to pull his wrist away, but no matter how much force he pulled, Dylan's grip was unbreakable. Dylan, now staring at Frank without blinking, uttered the words, "The lion, lion, lurks in the darkness to devour."

Frank, still startled, spoke in a voice now unsteady and broken. "What lion?"

"The lion that devours, the lion, lurks in the darkness." Dylan responded, not removing his eyes now firmly set on Frank.

Frank, hoping to continue making progress, regained his composure, no longer concerned with Dylan's grip. "You're saying that a lion did this?" Frank asked.

"1-5-8 Peter, the lion lurks and devours the goat, 1-5-8 Peter the lion lurks and devours the goat," Dylan continued uttering unbroken, "1-5-8 Peter the lion lurks and devours the goat."

Frank tried to interrupt. "What lion?"

"The lion not of the east, the lion who is a beast, 1-5-8 Peter, the lion devours the goat, 1-5-8 Peter, the lion lurks and devours the goat." Dylan continued to say, repeating repeatedly.

Frank once again interrupted. "What lion?" "What goat?"

"1-5-8 Peter, the lion lurks and devours the goat." Dylan continued in the same tone without breaking his line.

Frank becoming annoyed. "Why weren't you devoured?" he asked in a stern voice.

"The blood, the blood, the blood protects the sheep!"

"The blood, the blood, the blood protects the sheep!"

"The blood, the blood, the blood protects the sheep!"

Dylan continued chanting repeatedly, becoming more and more agitated. His voice rose until he began moving back and forth on the gurney.

"The blood, the blood, the blood protects the sheep!"

"The blood, the blood, the blood protects the Sheep!"

Dylan's voice became a yell. "THE BLOOD, THE BLOOD, THE BLOOD PROTECTS THE SHEEP!"

"THE BLOOD, THE BLOOD, THE BLOOD PROTECTS THE SHEEP!"

"THE BLOOD, THE BLOOD, THE BLOOD PROTECTS THE SHEEP!"

As Dylan continued yelling, someone threw open the door, and a nurse and doctor rushed in with a syringe, immediately injecting Dylan. This weakened Dylan's grip enough for Frank to break it.

The doctor then yelled, "Detective, you need to leave for now. This is not a good time!"

Frank responded, "I need answers. We have missing kids!"

The doctor, looking Frank in the eyes, said, "You can get them later. This is my patient, and this is too much for him. Please leave, or I'm going to call your chief. You can come back later when he is more stable."

Frank reluctantly accepted this for now. Dylan was succumbing to the sedation and probably would not be much use to him now.

Frank looked back, puzzled, trying to analyze the words that Dylan had uttered. It made little sense. *Nothing he said made any sense*, Frank thought to himself.

FRANK'S MIND CAME BACK to the present as he sipped his second beer. *I wish I had just left this case alone. It took everything, everything, from me.* He thought as he became overwhelmed with fear and sadness.

Frank sat quietly in the dimly lit house, remembering what had been before. An abrupt banging on the door interrupted the quiet. It was a loud banging that sounded urgent. This startled Frank, but he quickly got up to see who was breaking the silence of his somber home. As he opened the door, there stood David, who looked at Frank, full of rage. "Frank!" the chief yelled.

"What?" Frank responded, feigning ignorance.

"Frank, what have you done?" The chief asked, full of anger.

Frank paused and considered the check in his pocket. As he stared back at the chief, he questioned in his own mind, *What have I done?*

"Look at yourself. Do you think Autumn and Emily would want this life for you? You were one of my best officers. Now you're just a drunk and, worse, a mercenary who just betrayed everything you once stood for." The Chief Continued.

Frank stumbled over his words. "I.... I..."

"That's the problem. You were thinking of yourself. You know what that did to this town. People are just getting back to normal lives. Now all you've done is reopen wounds. You've damned us all with what will awaken, and you damned that outsider." The Chief continued as he berated Frank.

Frank could not even say anything but just looked blankly at the chief.

"Go back to your bottle, Frank, but know the blood is on your hands. It's on your hands, not mine. I can't even look at you anymore," David said as he turned around and angrily walked down the creaking stairs.

Frank looked down once again, fidgeting with the check in his pocket. On the one hand, he struggled with guilt, but it was not him who was a traitor. It was this town that abandoned him. Through his internal struggle with morality, Frank could not help but feel the coldness and dread in his heart. *What if he did just awaken something, something that would have its own life and the power to destroy? Something that had already destroyed him. There was not much else it could do to him.* He thought to himself as he went back to his chair.

Chapter 3

A Stranger in the Night

There were few lodging options in Anderson. Though Terrance was more accustomed to name-brand options and using his various rewards points, there were no such opportunities here. The only available option that Terrance could find was just south of the main square. It was a single-story former motor lodge that was now called The Inn at Magnolia Street. It appeared worn and nearly abandoned, like most of the town. There were no frills, and since it was the only hotel in town, there were no deals. Terrance just had to accept the price that was offered and hope for the best.

Terrance entered the lobby, which seemed to be stuck in the 1980s with darker lighting and old couches that reminded him of the one that once sat in his parents' living room. The air in the lobby was slightly stagnant and smelled as though it had been stuck in time along with the other ambiance.

The lady lacked Southern hospitality as she checked him in. She was an older woman whose skin appeared like aged leather. Though the complexion was different, the condition of her skin reminded him of his father. The sun and time had worn it. She was slightly pudgy and walked with a slight limp. Her graying dark brown hair grazed her shoulders, and thick-framed glasses covered her green eyes. She was cold in her demeanor, and there was nothing special about their interaction. Instead of a key card, she gave him a single key on a keychain with the number six hand-written on it.

Once he had finished at the front counter, he walked back to his car to retrieve his belongings. He was eager to review the file that seemed to cause Frank so much distress. It was a file that held many promises for Terrance's future success. A file that could serve as the next step in his ever-growing status and bank account. *Nine kids and one adult all vanished without a trace. This has to be good*, he thought.

As Terrance approached his room, he noticed how empty the hotel seemed. There were no other cars, and most of the rooms appeared to be closed, and some even boarded up. Terrance entered his room, and like the lobby, it appeared to be stuck in time. It had a decaying smell of mold. The carpet was green and somewhat dingy. The bed had a plaid bedspread that contrasted against the dark green floor and darkly stained wood panel walls. He sat on the bed briefly to test it out. It was no comparison to his designer mattress, but the creaky springs seemed to provide adequate support for his brief stay.

Terrance knew this would be his home away from home for only a night as he ran through his normal investigation to find the basic facts. He figured that when he returned after his mother's funeral that he would stay in a neighboring town with perhaps better accommodations. As he tried to ignore his surroundings, he imagined his next triumphant television interview celebrating his success. He had become used to appearing on the local stations in Atlanta, but he hoped this would be the catalyst to propel him to the national arena.

Terrance wasted no time in trying to unpack. Rather, he completed a few tasks to give him some comfort as he opened the file. There were several documents, but for now he wanted to focus on the beginning: the initial police report. Terrance sat quietly and read.

On October 14th, 2006, at 5:47 AM, I, Officer Jonathon Webb (Badge # 918) responded to Lake County High School, located at 606 Georgia Ave. in reference to a welfare check. Upon my arrival, I met with the complainant,

Miranda Roberts. Mrs. Roberts stated that her husband, Dr. Tony Roberts, was the principal of the high school and responded over an hour ago to investigate a fire alarm that was pulled in the front office area. Mrs. Roberts stated her husband had never returned home and was not answering his cellphone. Mrs. Roberts stated that when she arrived, she banged on the door to get his attention and that a student came with blood on his face and yelled at her before he ran off.

After speaking with Mrs. Roberts, I proceeded to the front of the school. I observed a red Ford Fusion parked in the fire lane of the school. I ran the Georgia Registration (110LLM) to confirm the registration. The vehicle did in fact return to Tony and Miranda Roberts. I checked the vehicle, and it appeared to be secure, and the hood was slightly warm to the touch.

I checked the front door of the school, but it was locked. So, I began a perimeter check of the building. All the doors appeared to be secure. Once I entered the campus quad, I observed some torn purple clothing on an adjacent rose bush. As I continued my walk through the quad towards the five hundred hall, I noticed small droplets of blood on the ground. The trail of blood abruptly ended with a small puddle on the ground near the koi pond. The blood was still wet in its appearance and appeared to be fresh. As I continued to check the area, I observed a shadowy figure run from an adjacent classroom window. Because of the circumstances that I encountered, I requested a second unit for backup. Since I was the only Anderson officer on duty, I had to await the arrival of a Lake County Sheriff's Deputy.

While I waited, I requested that dispatch contact another key holder so that we could check the inside of the property.

Dispatch advised that Vice-Principal Erin Gable would be at the school in the next ten minutes. At 6:02 AM, Deputy Jason Price arrived. While we were waiting for Mrs. Gable, we continued to check the exterior of the building. Once again in the quad, we located a black flashlight that was on the ground near the rosebush that I first saw in the purple cloth.

At 6:10 AM, Gable arrived and opened the front door. We instructed her to stay in her locked vehicle while we checked the building's interior. We initially began checking the front office area where the alarm had been activated. As we came around the corner towards the principal's offices, we located a white male, later identified as Dylan Davenport, sitting in a fetal position under a desk in the main hallway. He appeared to have injuries on his head and face, he was conscious, but unresponsive to any stimuli. Davenport continued to whisper the words, "1-5-8 Peter, the lion lurks and devours the goat." As he rocked back and forth on the floor. I attempted to ask him questions, but he would not break his chant. I requested that dispatch send paramedics to the scene to assist Davenport.

While I remained with Davenport, Deputy Price went to the front door to stand by and wait for the responding paramedics. Another deputy from the Lake County Sheriff's Office arrived to provide cover and support while I tended to Davenport. I should note that we heard running coming from an adjacent hallway while we remained in the front office. Because of the blood that was discovered and

Davenport's condition, we held and secured our current position inside the building. When the paramedics arrived, they transported Davenport to Cambridge Medical Center for further treatment.

At 6:36 AM, Sergeant Robert Early from the Lake County Sheriff's Office arrived and assisted us with checking the rest of the building. As we proceeded through the front office area, we observed a light on in an adjacent office. As we approached the office, later identified as Dr. Robert's, we noticed a chair was knocked over and several papers were scattered on the floor. There was also a silver Panasonic camcorder on the ground, still powered on.

We exited the office area and entered the main hall. As we walked towards the five hundred hall, we noticed some smeared blood on the floor that created a trail towards the opposite wall. Once at the wall, the trail of blood abruptly ended. As we checked the area, we heard a door slam on the three hundred hall. We immediately proceeded to that area to check.

As we walked down to the end of the Seven Hundred Hall, I noticed a crack in the door's window to room 720. It seemed an object struck and created the crack. As I inspected, I noticed that there appeared to be more blood in the cracks in the glass. Sgt. Earls and I entered room 720, while Deputy Price maintained a perimeter. Once in Room 720, we noticed a small amount of blood on the floor that abruptly disappeared.

Inside Room 720, we noticed that there were several cans of beer and what appeared to be some extinguished marijuana joints on the floor. There were also many chips and non-alcoholic beverage cans scattered throughout the floor. Another flashlight was recovered on the floor near the door to the hallway.

Following the check of Room 720, we re-entered the hallway. Because the rest of the rooms on this hall were locked and secured, we began checking the restrooms. In the 700 Hall Girl's restroom, we noticed a large amount of blood on the sink, forming a trail of blood into a closed stall door, directly behind the sink. Upon opening the stall door, we noticed it was empty and the blood, like before, paused at the wall. There was also a large splatter of blood on the wall itself directly above the toilet.

I noticed that there was a purse dropped into the sink. I checked the purse and located a wallet with a Georgia driver's license belonging to Katie Hartley. The wallet contained a debit card and $20.00 cash, along with a Nokia cellphone.

Continuing our check, we discovered another room (606) in the 600 Hall in which there were large amounts of alcohol.

During the search that followed, we could not locate any other persons on the property. After securing the scene, I tried to call my Uniform Patrol Commander, but I couldn't reach him because of poor cell phone reception in the building. I requested that dispatch notify him of the incident along with Detective Frank Sturgess. The interior and exterior of the scene were then secured until their arrival.

Terrance finished reading the report and noticed another version stacked underneath the report that he had just read. This report echoed the same as the first, but there was a slight difference that caught his eye in the third paragraph. The mention of the shadowy figure in the window was absent.

Why? Terrance thought, would there be two reports and with such a subtle difference?

Was there someone else on the scene somehow connected to someone? Was there another suspect in the case? And if so, why was this observation omitted from the second report? Terrance pondered.

Terrance stared line by line to find anything else. Perhaps he could find a time difference or one simple missing item, but the only other missing things connected to the unusual noises the officer reported. Terrance thought intensely about how things connected. *There had to be some significance here; otherwise, why would Frank have included two separate reports?*

Terrance looked over the crime scene reports and photos that were included. There, everything seemed to match the second report. The spatter of blood, the evidence of a party, all matched. *Shadowy figure, why is this significant?* Terrance questioned.

Terrance then read the investigative report written by Frank

On October 14, 2006, I, Detective Frank Sturgess, received a call about an incident at Lake County High School.

I arrived on the scene at 7:05 AM, and Captain David Pierce briefed me on the incident. Lake County Sheriff's Office Crime Scene Unit had arrived and was processing the scene. I was informed that a white male, Dylan Davenport, was discovered on the scene and transported to Cambridge Medical Center. After speaking with Captain Pierce, I left the scene to respond to the medical center and attempted to gather information from Davenport.

Upon my arrival at the medical center, I was directed to the East Wing, where Davenport was being held for observation and being kept in a containment room for his own safety.

Upon contacting Davenport, I observed he was staring at the ceiling and otherwise emotionless.

I attempted to speak with him, resulting in him, grabbing my arm, where he began uttering, "The lion that devours, the lion lurks in the darkness."

I attempted to engage him further, resulting in him chanting, "1-5-8 Peter, the lion lurks and devours the goat." He did this repeatedly.

I questioned Davenport about the lion, and he responded, "The lion is not of the east, the lion who is a beast."

I attempted to speak with him and asked, "Why weren't you devoured?" Davenport then changed his chant to, "The blood, the blood, the blood protects the sheep!"

I could not gather any further information from Davenport, who continued to grow agitated during our interaction. Medical personnel arrived shortly and administered a sedative. I left the medical center and returned to Lake County High School to further examine the crime scene.

Terrance pulled out his notepad and began writing the words that Dylan spoke:

The lion that devours, the lion lurks in the darkness.
1-5-8 Peter, the lion lurks and devours the goat.
The lion is not of the east, the lion who is a beast.
The blood, the blood, the blood protects the sheep.

Terrance pondered all the words that he had written on his paper. *What do they mean? What is its relevance?* He thought. Terrance pondered the name Peter. "Could Peter have been another person there? Perhaps an accomplice who had escaped. That shadowy figure?"

Terrance wrote the name Peter down and circled it. *Then the mention of the lion repeatedly. Lions are powerful predators from Africa, but why would he talk about lions in Georgia?* Terrance wondered.

Perplexing thoughts repeatedly consumed Terrance as he wondered what it all meant. In his deep meditation, he did not notice that the light that was installed on the wall above his nightstand flickered. The flicker continued and was again unnoticed by Terrance as he continued trying to decipher Dylan's words.

Terrance muttered softly, "1-5-8 Peter, the lion devours the goat." "The Lion not of the east, the lion that is a beast."

Just then, the flickering of the light gave way to a sharp pop as the light went out completely.

Terrance, startled, began looking for his phone so that he could again add some light to the now dark room. He soon located his phone, which provided just enough light for him to navigate to the light that hung by the chair in the corner. In a few moments, with the click of a switch, the darkened room was once again illuminated.

Terrance chuckled to himself that he allowed some old light to make his heart flutter. The silence then broke again, this time with a knock at the door. It was a gentle tap, but one that surely let him know that someone now stood on the other side of the door.

Terrance walked over towards the door and observed a woman with long dark hair, wearing dark jeans and a black blouse. Terrance, not taking her presence as a threat, opened the door slowly and asked, "Can I help you?"

The woman, who had striking green eyes and stood about five foot seven inches and had a voluminous appearance despite her conservative dress.

"Mr. Greene?" The woman asked.

"Maybe. May I ask your name?"

"Hi, my name is Dr. Abaddon," she responded

"Well, I don't think I need a doctor right now."

"I'm sorry. I don't mean to be so formal. I'm Lilith Abaddon. Please call me Lily," the woman responded.

"Okay, Lily, a pleasure. May I ask why you are here and how you know my name?" Terrance responded in a suspicious tone.

"This is a small town, and news travels fast when there is a local celebrity in our midst." She responded.

"I appreciate that, but I'm no celebrity."

Lily smiled casually at Terrance. "I am from Charlotte myself. I've been doing research here for the last few months. As one stranger in this town to another, I wanted to introduce myself."

"What are you researching?"

"Same as you, the high school and the missing people." She responded.

Terrance now grew concerned that he had a competitor for this story, so his demeanor changed from one of curiosity to one of greater suspicion. *This was his story, and he really did not like the idea of a competitor.*

"So, maybe we are looking at similar things. What do you really want?"

Lily looked down at the ground, then smiled once again at Terrance as she looked at him. "I was thinking we could work together on this one."

"I typically do my work alone."

Glancing back down toward the ground, she looked away. "I get that, as do I, but this one is a little different. I have a lot of resources that I have gathered through more questionable means, but there are still things that make little sense. But you met the detective who worked the case. He has no interest in meeting with me, like, at all. I figured we could just share each other's information, so we get a better picture."

Terrance remained firm in his response. "I appreciate it, but like I said, I usually work alone. In fact, I always work alone. It is much easier that way because sharing can quickly turn to fighting over resources."

"I get it, but I'm not a competitor to you. In fact, I think we are both looking for different answers that will not pose any risk to each other's work." She said once again, looking him in the eye.

"Like I said, I'm not interested, but I thank you for your time."

"Mr. Greene, do you have the tapes from the school?" she asked

"I will not reveal what I have and don't have." He responded.

Lily grinned and gained some confidence. "I'm going to assume that you do not."

Terrance knew he didn't have these tapes, but the fact she brought them up intrigued him. *Perhaps she may be useful,* he thought to himself.

"I assume that you have all of this?" Terrance questioned.

"Oh yes, now don't ask how I got them, but I do." She responded.

"So, what do you want in return?"

"Mainly just your presence. There is power in numbers, and this town is not as safe as you would assume." She responded.

"So if we work together, I'm assuming you want a cut?"

"No, I just want cooperation so that I can get what I need. I don't think you understand. Our interests are not competing. In fact, I think we can both benefit from working together." She responded.

"What kind of doctor are you?"

She replied, "My specialty is what you would call parapsychology."

Her words quite surprised Terrance. *Great, this is all I need to get involved with.* He thought.

"I don't really buy into all that kind of stuff. Sorry, no offense."

"None taken. My line of work is not for everyone, but it is my passion." She responded.

"I really don't see how this is going to work."

Lily shuffled in her purse and pulled out two old mini–VHS tapes. "But I have these," she said as she made the tapes visible.

"Okay, you have sparked my interest a little. I have to tell you, though, I don't buy into supernatural things."

"That's alright, I love skeptics. They always add a little something special to my work." She said with a smile.

"Would you like to talk more and look over what we've got?"

"Not now; I merely wanted to introduce myself," she responded.

"Okay?" Terrance said, with a confused look.

Lily handed the two tapes over to Terrance and said, "I must go for now; it's not safe for me to hang about too long, but take these and see what you think. We will meet again soon. When we do, I will answer what I can after you watch these tapes."

Terrance accepted the tapes, but her apparent generosity confused him.

"Until next time, my new friend," Lily said as she walked away.

"How will I know how to find you?"

"No worries, Mr. Greene, I will find you when it is safe, and the time is right." Lily responded as she walked into the shadows down the exterior corridor of the hotel.

Terrance was never a person to turn away things that might benefit him. Her willingness to trust him puzzled him. He wasn't used to this happening during his investigations. Although accustomed to conflict, he was unfamiliar with selfless help or sharing. He accepted them and would deal with whatever came later. Terrance walked back into his room and added the tapes to his collection of items on his bed. He was a little intrigued, and he thought to himself, *This woman, Lily, was a mystery. She was also very attractive, so at the very least, this made the potential for this investigation to be much more interesting.*

Chapter 4

Woken in the Dark

Frank had a sleepless night; it took what seemed like hours to fall asleep after his interaction with the chief. However, the increasing stack of beer cans that littered the floor under the seat of his recliner did its work, and Frank finally drifted off to sleep. Challenges plagued his sleep, preventing him from getting much-needed rest after such a stressful day.

On one hand, Frank now had enough money to leave Anderson, but he was worried about the cost. *Did he in fact open wounds that once festered? Wounds that took so long to close, even though some never fully healed.* Frank lay passed out in his recliner, but he was not still nor calm. Sudden jerks and head movements interrupted the calmness of his body as his dreams bore a life, one that he wished would die.

His dreams replayed events from his past and one night that forever changed him. Like a slow-motion flashback in some movie, he relived the days leading up to December 14th. In the years and months that had preceded, Frank had long since given up on his younger days of drinking. But now he found himself once again latched onto the bottle or can. Since he began his investigation of Lake County High School and those missing teens, he found his life and dreams haunted by mystery and unseen visits by dark shadows that seemed to dominate all moments of his life, including his dreams. The only escape that he found was malt and liquor beverages that seemed to calm all that tormented him.

His dream tonight centered on one night. It was a stressful night, but he had chosen not to drink. He knew he had father and husband duties. It was the night of his daughter's Christmas concert at Oakbrook Elementary. He was so proud of her; she had practiced long and hard for the solo that awaited her. Emily provided him with some grounding amid a sea of chaos. Even on the worst days and worst nights, her calming smile and innocence from the world seemed to give him hope that no matter what, there was good.

"Oh, Holy night", she sounded like an angel as she would practice her lines throughout the house. His wife had the camcorder ready, and Frank was going to be tasked with taking the pictures. He needed this. He needed to see his daughter's light shine and her voice radiate with the sounds of peace. This year Frank had been little in the Christmas spirit. This case seemed to dominate everything, but perhaps tonight that spirit would pay him a visit. There was hope and the potential for one night of peace. Frank and Autumn had made plans to take Emily to one of her favorite restaurants in town, a local pizza place called Nick's. In the present, like many of the storefronts, it sits as a skeleton of the past. A relic of a bygone era before a curse cast its shadow on what once had been a peaceful town. But now in this dream, it was alive and, as Emily said, "They have the best cheese sticks!" It was a time to celebrate! The world was about to hear his angel's voice.

Emily wore a white dress that night, and her mother had helped her add some makeup that highlighted her blue eyes. Emily had blue eyes not so dissimilar to Autumn. They were blue as the sky on a bright summer day. They seemed to twinkle as though they were lights in the darkness. Deeper though, the eyes provided a gateway to Emily's soul. They were kind, caring, and forgiving, as Frank had often looked in her eyes when we had to disappoint her because of his chaotic work schedule and events that were long missed.

Tonight was different though; he would not miss this! Emily bounced up and down, almost shaking the old white house to the foundation. She was so excited! Frank remembered walking out of the house that night. He glanced up at the gables covered with icicle lights and looked at the twinkling Christmas tree that beamed all colors in the window at the front of the house. As they got into his truck, he remembered her voice, so filled with excitement for the concert. He remembered backing out of the gravel driveway and thinking, *Things are going to get better, things are going to get better.*

It was not quite the white Christmas that many Georgians had wished. In Georgia, winters shift from moderate to cold, but sadly, things rarely align for snow. Instead, especially in south Georgia, residents are met with a cold rain. The hazard that comes from this cold rain occurs when the sunsets and the puddles turn into more hazardous conditions that a driver must navigate. Today there was chilly rain, but the temperatures had cooperated just enough to prevent the latter.

Frank had watched intently, hoping that the weather would not affect tonight's concert. Fortunately, everything looked good. It did not mean that it was comfortable. The temperatures had dipped just above freezing and made for a cold walk to his truck. The warmth of the moment that was at hand seemed to keep the family just warm enough.

As they pulled up at the school, Frank spoke with some other parents before they all entered the elementary school cafeteria to watch the concert begin. Frank needed this; it was like a choir of angels singing songs in the exaltation of this wonderful season. Frank felt lost in the innocence of this world at that moment. It was a stark contrast to Lake County High School, and the case that still seemed to baffle him. Then the moment came, and Emily stepped forward into the spotlight. The stillness of the cafeteria, now concert hall, seemed to make this moment even more special. Emily stepped forward with her eyes sparkling, complimenting the paper snowflakes and winter décor. Then she sang, just like a cherub sent from Heaven itself. She sang. It was perfect. Her voice filled the room with a gentle, sweet celebration. At this moment, Frank was at peace. Regardless of the noise out in the world, everything stood still, and he was at peace. It was a peace that he had not felt in several weeks.

Following the concert, Frank met Emily with a bouquet of white roses, something that he had hidden from her sight somehow throughout the night. She felt like a princess at her coronation; it was her special night, and Frank felt a sense of warmth in his own heart. A warmth that seemed to keep him warm as they walked back to the truck.

During dinner, Emily was so excited! She stopped talking only to place a cheese stick in her mouth, even talking around the chewing of it as some particles escaped and struck the table. No one seemed to care. It was a good night.

The temperature outside didn't improve as the night progressed. An arctic wind blew through the trees, striking the ground and all who dared to venture outside. One unseen benefit of this miserable wind was that, though cold, it dried the surfaces, making the concern of ice on this chilly night less of a threat.

Frank and his family left the restaurant and walked into the now dried parking lot. The bone-chilling cold in the air cut through the family. The emotional warmth of the concert and celebration is now being replaced by a cold that almost seems supernatural. Inside the truck, the slowly warming heat blew around them, eventually giving some warmth to the truck's occupants. The high energy and excitement of the night now gave way to tiredness as the concert and celebration ended. It was like the euphoria was now replaced with the need to rest.

The drive was uneventful; the family took in the sights of the Christmas lights that were wrapped around the trees lining the short downtown streets. They twinkled in the windows of the closed businesses, almost making one feel surrounded and entombed by the glittery lights. As Frank continued to drive home, they traveled further from the streetlights of the downtown, and now the stars took the place of the sparkling Christmas lights, seeming to keep the atmosphere alive.

As Frank continued his drive home, he drove slowly past the entrance to Lake County High School. He had avoided this previously since the elementary school was on the opposite side of town. As he approached the school, he felt all the warmth that had filled his heart and the truck earlier now being replaced with dread. Even the stars that had peered behind the clouds seemed to disappear, leaving only darkness. The building seemed to have its own presence, one that was devoid of all that was joy. Frank drove slowly past it to involuntarily torture himself by prolonging the time he had to spend in its presence.

Frank glanced slightly to the left to glimpse at his foe as he drove past. In life, it only takes a millisecond, one millisecond of something that goes unnoticed throughout one's days, to change everything. In the moment of that fleeting glance, a millisecond happened. The wind that was keeping the roads clear tonight had also placed stress on the trees that lined the street and, in that precise moment, though with the precision of some evil surgeon, there was a snap.

The snap of a collapsing branch followed by a thud as it struck the roadway directly in front of Frank's approaching truck. Frank saw the motion and reacted as his training dictated. He tried with all his might to avoid the menacing branch and its limbs. He did it quickly, as though it was an involuntary reflex. Frank narrowly avoided the branch and the limbs that threatened to burst through the windshield of his truck. Though as the truck skidded to the left, the laws of the universe were not in his favor. The momentum and the weight caused things to shift.

In that moment, the truck became like the inside of a tumbling dryer; bags, toys, and those white roses flowed freely through the cabin. The petals of the roses were now broken apart as they littered the inside of the truck as though they were that elusive Georgia snow. The time seemed to move at a snail's pace as the world inside the truck entered a state of violent turns and spins. Despite the violence of the force at work, it seemed like there was no noise, just silence. At that moment, time stopped amidst the turmoil and violence. Life was stuck, stuck in one moment.

The truck finally settled onto its roof. The moment was no longer paused, and the senses returned. Silence still existed, but within that silence there were sounds. Sounds of moaning and crying, sounds of fluid dripping striking the pavement. The sounds of a still-roaring engine and tires that spun with no hope of gaining traction.

Frank felt pain but ignored it as he took stock of the welfare of his family. Autumn was conscious and told him to take care of Emily. She began pulling at the seatbelt but was having challenges freeing herself from the confines of the truck. Frank worked quickly, freeing himself so that he could tend to Emily. She was conscious but crying. He gently removed her seatbelt and pulled her from the truck, laying her on the ground. Frank removed his jacket and made a pillow to support Emily's head.

Frank felt relieved. She was breathing; she was crying. He knew this was good. It was good that she was conscious. As Frank took stock of her condition, he looked down from her head and he saw the once white dress that was a symbol of her innocence and purity in this world was stained crimson with blood. As he glanced down further, he noticed that the bright red color increased as he looked further down her abdomen. His heart sank as he looked near her stomach, there a six-inch shard of glass from the vase that was in her lap. Frank was fearful but did not let Emily see his emotions.

Emily grabbed her father's hand and said, "Dad, it doesn't hurt anymore." She looked her father in the eyes with those blue eyes and said, "It's going to be okay, Daddy. I'm still your princess". In that moment, she coughed with blood coming out of her mouth, and the eyes that were bright as a summer sky lost all their life. The light that had shone so brightly through the night was now extinguished.

"No!!! God no!!!" Frank shouted repeatedly. Then his attention went back to his wife, who was still struggling to free herself from the seatbelt. Frank jumped up and went to help her, but he was met with a greater force as the fluid that dripped from the overturned truck ignited and the truck exploded. The explosion threw Frank backward, his head striking the pavement. He landed with a thud beside his now lifeless daughter. As he looked at her lifeless body. All he could do was hold her hand. His eyes then turned to the truck now buried in a sea of flames. He could not move. Tears filled his eyes. Despite the liquid that now obscured his vision, he saw something.

A strange shadow on the other side of the flames that engulfed his truck and Autumn. He could see only a shadowy figure that seemed to move slowly, just beyond the reach of the flames. In his mind, he recognized the figure that lurked in the shadows. It was the same figure that had tormented him on so many nights. Frank's consciousness slowly faded, and darkness overtook his body. He hoped he would never awaken again.

Frank awoke in his chair with a jolt from his nightmare. He was breathing deeply, and his heart was racing. Though he was miles and years away, he could still smell it. The fire, the rubber, the blood, and the trace of Emily's perfume. He leaned forward in his recliner and wept into the palms of his hands. Frank lost everything! In that one millisecond, his life changed forever. Dreams became nightmares. Hope and happiness became an elusive feeling that he would never feel again. Frank's face emerged from his palms; his eyes were still filled with tears. As he looked to the kitchen, he saw it. Just like that night and so many others. Barely visible in the kitchen's darkness with the naked eye was the shadowy figure. The alcohol no longer concealed the demon that had haunted him for so many nights and so many years. Frank wished it would just kill him and end his torment once and for all.

Taking a deep breath, he looked again towards the kitchen, and the figure was gone. Frank felt in his pocket. He felt the paper of the check. The check was supposed to free him from Anderson and the torment of his dark shadow. He wondered whether any distance would ever truly free him in this world. Free him from the pain, the hurt, and the guilt that he felt. Frank sat up in that moment of despair, having relived the millisecond as he had many times once again. He reached into the drawer of the table that sat beside his chair and retrieved his salvation.

The silver of the metal seemed to be the only hope he had. His only light in the darkness of his life appeared to be the shining silver. The alcohol, the drugs, they numbed him, but the pain never went away. Like the dreams, it always returned. No matter how far he went or how much time passed, he would never be free. He nervously examined the tool in his hand. Despite what the tool in his hand meant, his hands were stable. Hope returned in that moment to him. In one millisecond, it could end. Just like the millisecond that took everything. He could finally be free of his oppression.

Frank rubbed his fingers on the cold silver surface. He looked at his reflection on the side. This was not him. He once was very different from the overweight, dirty man that stared back at him. He slowly brought the tip to the side of his right temple and took a deep breath. One millisecond could free him from his torment. He placed the cold tip right against his temple. At that moment, it was surprisingly not cold but perhaps had a warmth to it. He took one more breath and began applying pressure to the trigger.

Just before adding that final pound of pressure, something startled him back to reality. There was a knock at the door. Frank pulled the gun away from his head, staring almost in disbelief. *What am I doing?* He thought. He quickly put the gun back in the drawer and stumbled through the maze of beer cans and pizza boxes to answer the front door.

TERRANCE TRIED TO GET comfortable. He had misjudged the comfort of this old hotel bed. Perhaps it was the old springs or perhaps it was all the thoughts that raced through his head that kept him from reaching that vital point of slumber. He would get within reach, but something would bounce him back awake.

This was not a new challenge for Terrance, as he always got like this during an investigation. His mind would race as he analyzed in his mind the outcomes. He was extra restless this night. His mind wandered about the stranger who had visited him. Being the pessimist that he was, he wondered about her motivations. *Why would she freely give him something, yet not ask for anything in return?* He wondered as his mind continued to race.

Eventually, as the clock crept into the morning hours, his brain slowed, and the sleep that had so far evaded him appeared within reach. The last time he looked at the clock, it was half-past one o'clock. In the next few minutes, Terrance began to dream. His dreams took him to comfortable places, newly found fame that bounded past the local esteem that he had garnered in the Atlanta area. He dreamed of national appearances and book tours. He dreamed of that recognition, of the notoriety of being the "Destroyer of Corruption". His dreams took him to parties in Los Angles and New York. With the music, he could almost feel the beat of the music in these high-end clubs. He felt as though it vibrated throughout his whole body. The women in these clubs were beautiful, something out of a magazine, and they followed him. He was a hero; he was famous; he was rich.

His dreams shifted to one woman in particular. Though he could never focus on her face, what he could see sparked his interest. She had a body full of curves in all the right places, and her skin was just sun-kissed enough that it provided a pleasant contrast to her outfit. Her tone looked as though she had spent hours on the beaches of Miami. She seemed exotic and foreign.

It was not just her looks; she was passionate and empowered. They danced close, bodies becoming one on the dance floor of some club in South Beach, Miami. They danced under the lights and palm trees. He became intoxicated with her body and her moves. He had seen no one move so perfectly. Where she went, he followed, and their bodies continued to become one on the dance floor. He still never saw her face, but in the dream, he didn't care; he was hooked on this girl. He just could not get enough of her. She was addicting.

Though it was a dream, he could feel her body, her touch, her breath on his ear. He then could feel her firm wet kiss. She was more aggressive than the women he had dated; she was pressing into him. He couldn't seem to escape her, and in that moment, he was completely fine with that.

Her touch was driving him wild. He had never had a dream like this before, nor met a woman like this before. The dream was exciting; he felt as though he were a teenager again, dreaming of some model, but this felt so real. It was almost freeing to become totally hers.

The dream continued; they continued becoming one, and her body never left his on the dance floor. He was in a state of bliss, and he focused on her features, her arms now wrapped around him. He was hers in this dream; she had taken possession and wrapped him within. As the passion continued, he felt a pain in his back. It distracted from the experience of the dream. His senses returned, and pleasure began giving way to a trapped feeling. He struggled to become free of her grip. The heat of the moment grew cold. She was cold. The warmth of the moment had escaped, and now she was like ice. His eyes focused on her closed eyes. Her face remained out of focus for him. He could see those closed eyes, though. She made noises; but they were no longer noises that were normal; they seemed almost animalistic. He kept trying to escape, the fingernails firmly implanted in his back, but her grip on him was unwavering. As he panicked in his dream, her eyes opened.

Nothing but her eyes were in his field of vision. When they opened, they were colder than the touch of her skin. They reminded him of the videos he's seen of a shark in the wild. Black, devoid of life, with no emotion, just coldness. He thrashed to escape the pain and fear, but he couldn't. The grip was too strong. Then that laugh — something inhuman about that laugh. *What is she?* He thought as he panicked.

In that moment, he felt a jolt as he jumped awake in his bed. He was sweating, his heart racing, and he was nearly hyperventilating. Though he was sweating, he felt cold. The room was so cold. He felt as though his breath would become visible at any moment. As he continued to come back awake, he also felt something else. It was a pain, a burning coming from his back. Terrance jumped up and went to the vanity, which stood outside the bathroom. He turned on the light and turned slightly to face his back to the mirror. He stood in shock; there were three lines of scratches stretching from the top of his shoulders and going toward his mid black. Terrance knew these weren't here before, but he wondered, *Where did they come from? Surely, they did not come from the dream. That's not possible.* He assured himself.

Terrance tried to shake his uneasiness; he left the vanity and returned to his bed. Looking around, he sought an explanation for the scratches. He was in disbelief, but now so awake that he could not fall back asleep. He decided to get back to work and review more of the files that the folder contained. Checking his bedside alarm clock, he quickly determined how much time remained before he could begin his legwork. The red numbers across the clock read 3:36. He sighed, as he knew he would have hours before he could do much in the town. As he looked through the files and papers, he tried to put away thoughts of the dream or of these mysterious scratches on his back. The temperature of the room seemed to return to normal, and his uneasiness faded as he became lost in the files.

Chapter 5

The Sun Rises

Hours seemed to pass by unnoticed to Terrance as he continued examining the files that Frank had given him. The more he read, the more curious he became. *Why were no charges ever filed against Dylan?* He thought to himself, *Perhaps the answer lies with Dylan's family. After all, his father was the pastor of the largest church in town and surely a community leader. Was this some type of cover-up?* Terrance continued to wonder as he took another look back through the files.

The second round of analyzing the files brought him more questions than answers. *Dylan was not the only member of his family who was at Lake County High School that night. He had a brother two years older named Chase.* Terrance examined more intently through information on Chase. From the information that he could uncover, Chase was the quarterback for the school and probably the most popular student in his class. He had a promising football career, attracting scouts from several universities. He was all set to have a full ride to Florida next fall and had options at two other schools.

Terrance pulled out the pictures of the teens, and he looked over Dylan. He was a very slender teenager with dark brown hair. He lacked visible muscles and was even short for his age. It looked as though Dylan had never stepped foot on a sports field of any kind. In fact, the report showed that he was a member of the chess team and audio-video club.

He sat down the picture of Dylan, then compared it to Chase. The contrast between the two brothers was obvious from the start.

Chase stood at least a foot taller than his younger brother. Chase was athletic and reminded Terrance of the jocks who once tormented him in his own school. *There is no way that Dylan could have overpowered his brother.* Terrance thought to himself.

There were never any weapons found in any search conducted at the school. Searches of the school never recovered even blunt objects used as improvised weapons. It just made little sense to Terrance. *Dylan would have had to have somehow overpowered Chase and two other senior football players.*

Terrance thumbed through the stack of pictures and located the pictures of the other two young men. Eric appeared huge in the pictures; the descriptions matched. He was the center and stood like a brick wall on the offensive line. Matteus, who was called Matt, was the third player there that night. He was a running back, and once again he would have physically outmatched Dylan.

Terrance couldn't understand how Dylan overpowered all the players, let alone the principal, a former college football player, without a weapon. He continued his meticulous review of the files, trying to make connections. Many times, investigators suspected Dylan, but never charged him, and the disappearance of the nine people that night remained a mystery. Aside from blood, there were no bodies and no weapons. It was like the bodies never left the school, but the school was searched multiple times; cadaver dogs even searched the school twice. However, all these searches yielded the same result — nothing.

Taking a pause, he looked up and tried to clear his head. Terrance then looked down at the VHS tapes he had been given the night before. *Perhaps these hold some type of evidence of what happened.* Terrance thought to himself. Despite the age and retro appearance of his hotel room, there was not a VCR to accompany the old tube television that sat on top of the dresser. Terrance wondered where he would find one of those old things in this small town.

Sitting up, Terrance rubbed his eyes. Time had gotten away from him as he lost himself in the files. Once the sun rose, he decided he would go to the office and ask the front desk worker if she could point him in the right direction to find a VHS player. Realizing that he had not yet showered, he decided he needed to freshen up and shower before leaving his room.

As Terrance got ready for his first full-day in Anderson, a lone figure hidden in the shadows sat in a black Ford truck. The truck was backed into a parking space just behind Terrance's Mercedes. Fresh mud covered the lower side of the old truck. The silhouette of a rifle rack was just visible through the back glass of the truck. Two empty beer cans sat on the ground just under the driver's side door, and dip stains ran down in lines from the driver's window until they met the reddish-brown mud. A third beer can fell on the ground before the truck cranked and slowly drove out of the hotel parking lot. Terrance never heard the truck crank, nor did he suspect someone had parked behind his car. The truck slowly disappeared from the horizon, and Terrance was none the wiser as he got ready for his shower.

Hoping for a hot shower, Terrance jumped into the shower. The shower itself was part of the tub. Like most of the hotel room, the bathroom seemed to be lost in time. The tub, with its avocado-green color, matched the adjacent toilet. As Terrance stood in the back of the shower, waiting for the water to warm, he looked around. Everything around him seemed to be stuck in the 1980s or in disrepair. Floral wallpaper was peeling off of the wall at the seams. The ceiling had brown stains that showed a previous leak. As he took in his surroundings, he remembered how unfamiliar such motels were to him. This was definitely not the flag chain hotels he was used to staying at.

His hopes for a hot shower seemed to disappear with his hope of a decent night's sleep. The water warmed, but never got as hot as Terrance liked. Despite the cooler temperature of the water, his back burned as the water touched the series of scratches on his back. At first, he had forgotten about them, but the sudden jolt of pain brought them back to his thoughts. *Did I scratch myself during that dream?* Terrance did not believe in things he could not explain, so to him there had to be some logical explanation for the scratches and the connection to his dream.

Logic dictated his life, and he allowed the world of fantasy to escape his life at the same time he abandoned his parents' church and his faith. The only acceptable answer that he could muster for the scratches was that they were self-inflicted during an insane dream. He knew he had been working very hard lately, barely giving himself a break. In his mind, he knew exhaustion could cause the brain to do some unusual things, so he became comfortable accepting that extreme exhaustion was behind everything.

He continued lathering and rinsing in the lukewarm water, trying to focus his brain on the work ahead. Finally, he focused away from the scratches and on the to-do list for today. As he relaxed in his thoughts of how best to tackle this investigation, something distracted him. He thought he heard something; it was light, a gentle scratching. *Probably a rat or mouse in this dump,* Terrance thought. Then, suddenly, a loud crash interrupted the sound of the running water.

Terrance jumped, almost slipping on the slick surface of the cold iron bathtub. He quickly finished rinsing and grabbed a towel to see what could have produced such a sound. *That was too loud to be a rat,* he thought to himself. Coldness met him when he exited the bathroom. The room, like last night, was cold, almost frigid. He ignored the temperature for now and looked for the cause of the sound.

His eyes slowly scanned the room until they located the culprit. It was the picture that was on the wall beside his bed. It was now lying face down on the floor. Terrance reached down and picked up the fallen painting. He looked at the painting; it was a small country church, an old building that reminded him of his parents' church. He hadn't noticed it before as most of the pictures on the wall appeared like an afterthought and just seemed to create breaks in the dark wood paneling.

After his heart stopped pounding and he became comfortable with the cause, he simply leaned it against the wall and tried to pick up some of the glass, leaving the rest for whoever cleans the rooms. He continued to get dressed and get ready to leave the motel. *Man, this room is cold.* He thought to himself as he walked over to adjust the temperature on the thermostat.

Terrance left his hotel room with a rumbling stomach. He walked towards the office, expecting to find some sort of continental breakfast, but the only thing that greeted him was a pot of coffee. Slightly annoyed, he decided to take advantage of whatever amenities they provided. He fixed his coffee and added his cream. "Blah," he almost said out loud as he took his first sip of coffee. It was bitter despite the addition of the sweetener. It had an almost burnt taste. Despite his aversion to the taste, he sucked it up to get caffeine into his system. He knew it was going to be a long day, and he needed every bit of energy he could gather.

After taking a few sips of coffee, he walked to the front desk; the same woman with the flatline personality who had checked him in greeted him. "Good morning," Terrance said with a smile.

"Can I help you?" The woman responded in her raspy voice.

"Yes, I was wondering if you guys had a VCR that I could borrow?"

"No, what you see is what we got." The woman answered abruptly as she began coughing.

"Do you know if there is any place in town that may have one I can use?"

After she stopped coughing and spat the results into a napkin, she looked up at him with an annoyed look. "You can check the library."

"Okay, thank you", Terrance responded.

The woman simply responded with a murmur that sounded more like a growl than an actual response.

"Oh, can I ask if someone can check the thermostat in my room? It keeps getting freezing cold in there." Terrance asked as he started backing away from the front desk counter.

The woman responded with a similar murmur as she nodded her head.

Terrance took the rest of his remaining coffee and left the hotel and traveled to the library. The library sat across from a small park that was mostly empty except for a familiar face sitting alone at a picnic table reading a book. Buried in her book, she didn't notice him. Terrance looked towards the library; the parking lot was empty, and as he looked at the door, he found the reason. The library was open only Monday through Wednesday. The most recent roadblock frustrated Terrance.

Since he could not go into the library, Terrance made the most of his journey to this part of town and walked over to the picnic table.

"Lily? Isn't it?" he asked as he approached the woman at the picnic table.

"Good morning, Mr. Greene," she responded as she glanced up from her book.

"I wanted to thank you for the tapes, but I'm having a hard time finding a VCR."

"Yeah, those tapes are a little old school." She responded.

"Do you have one?"

"Sorry, I always travel light when I come down to Anderson, but I do have something else that may help," Lily responded as she handed another envelope to Terrance.

"I get it, thanks." Terrance said with a smile as he accepted the new gift.

"So, other than having no video player, how are things going?" Lily asked.

"Getting interesting." Terrance said with a flirtatious smile.

He saw more of Lily in the sunlight, and he was impressed by what he saw. She was wearing tight jeans that hugged her curves around her shapely hips. He always enjoyed meeting women. Normally, the women he would meet on these trips were locals who were common and uninteresting. They served more as something to kill time, but she was different.

"This is an interesting town." Lily said, returning a smile.

"So, I'm curious, what brings a specialist in the occult to this town and this case?" Terrance asked, maintaining his smile and eye contact with her.

"You aren't into history, are you, Mr. Greene?" Lily asked.

"Please call me Terrance. I look at the history of a case, but that's about it. Unfortunately for people like me, history hasn't been so kind. So, I would rather leave it in the past."

"You know, the strange thing about history is that it is cyclical. Humans are so stupid that they just keep repeating the same mistake over and over again. Sometimes it is good to identify the cycle." Lily said with a hint of arrogance.

"Maybe," Terrance responded.

"Anderson is rich in history, Mr. Greene. Do you know the history of the land that the high school sits on?" Lily responded.

"Just what happened that night." Terrance said.

"That's a very narrow way to look at things, Mr. Greene. I'm surprised you have fared so well on your other articles," she said smugly.

Her remark took Terrance back.

"See if you look deeper at the location, you would learn that a high school should have never been built there." Lily continued.

"Why is that?" Terrance inquired.

"Before the white man occupied this land, it was home to the Creek and Muskogee Indians. This town was one place they would not venture; they called it the Land of Night. They believed it was tainted and home to a Trickster. It was an evil spirit that would prey on the souls of those who were dying, tormenting them until death, and then it would consume their hearts." Lily shared.

"Interesting," Terrance responded, feigning an interest.

"When the white man first settled this land, strange illnesses plagued them, and people would vanish from the fields without a trace. Even the white man left and viewed this as a cursed land until years later when they returned. Like I said, history is cyclical. No one paid attention, and eventually you got Anderson," Lily said.

"What does that have to do with the school?

"Many in my field believe that when bad things happen, when negative energy centers on a place, that a portal to the other side can be created or at least the veil between worlds can become thinner." Lily said in a serious tone.

"I'm sorry, I don't buy into all this. There is one world, and we are living in it."

"Perhaps, but like I said earlier, I like skeptics, maybe this town will make a believer of you yet. Anyway, that is what brings an expert in my field to Anderson," Lily said.

"No offense, but if my grandmother and momma couldn't make a believer out of me, I doubt this town has any hope," Terrance said, rolling his eyes.

"I'm assuming you mean a believer in God?" Lily asked.

"Yeah," Terrance responded

"Well, I'm not talking about God, Mr. Greene, I'm talking about something very different," Lily said with a smile.

"If I don't believe in God, I definitely don't believe in a man in a red cape or other evil spirits taking souls," Terrance responded.

"The devil or something like him comes in many forms, Mr. Greene, many forms." Lily said as she closed her book and packed it into her bag.

"I didn't mean to offend you." Terrance said, feeling that he was killing his chances of getting to know her a little more.

"No offense taken, Mr. Greene, but let me give you a suggestion though. You need to look deeper into the past if you want to know what happened to those kids. When you can look at the article that I gave you on The Carmichael Textile Factory or the Carmichael family." Lily said as she got up and walked away.

Before she departed, she patted Terrance on the shoulder, saying, "Good luck, Mr. Greene."

Her touch caused Terrance to wince as she touched his right where the scratch began. "You okay, Mr. Greene?" She asked.

"Yeah, I just scratched myself last night."

"Oh, must be a nasty scratch. Stay safe, Mr. Greene." She said as she began to walk away.

Seeing an opening to stay connected with her, Terrance called out, "Hey, think I can I have your number? You know, just in case I have questions?"

Lily turned around and said, "I'm sure we will see each other again, Mr. Greene." She then turned around and walked away. "I look forward to our next meeting, my unbelieving friend," she said as she smiled and continued to walk down the sidewalk.

This woman perplexed Terrance, and he kind of liked it. A challenge always seemed to pique his interest. Thinking to himself, *perhaps next time I will at least attempt not to rebuff her beliefs so quickly*. As Lily disappeared down the sidewalk, Terrance's thoughts returned to the library and what he could do now to move forward in his investigation. He sat his book bag down and fumbled through its contents, eventually pulling out a notebook. As he scanned the contents, he stopped upon pulling up Frank's address from some previous correspondence. *It's time I visited the detective,* Terrance thought as he once again had to figure out the location without the ability of relying on modern technology.

Chapter 6

Unanswered Questions

After struggling for some time, Terrance eventually found Frank's house or at least what Frank considered to be his home. Terrance pulled up at an old rusty trailer just outside of town. Dense walls of trees surrounded it. It seemed so isolated, it almost made Terrance nervous to make an unannounced visit. He took a deep breath and decided it was now or never. As Terrance stepped onto the porch, his concern shifted to the rickety structure and whether it could actually support his weight. As he finally reached the front door, he was happy to realize that his concerns were unfounded. Once he was at the door, he took a deep breath and knocked.

No one seemed to respond at first, but then he heard some rustling and footsteps moving toward the door. The door creaked open, and Frank stood on the other side with sweat covering his forehead. Frank looked at Terrance and asked, "Why are you here?"

"I've been looking at what you gave me, and I need some help. Some things just don't add up?" Terrance asked in a gentle voice.

Frank popped his head out of the door and looked around. "Did anyone follow you?" Frank asked.

"No, it's just me."

"We don't need to talk in the open; come inside," Frank said as he opened his door and motioned for Terrance to come in.

"I don't get many visitors, so excuse the mess." Frank said.

Terrance paused for a moment, then accepted Frank's invitation. The smell of stale cigarette smoke and rotting food took Terrance back. He needed answers, so he accepted the conditions and walked further inside Frank's trailer.

Frank came alongside Terrance and shifted some papers and junk from a spot on his couch and invited Terrance to sit. Terrance accepted and sank into the old, stained couch.

Frank kicked some beer cans away and sat back in his chair. "I really don't like the idea of you coming here. I did my part; I gave you what I had," Frank said.

"Those pages only give me so much. There are so many things that just don't add up. I just need to ask you some questions, and then I will never bother you again."

"Fine, but make it quick," Frank responded.

"So, I've been looking over the files. Why are there two different reports?"

"The first one was the original; it was redacted and merged, but I kept the original." Frank said.

"But why was it changed?" Terrance asked.

"The chief at the time didn't think it was relevant to include some of the stuff." Frank responded.

"But why?" Terrance followed up.

"You would have to ask him; we just followed orders." Frank said.

"Why was Dylan never charged? How did you guys pin it on him without him ever being charged? I don't even see anything where there was a hearing to even lock him away in the hospital." Terrance said.

"Dylan was a very disturbed individual. He had a breakdown and never came back." Frank responded.

"Did you ever figure out what he meant by 1-5-8 Peter the lion devours the goat or anything else he said?"

"Are you religious, Mr. Greene? I mean, do you have any religious upbringing?" Frank asked.

"I grew up in a church, but I'm far from believing in made-up characters." Terrance retorted.

"First Peter 5:8, Be sober-minded and alert, because your adversary the devil prowls around like a roaring lion, seeking someone to devour. Mr. Greene. It comes from the Bible." Frank said.

"Okay, so he was a preacher's kid, but what about the goat?"

"In the Book of Matthew, there is a parable where Jesus divides the sheep from the goats. Jesus admits the sheep to Heaven, but forsakes the goats," Frank said.

"So, he was saying the Devil devours those who Jesus separated?" Terrance asked.

"Your guess is as good as mine. I'm no theologian, and like I said, that boy was very disturbed." Frank responded.

"Do you believe in this religious stuff?"

"I've already been forsaken. I'm what you call a goat, Mr. Greene; it does not matter what I believe," Frank responded.

"So, this kid Dylan is really messed up. Maybe some religious nut, but where's any documentation?"

"All of that is above my pay grade, Mr. Greene. I've given you all that I have." Frank said with a hint of agitation in his voice.

"Did anyone ever figure out why the kids were in the school in the first place?"

"To party. They snuck in after the dance, drank, smoked pot, did what kids do." Frank responded.

"Dylan wasn't like the rest, so why was he there?" Terrance asked.

"This is where it gets odd. Some of Dylan's friends on the chess team said that he went there with a new girl. He was the president of the audio and video club, and this girl was into those paranormal shows. You know the ones where a team goes in and captures some crap on video. They said she convinced him to go with her, and to keep him quiet, Chase let him join the group." Frank responded.

"So, who was this girl?"

"No one knows. Some kids said her name was Hailey, but there were no records of her attending that school. Outside of a small group of kids, no one ever saw her or knew who she was. There was not even any evidence at the scene to show that she had ever existed," Frank said.

"So, was she even there or was this some kind of rumor?"

"I don't know." Frank said.

"Well, what do you think?"

"I don't even know what to think anymore," Frank said.

"I mean, seriously, do you think there was another person there? An accomplice?" Terrance asked.

"A person? No, but there was something." Frank said.

"Like what?" Terrance questioned.

"I don't know. Something that shouldn't have been there. Look, please leave me alone. I just want to be left alone." Frank said, becoming agitated and angry at Terrance's continued questions.

"Why did you reach out to me? Why did you get me down here if you will not help me?" Terrance asked.

Frank Snorted "I wanted the money; I wanted to just get away and have a fresh start. I thought you would do your little thing and just go away." Frank paused and started to cry, "I just want to get as far away from here as I can. I needed the money to give me a chance." Frank continued.

"Can I ask you just a few more questions? Then, I promise I will leave you alone."

Frank nodded while placing his face in the palm of his hand.

"Was there something on the school property before the school?" Terrance asked.

"Yes, an old textile factory," Frank responded.

"What happened to it?" Terrance questioned.

"You need to leave. Mr. Greene, please leave my house and don't come back. I've done my part." Frank said as he got up.

"Fine!" Terrance said, frustrated that he was not getting any of the answers that he needed. As Terrance stood, he winced as he struggled to get out of the sunken couch and his back rubbed against the backrest.

"What's wrong?" Frank asked.

"Don't worry about it, I scratched my back." Terrance said as he got up and walked to the door.

As Terrance walked towards the door, Frank got up and lifted the back of Terrance's shirt.

"Yo, man," Terrance yelled at the violation of his personal space.

Frank turned as white as a ghost as he stared at the marks on Terrance's back. There were three vertical scratches on both sides of his shoulders stretching down to his middle back.

"I've damned us both," Frank said.

"What are you talking about, damned us?" Terrance asked in anger.

Frank took a deep breath and asked, "Did anything strange happen last night?"

Terrance was silent as he stared back at Frank with a shocked look.

Frank grabbed the check that was meant for his salvation and handed it back to Terrance.

"Leave! Leave this place and forget everything. Go back to Atlanta. Go back to your life. Just get out of this town." Frank said, thrusting the check towards Terrance.

"Man, don't be trying to scare me. I scratched myself in my sleep, that's all." Terrance responded with a scowl on his face.

"You need to leave!" Frank said with a scared look on his face.

"I'm not going anywhere!" Terrance said as he hastened his pace to the front door.

"I've killed us both; please forgive me, God, please forgive me!" Frank called out.

Terrance ran down the weak stairs of the porch and jumped in his car. He wouldn't openly admit it, but he felt scared. The supernatural did not scare him, but from looking at Frank, he knew Frank was terrified of something. He thought of the stories that he had heard as a child about these small towns, and now he was all alone in one.

Terrance backed his car out of the driveway and turned around, leaving the rusty trailer in his rearview mirror. He stopped at where the driveway ended on the roadway. There was no traffic, just a black truck parked down the road a bit on the side. Terrance didn't pull out right away. Instead, he considered his options. Turning left would send him back to town, and turning right would take him back towards his mother's house.

He paused for a moment. *Am I in danger here?* He thought to himself. He had done a lot of investigations, but this one was strange; it was stranger than anything he had ever seen before. Staying in Anderson meant he was alone. The lack of allies, especially in an unfamiliar area, poses a risk, especially when investigating a story that so many have covered up something. Terrance took a deep breath and once again weighed his choices. After a moment, he turned left. *If it was this challenging in the beginning, the reward must be worth it.* Terrance thought to himself as he turned and headed back to town.

Chapter 7

History Revisited

Terrance knew he had limited options today. His wasted afternoon frustrated him because he knew his time was limited. He still had eaten nothing, and his stomach was reminding him of that with low rumbles. In order to put his stomach at rest, he decided to grab a quick bite from the cafe, then return to the hotel. Terrance drove back down the nearly abandoned downtown and parked in front of the cafe. Despite being the only restaurant, it was fairly empty. *Perhaps I'm early for dinner*, Terrance thought as he entered.

The restaurant was clean, but there was a strong burning odor. There was only one employee who was visible, and she greeted him smugly. She was a plump, middle-aged woman with graying hair and what appeared to be scars from burns just above her right eye and along her right arm. She had a gruff voice that made her sound as though she had smoked two packs of cigarettes a day most of her life. Her skin was worn and leathery. Her demeanor was pleasant, but not over the top friendly. As he took his seat at a small table, he glanced towards the glass counter that featured an abundance of what seemed like freshly baked desserts.

Terrance ordered a burger and fries and then pulled out his laptop. He searched for an internet connection, only to find there was no Wi-Fi available. Despite his attempts to use the internet in his hotel room, it yielded the same result. He was becoming frustrated with this town's lack of internet, coupled with the lack of proper cellular reception. Since he could not use his technology, he began looking at the contents of the new envelope that his new friend or foe had recently shared.

Inside there were newspaper clippings, and he came across a few interesting headlines: "Mill Closes Amid Unfortunate Events", "Suicide at Carmichael Textiles", "Murder at Carmichael?", and "Occult Activity Suspected in Carmichael Murders". Terrance dove into the articles one by one. He started with the first, "Factory Closes Amid Unfortunate Events".

The article mentioned a series of tragic events that seemed to strike both members of the factory workforce and Carmichael's family. In six months, ten workers and a teenage girl had either died or were missing from the factory. One night, the entire Carmichael family and the maid turned up dead, with one missing. Following William Carmichael's suicide, with no heir, the factory closed and many of the townspeople moved off to find better opportunities.

The second article highlighted a series of accidents that claimed the lives of workers at the factory. Some were gruesome, like the story of Rhett Talmadge. Talmadge was a supervisor and had worked at the mill for over a decade. His safety record was impeccable, but one afternoon he slipped on something on the third-floor catwalk. The slip caused him to slide right through the railing and into the machine below. When they looked for the cause of the slip, nothing was ever located.

Other accidents involved objects falling from shelves and crushing an employee below. There was also a collapse of some scaffolding that killed three employees at once as they were walking from their cars and entering the factory. There were also reports of employees clocking in at the beginning of a work shift but never clocking out.

Terrance continued his search of these accidents; it all seemed to circle back to October 1967 and continued until April 1968 when the factory closed. Prior to October, there were no negative stories about the factory. The Carmichael family was "The Family" in Anderson. They were donors for many local charities, and the factory itself employed about half the town with decent-paying jobs. There was nothing negative about the factory or the family until after 1967; then, it all unraveled.

As Terrance continued to eat his burger, which was surprisingly good today, he continued diving into the information in front of him. This brought him to the next two articles. In March 1968, something else happened that seemed to shatter the quiet of Anderson; the family that was once placed upon a pedestal fell. Following his suicide, people accused Carmichael of murdering his whole family and the maid. Police could never locate his eighteen-year-old daughter's body, but someone brutally murdered the rest of them at the Carmichael House. At the factory, there was another teen's body found, but instead of his daughter's, it was Mary Pierce, her best friend from high school. Carmichael apparently shot himself that night in the factory office, but he did not leave any notes or clues. Since the suspect was dead, there was no trial, and nobody ever found a motive. It became a town mystery that haunted it for decades; that is, until fresh growth led to the bulldozing of the factory and a new high school being built.

Terrance read the final article that Lily had given him, "The Occult Suspected in Murder". It was a brief article, one that was probably discarded at the time it was written. This article seemed to point to the Carmichaels being involved in the occult and dark magic. There was even speculation that Mrs. Carmichael had started some sort of local witch coven. The article described strange symbols being written and inscribed at various locations in the factory and even in the room of Hailey Carmichael, the eighteen-year-old daughter. Police at the time seemed to discard these notions much as they would today.

Terrance took a pause. *What is wrong with this town?* He thought to himself.

He investigated further into the Carmichael family. They were founders of the community, and the family had a sprawling mansion two blocks from where he was sitting. *Interesting,* he thought as he wondered if the mansion still stood or if something had destroyed it, as it had destroyed the factory. He began trying to figure out where the house was in relation to the cafe. He was staring to analyze one clipping that showed the house for any signs of its whereabouts.

From what he could tell, it looked like an old Southern plantation. The image brought back memories of similar houses that once stood to deprive his ancestors of their freedoms. Now, there stood another, but this one had become a tomb for an entire family. The house in the picture had four large columns that supported a large gable. If this house still stood, Terrance knew it would not be difficult to find since it would be a giant mixed among farmhouses and ranches.

As Terrance was studying the image, the waitress appeared behind him to present him with his check.

"I would stay away from that place if I were you," the woman said in her rough, nearly robotic voice.

"Excuse me?" Terrance replied.

"That's the devil's house; I would stay away from that place. No one goes near it; folks here were even too scared to tear it down." The waitress replied.

"That's the old Carmichael House; why did you call it the Devil's House?"

"Because that's who lives there. It's tainted by evil; nothing good comes from that place, and never has," she replied.

"I don't believe in the devil," Terrance scoffed.

"Well, whether you believe in him, he's out there," she replied.

"What happened there?"

"Bad things." She replied.

"I've been to a lot of towns, and they all seem to have their ghost stories."

"You ever thought that, out of all those stories, maybe some are real?" The woman questioned as she placed his check on the table and walked away.

"So where is this house?"

The waitress stopped and turned back, looking at Terrance with a look of disbelief. "Weren't you listening? You just need to stay away." She said.

"I just want to drive by it. I won't do anything else, just want to see it."

"Well, if you're so stubborn, it's down off 3rd Street on the corner of Maple. You can't miss it. I would do nothing more than just drive by, don't even get out of the car." The waitress said.

"Yes, ma'am."

"I suggest you believe in this one," she continued as she disappeared behind the counter.

Terrance's grandmother was superstitious and often warned about spirits and things that wandered the earth. He always thought of her as crazy. Not since his grandmother had he seen so many people so focused on this stuff, much less in Georgia. Now he had been to Savannah, where part of the tourism industry centered on ghost walks, storytelling, and amateur ghost hunts. To Terrance, Savannah was simply a tourist trap, a money-making scheme, but here in Anderson there were no tourists. *So why are people so obsessed here?* Terrance pondered.

Terrance looked out the window. There was still a little daylight left, so he decided to take a trip a few blocks down the road and look at this old house himself. If the Dylan case was tied to the past, it was at least worth a look. *Maybe it was some type of copycat killings?* Terrance thought to himself.

He paid his check and walked out to his car. He sat in his car for a moment and gathered his bearings. There was only a small grid of streets in this town. He was currently on Main Street, with First Street being just one block up. After a quick and detailed look at his surroundings, he decided it would be a short and simple trip to the house.

Terrance made his way through the quiet streets of Anderson. He drove slowly as he calculated each turn to get him to the house. As he pulled down Third Street, he kept his eyes open, scanning for Maple Street or some grand mansion. He felt disappointed at first as he approached Maple Street. He found the lot where the house should have been, but all he saw initially was an overgrown lot with a large shadow of a house buried behind the trees and growth.

Terrance remembered the chief's warning about the school property, so he decided that parking his car on a side street would be the best choice. Just in case the threat carried over to this house, he wanted to take the extra precaution. Once parked, Terrance carefully walked over to the house itself. You could barely see the house itself through the overgrown woods that blocked it from view. However, he could see its silhouette, the columns and the gable, just like the picture he had seen earlier. He examined the best path to get to the house and finally found the easiest path with the fewest obstacles. Even better, this path led to the back of the old mansion, which would better hide him from view.

The back of the house was much like the rest; overgrowth, weeds, and trees covered nearly every square inch. He noticed what had once been a large pool in the backyard. Imagining the parties that once must have surrounded the pool, he walked slowly, examining the once beautiful backyard. There were also other structures with columns positioned around the pool that further illustrated its grand past.

He pictured the mansion when it was alive. But the picture in his mind was met with the reality of the backyard's current state. In the middle section of the pool, the once clear water was now filled with brown murky water that reminded him more of a sewer than a pool. Amid the brown muck stood a massive statue that was most likely a fountain.

Terrance imagined how he could one day perhaps own a similar estate, but his would be very much alive with parties and life that would extend well past the late-night hours. He was not typically sentimental about such things, but it brought him some sadness to see the shell of grandeur that now stood like a relic in this dying town.

After he stared at the pool and what perhaps used to be tennis courts at the far end of the backyard, he looked for a way into the house. He wanted to see for himself what secrets lay within. He found his answer with a rotten French door that had collapsed some time ago and now left wide open for anyone to enter. Terrance felt scared, not of ghosts but of wild animals and weak floors, as he began his quest by crossing the threshold.

When Terrance was a child, Lamar, his cousin, who was just a year older than him, had a treehouse in his backyard. Terrance, Lamar, and some of his other cousins would spend all day in the treehouse during hot summer days. Lamar's grandfather built the treehouse, and it seemed as old as him, but as kids they didn't care. That all changed one summer afternoon, just as Terrance climbed up the steps and hoisted his body up onto the treehouse floor. One moment he was in the treehouse with his cousin; the next he was on his side staring at tall grass in immense pain. It was the only time he broke a bone, but it is something that he has never forgotten. Since that summer afternoon, Terrance has always been very cautious, if not scared, of rotten floors. As he ventured into this house, the creaking sounds of the treehouse floor echoed in his memory.

Despite Terrance's concern, his future article motivated him to step further into the house. Once inside what must have been a family room, Terrance looked around. The smell was terrible; the odor of mildew now filled his nose. He saw furniture, or at least what used to be furniture, placed about as though it waited for the owner's return. There was even a grand piano in the corner. Terrance imagined the enormous parties that people must have once held here. Now, though there was silence, the sounds of people talking and music playing were distant memories, and only silence remained.

He looked over at the stacked-brick fireplace. The bookshelves that once stood beside it now collapsed, and a large stain of mildew seemed to grow along the wall. He carefully continued his walk inside the house, further venturing into the inner workings of this once great manor. As he walked towards the front, he noticed the grand staircase, which was now covered by spiderwebs and decades of accumulated dust.

He looked at the stairs, and he knew he wanted to make his way up them eventually, despite the hazards; he hoped to find something that explained the articles. For now, though, he kept his exploration to the bottom floor, which had already creaked and cracked enough to cause his heart to beat faster. He tried to envision where the beams and supports were underneath the floor, carefully planting each foot with precision to avoid any type of collapse.

As he continued, the smell of mold and stagnant air almost grew unbearable. Fleeting thoughts about the air quality concerned him, but his inquisitive mind kept pushing him forward. He discovered another living space, which was most likely the formal living room. Carefully, he walked to the portrait that hung over the fireplace. He could barely make out the figures in the painting because of the layers of dust, but he could see enough. It was a family picture; it looked like a happy family. Someone had posed them along some sort of couch. The man stood proudly with his woman beside him, both staring forward. On the couch sat a young woman. *Hailey,* he thought. She must have been at least sixteen in the picture. She was a brunette with long brown hair. Her face was olive complected.

Beside what he presumed to be Hailey was a younger male, probably in his preteens. He looked like an average young man of the 1960s. All-in-all, they looked like the perfect family. As he analyzed and stared at the painting, a slight noise interrupted the silence of the slumbering house. Terrance paused, and his heart sped up, accompanied by his breathing. He listened intently to identify the source of the sound. It would continue, then stop, continue, then stop as the cycle continued. The sound reminded him of what he had heard earlier when he was in the shower in the hotel room. It sounded like clawing or scratching. Then there was a silence that once again covered the entire estate. It was almost an eerie silence, not one that someone would seek for relaxation.

He backed away from the fireplace, and then the sound returned. It sounded as though it were right there with him. His heart raced again, and he tried to take in what was happening. Then, with a sudden pop, dust and some type of flying creatures poured out of the fireplace. Terrance startled, fell backwards, and his bottom struck the floor with a load thud. Now, all he could hear was flapping and his own heart racing.

"Bats!" Terrance yelled. As he stood up, he kind of laughed at himself. His heart calmed as he continued his exploration of the abandoned estate. Terrance left the living room that nearly gave him a heart attack and ventured past the dining room and stepped into what appeared to be an office. There was an old wooden desk with papers scattered about. The sun was setting, and the rooms were getting darker. So, he dug into his backpack and pulled out a small flashlight. Using the flashlight and being careful near the windows, so as not to give his presence away, he glanced down at the various papers.

Most of the papers in front of Terrance appeared to be financial records for the textile factory. Based on what he could see, the numbers looked good. There seemed to be good cash flow compared to what was outgoing. So at least whatever happened did not appear to affect the company's bottom line. Terrance looked at a few more things on the desk but could find nothing that benefited his search.

He knew where he wanted to go next, and he wasn't so eager to attempt the climb to the second floor. Everything inside him told him to stop and return to his car, but it was as if he was being led by some unseen force. He took a deep breath and ascended the staircase slowly, one step at a time. The higher he climbed toward the first landing, the more his body felt uneasy. He ignored his feelings; he was driven to find Hailey's room. Maybe there he would find some answers.

Step by step he took, treading lightly with each new ascent, slowly making progress. As he neared the top, the smell of the mildew grew thicker, and the musky air seemed to threaten to overtake him with each breath. When he finally made it to the top of the stairs, there was a short balcony that led to halls in two directions. At first, he went to the left. As he began this walk, each step he took caused the floor to creak. His heartbeat more with each step. Besides this unexplained uneasy feeling, he was also fearful that the wrong step would lead to his going back to the bottom floor by a route that he was not planning to take.

This hall ended at a set of double doors. He peaked inside, and it was the main suite with another grand fireplace, moldy ceiling, and a four-poster bed. This was not the room that he was looking for, so he turned carefully and went back in the direction that he had come. Again, taking each step with caution and ease. He once again crossed the balcony, where the stairs began and continued down the other side. There was a room on the right. He glanced inside, and it appeared to be a boy's room based on the remaining items that were scattered around.

He thought to himself as he continued to walk, *There are no signs of vandalism or anything. It seemed as if time froze it.* Coming from Atlanta, this surprised Terrance. Terrance thought an abandoned house, much less one this big, would have become a teenage hangout or home to the homeless seeking shelter, but in this house, there seemed to be no evidence of anyone's activity since they abandoned it all those years ago.

To the left, he noticed another room. *This had to be it!* He thought. As he crossed into the room, the smell changed from just the musty mildew smell to a slightly rotting smell. It smelled heavy and almost as if someone had passed gas. He couldn't quite place the smell, but as he continued walking into the room, his uneasiness continued.

It looked like a typical teenage girl's room, at least for the 1960s, he thought to himself. Flowered wallpaper differed from the peeling wallpaper in the rest of the house. Shining his flashlight on the walls, he looked for odd symbols, but there was nothing. He scoffed to himself, thinking back about the last article he had read. Glancing at the dresser, he noticed several trophies still sitting on top. He walked over to look more closely at them. *She was quite an accomplished gymnast and swimmer with multiple trophies and ribbons;* he thought to himself.

Beside the dresser was a desk with a math book still open to a page containing algebra equations. He looked around the desk more; there was nothing unusual. He slowly opened the top drawer of the desk. Instantly his heart skipped a beat as out of the darkness a small gray mouse leaped in his direction. As the mouse quickly scurried off, Terrance nearly lost his footing, but held his own. This was his second scare of the day. He was thankful for his running and good cardio health; otherwise, these scares might have given him a heart attack by now.

Once his heart calmed, and his breathing slowed, he began looking through the contents of the drawer. It contained various papers that really weren't relevant outside of the typical teenage girl's life. Then, he saw something. It was a drawing or, more of a sketch. He pulled it out and brought it closer to his flashlight so he could see it more closely. It was quite odd in the bedroom atmosphere. Everything else was upbeat, but this drawing was much darker. On this yellow faded paper that seemed to risk turning to dust just at his touch, there was an image. He could still see the sketch, though mold covered and discolored it. What he could best make out appeared to be a whirlpool, a black whirlpool, and in the center there was something coming out of it. It looked like some sort of person. *Was it a female?* He thought. The more he examined it, the more he heard something. A creak. *Was someone else here?* He thought to himself as he scanned the room.

The more he looked and shone his light about the room, the more the sound — a creaking — and the creaking increased. He couldn't see anything or anyone except himself. But the noise wasn't coming down the hall; it was right in the room with him, and it was growing loader. His heart beat again, more and more, and then without warning, there was a loud crash.

His greatest fear came true as the floor beneath him gave way, causing him to drop the picture and his flashlight as he tried to reach for anything to keep him from falling through the floor. Although he gained some traction with his arms, his feet now dangled from the hole. He couldn't feel anything underneath him, just air. He tried pulling himself up, but each time he moved again, the floor creaked more, threatening to swallow everything around him.

Now panicked, he looked down the hole and saw nothing but darkness under him. He had let the sun set while he was exploring, and now he couldn't even see where he would land if he fell. Having dropped his phone, he could see it just out of reach. He was alone; there was no one to save him, not one person he could call. Picturing himself with fractured legs rotting with the rest of this house terrified him. *No one will ever find me*! He thought to himself. His panic now grew into despair. He tried once more to use his upper body to climb, but that caused the remaining floor around to drop an inch. He stopped; he knew this might actually be his end. All he could do was hold on, but any second the rest of the floor could give way.

Suddenly he heard another creak. He closed his eyes and braced for the floor to give more. But instead of the floor collapsing, he felt a hand reaching out to him. It startled him instantly since he knew he was alone. He looked up to the unknown person now offering to help him. It was Lily! He didn't question her presence; instead, he reached for her hand. She helped him get the grip that he needed, and he dragged himself out of the hole.

"Thank you," he said, out of breath and barely able to even say the words.

"I saw your car around the corner. I had hoped you weren't foolish enough to walk into a condemned house, but here you are." She said with a smirk.

"I can't thank you enough." Terrance said, still out of breath, as he began to carefully stand back on his own two feet.

"I didn't think you believed in this kind of stuff." She said in an arrogant tone.

"I don't, but some things don't add up."

"Well, regardless, you have to be more careful. You're no good to me dead." She said, almost mocking him.

"I just want to get out of here!"

"I couldn't agree with you more," she said.

Terrance collected his flashlight, and the pair carefully walked toward the stairs and out of the back door of the house. In his haste, he forgot about the picture, but once he remembered it, he decided a sketch wasn't worth the risk. It was now fully dark outside, so they walked carefully through the brush back to the front. As soon as they walked around the front, they were blinded by a spotlight. Terrance initially thought someone had busted him, but it wasn't a police car. Rather, a pickup truck. The light moved over Terrance and stopped on Lily. Then it turned out, and the truck quickly drove away.

"I'm over this town!"

"You get used to it in time." Lily said.

The pair walked down the sidewalk and towards where Terrance's car should have been parked. As Terrance walked closer, he said, "You've got to be kidding me! Those inbreds!" The car was missing, and he was sure this was where he had parked. Lily had also confirmed it. Lily tried her best to calm Terrance down, but between his near-death experience and the now-missing car, he was furious. Terrance tried to call the police on his phone, but the signal was too weak to make any outgoing calls.

Terrance, ever frustrated, sat on the adjacent curb and just placed his hands on his face as he looked down, nearly in tears from the frustration that the night had caused. Lily sat behind him and placed her hand on his shoulder to offer him comfort.

"It's going to be okay, Terrance." She said.

"The hell it is!" Terrance responded.

"Hey, let's just go to the cafe. You can use the phone there, and we can get some coffee or something," Lily said.

"I'm really not in the mood." Terrance responded.

"Well, we can sit here and give up, or we can walk over to the cafe and call the police. At least then they can start looking for it. There aren't many Mercedes around here, so I'm sure they will find it." Lily said.

"Yeah, I'm really confident with the police here. I met them earlier." Terrance said in a sarcastic tone.

"Well, I have had my fun for the night. I'm heading to town; it's up to you," Lily said as she stood up from the curb.

Terrance looked up. "Where is your car? Can we ride in your car instead of walking? My legs are a little sore from almost dying!"

"I prefer to walk and get fresh air since everything is close, and it's back where I'm staying." Lily said with a smile.

"Where are you staying again?" Terrance asked.

"Well, not that dive of a hotel that you are enjoying right now," Lily said sarcastically.

"Where else is there?" Terrance asked.

"I'm at a family member's house down the road." Lily said.

Frustrated in the situation, Terrance said, "How am I going to get to the funeral now?" He became frustrated when he realized he had focused so much on investigating and following this story that he had nearly forgotten his family.

"Funeral?" Lily asked.

"Yes, my mother passed away. I came down here for the funeral, but I couldn't pass up checking this place out." Terrance said.

"I'm sorry to hear that." Lily said, looking down on him with compassion. "I lost my mother several years ago. It is hard." Lily said.

"We haven't been close in many years. I haven't even been home in over a decade." Terrance said, looking down towards the ground in defeat.

"I wasn't close with my mother or family either, but it is still hard. Come on, let's get off the street and go call the police about your car," Lily said while extending her hand to Terrance.

Terrance finally accepted, and the two began their walk back into town.

"So, how did you start studying the occult?" Terrance asked, trying to make small talk and deflect his frustrated feelings.

"Do you ever wonder what happens when you die?" Lily asked.

"Not really, I mean it's just lights out."

"No, it's much more than that, Terrance." Lily said.

"I told you; I'm not really into that religious stuff."

"It's not about religion, Terrance, but it is part of it. Even one of the greatest scientists said that energy never ceases, but changes form. There is more, and I've seen it. I'm just trying to bring it all together." Lily said with a hint of excitement.

"So, what do you believe?" Terrance asked.

"When we die, our bodies release our energy. We are no longer bound by physical form. What happens next is a mystery. I think some spirits move to the next plane, rather it is heaven or hell, who knows? However, there are other spirits who are damned to remain here. They simply repeat the cycle of their life and death over and over again in a form of personal hell. That's what your typical haunting is, merely the ghosts reliving the past in an endless loop." Lily said.

"So, you've seen stuff to back it up?"

"Yes, many times," Lily said.

"And you said this town is some type of hot spot?"

"Yes, the stench of death and trauma has tainted this area. It is the perfect place for my studies." Lily said.

"I would say it's tainted all right." Terrance said with a hint of frustration.

"Have you experienced anything while you have been here? Something that you can't explain?" Lily asked.

"Not really, nothing that can't be explained."

"Well, buckle up, Terrance. You're investigating things that will open you up. There are good spirits and some bad, just like they were in life. But be warned, there are some who have much more sinister goals. And you're just so scrumptious one of those evil spirits might want to just gobble you up," Lily said jokingly while grabbing onto his arm.

Lily somehow had placed Terrance at ease. Her presence, her personality, had somehow caused him to misplace his anger over the car. The two continued to walk, making small talk. As they walked, they continued to hold hands, and Terrance got to see a different side of Lily. Instead of being shrouded in mystery, she had a fun personality. So far, Lily had been the only person who had seemed honest with him. There was still some mystery about her, but tonight she had removed some of that veil and revealed herself. She even saved him from death, and now she was trying to help him and comfort him. He felt a veil being lifted away from his own heart. He felt comfortable with her and safe. It had been years since he had felt this way with a woman, but he was now ready to let her in.

They finally made it to the cafe. It was mostly empty like earlier, and the waitress looked up at Terrance as he returned and rolled her eyes. "My food so good that you back again?" she asked sarcastically.

"Someone stole my car. Can I use your phone to call the police?" Terrance asked.

"Yeah, it's around the corner by the bathrooms." The waitress said as she pointed in the general direction.

As Terrance walked around the corner, he noticed it was a payphone. He didn't have any change, so he walked back to the counter and asked, "I don't have any change. Is there a regular phone?"

"Just dial zero and ask the operator to connect you to the police." The waitress said.

"Thanks," Terrance said as he glanced over and saw Lily smiling at him, sitting at a small table in the corner.

Terrance walked over to the phone and began using the operator to contact the police. At first, the phone wouldn't even connect, but eventually he got through and reached the police department.

Though they seemed annoyed when they answered, the police assured him someone would come shortly and take a report.

Terrance came back around the corner to let Lily know the police would be there shortly, but when he glanced over to the table where she was sitting, she was gone. At first, Terrance thought maybe he had missed her walking to the bathroom, but he was sure he would have seen her pass. Something caught his eye at the top of the table. It looked like a notebook of some sort. The closer he looked; it was a diary! There on the front was a handwritten note on a napkin. *Looking for this? Good luck, L.* With nothing else to do but wait, he took the diary and settled into the seat and opened it.

The waitress walked over to ask if he wanted anything, and he ordered a coffee. As the waitress walked away, he asked, "Did you see where the young lady sitting here went?"

"I didn't see a lady, but I wasn't paying attention." The waitress said as she walked off.

Why didn't she say anything before she left? Terrance wondered. *"Lily was a different person tonight, much warmer. Did I say or do something?"* He thought to himself. Without thinking about it anymore, he continued diving into reading the diary.

Chapter 8

The Diary

As Terrance sat at the table waiting for the police and drinking his bitter cup of coffee, he looked at the time on the phone; the passing time seemed like an eternity as he waited. He adjusted himself at the table and opened the diary. *How did she get this?* He thought to himself. The book itself was in good shape. Despite the overall condition, it was old, and the pages seemed brittle. The same odor from the house permeated his senses as he opened the pages of the book. He was careful in turning each page, not knowing if each turn would cause it to fall apart. It was stained by time, and each touch could be its last.

Terrance carefully flipped through the pages, and most of the content focused on typical teenage issues. Terrance remembered his own teenage years as he scanned the content. Memories of bullying and the feeling that he was never good enough rose to the surface. He was a social outcast, never included in parties or the hijinks that made high school memorable. Instead, he was in the shadows, thankful for each day that had passed. The pages that Terrance read painted Hailey's experience as very different. She seemed to be popular and at the center of everything. It seemed like the perfect life, with not a worry outside of what to wear or which date to accept for an upcoming dance or social. Terrance was growing discouraged that the pages would reveal any secrets. As he turned to the date September 18, 1967, his reading slowed and became more intent.

Eighteen years old! I'm finally an adult! I don't feel any different, but apparently, I am an adult now. My birthday was all that I could ask for! Mary was there with Wayne. I really think that Wayne likes me, but I would never act on it. I think he's cool, but Mary has been my best friend since first grade. I think he flirted with me some, but who knows? It could be my imagination. Well, today's been a great day! I'm hopeful though that now I'm 18, the visits will stop and my torment in the shadows will end. I pray to God that things go differently. I'm an adult now! As I end my day, I pray the night brings joy.

Demons in the Night

THE EXCITEMENT OF THE house had finally drawn to a close; the faint smell of cake and ice cream still hung in the air. Hailey had just celebrated her eighteenth birthday. She stood in the driveway waving to her departing friends. Her eyes then turned to the red Ford Mustang that sat in the driveway. It was a gift that her parents had given her. Earlier, Hailey's father had hidden the keys in a box that was at least five times the size it needed to be, but it provided a challenge for Hailey to open. She was excited when she realized that embedded in two boxes within the box and through piles of shredded papers there was a key.

Now, the olive complected brunette girl with green eyes stared at her new car. The crimson red reflected in her eyes as she stood in the driveway. After her friends departed, the joy faded, and she looked at the car as more of a peace offering rather than a gift without strings attached. The relationship between her and her parents had become strained over the last few years. She felt so isolated in that house. No one to talk to and no refuge. Her parents mostly stayed out of her life. Her father was always so busy with work and the factory. She grew to resent the factory more than anything else in her life. She felt it was her father's special child and no one else could ever compete. Her mother was not much different; she was so focused on Anderson Social Life and more about what people thought outside of the house than what occurred within the cold, closed walls of the mansion.

Hailey considered the gift more show that her parents put on, rather than a present given out of love. It would not fix years of neglect, nor make things better for her in the house. It was just for show, like so much of their life. However, within her own mind, she wondered if her parents even knew what love actually meant. Her eyes moved from the car to the house; she did not like the house. There were secrets. There was a shadow, a dark shadow that had tormented her, making her life one filled with dread, shame, and hopelessness. Eighteen, maybe things would be different since she was an adult was the theme that filled her head. Maybe as an adult childhood terrors would cease just like the joyous things of a child's imagination, but this shadow was anything but joyous.

Hailey walked into the house. In the family room, her parents commented on how well the party had gone that day and who from the town had been there. Hailey walked past and ignored their commentary. She walked toward the kitchen. Inside, Bea cleaned dishes and put things away, so that everyone forgot about the party and the household could continue to operate normally. Bea was an African-American woman in her late forties. She had been with the household as long as Hailey could remember. She was plump, but her round plump face was always bearing a smile. Bea had become Hailey's confidante over the years. With Hailey's mother so focused on the social life of Anderson, Bea had been much more of a mother to her. She listened, she offered advice, and she always seemed to care. She kept the household running, but she also seemed to be the glue that kept it all together.

Hailey entered the kitchen and leaned against the counter right beside Bea.

"The cake was amazing, Bea!" Hailey said with a smile.

"Thanks, Ms. Hailey," Bea said with a returned smile.

"You always cook so good!"

"Thank you! I always put a pinch of love in it." Bea said, pinching her fingers together as she winked.

"Maybe one day you can teach me."

"Now, I don't think Ms. Hillary would like you working in the kitchen. That's not the place for a girl like you," Bea said.

"A girl like me, I wish people would just let me be a girl."

"You are a woman now, Ms. Hailey. You're a beautiful lady now." Bea Said.

"Yeah," Hailey responded.

"Why do you look so sad? All your friends left?" Bea asked.

"I don't like the night."

"Well, the sun is always going to come up, Ms. Hailey." Bea said.

"Sometimes the night is just too long."

"Is it still bothering you?" Bea asked.

"Yes," Hailey responded.

"Just keep praying; praying will keep it away. I wish you never opened that door," Bea responded.

"I've been praying; I don't think God listens anymore. At least to me," Hailey said.

"God is always listening, Ms. Hailey," Bea responded.

"I just don't know anymore. I just feel numb."

"You've been staying out of that book?" Bea asked.

Hailey looked away from Bea. "Yes," she replied.

"Ms. Hailey, some books are better left unopened." Hailey and I worry about you. My grandma used to tell me stories of what you've been reading. She told me about some family using things like in that in the old days. It's not God's book. It isn't a book you should have ever touched." Bea said out of concern.

"Thank you, but I'm good. I promise." Hailey looked defeated as she stood in the kitchen talking with Bea. Remembering the young lady who used to be so happy and full of life brought sadness to Bea. Hailey had a rough home life, and it had gotten especially difficult during her teenage years. She loved Hailey just like she was her own. She wished so many times that she could save Hailey, but she was limited by her color and station in life.

"I'm afraid that book has a haint or at least that's what my grandma used to call it, and when it comes through the door, it's hard to get rid of. That's why you need to be reading that Bible I gave you," Bea said.

"I'll be fine. I don't even read it anymore." Hailey said.

"But it's still bothering you?" Bea asked.

Hailey's mom walked into the kitchen, looking at the two in deep conversation. Hillary was not a warm or loving mother. She could be quite cold in her treatment of others. She did what she felt was best for her family, at least in the public eye. Maintaining a certain image was a top priority for her.

Hillary was always envious of Hailey and Bea's relationship and had been since Hailey was a young girl. As she came further into the kitchen, she began glaring at Hailey. Her eyes pierced through Hailey before she ever said a word.

"Hailey, leave her alone. She has work to do, and you're keeping her from it!" Hillary said as she glared into her daughter's eyes.

"Oh, she is no bother, Ms. Hillary," Bea said.

"I said you need to leave her alone, Hailey," Hillary said.

Hailey returned a similar look to her mother. "Yes, ma'am," Hailey said as she told Bea, "Goodnight" and walked out of the kitchen.

Once Hailey had left the room, Hillary turned her gaze upon Bea. "Know your place. Never try to undermine me again, is that understood?" She said with a firm tone.

"I'm sorry, I was just." Bea said before Hillary interrupted her.

"If you ever interfere with my orders for Hailey again, it will be your last day." Hillary said before she turned around to leave the kitchen.

For the rest of the evening, Hailey talked on the phone with Mary. They shared normal teenage gossip, talked about boys and who was there at the party. Mary and Hailey had one of those once-in-a-lifetime friendship. The ones where you connect with a kindred spirit. You become so synced that you know what the other person is thinking without them saying a word. It is one of those unbreakable bonds that can last a lifetime and weather many storms. Mary was the person she was closest to, and the two could talk all night despite seeing each other all day at school. Hailey tried to keep the conversation going as long as it could, to drag it on in the evening, but eventually bedtime approached. Both families went to church the next day, and even though it was the weekend, an early bedtime was the rule of the night.

Nights at Carmichael House were cold, not physically but emotionally. There were no drawn-out goodnights or bedtime stories. Hillary gave instructions for the morning, and then the door shut. Hailey dreaded most of all. This was when the house grew quiet, so quiet that each step, each settling motion would radiate through the upper floor.

It took a while, but eventually Hailey ignored the sounds long enough to fall asleep. Hoping for a peaceful night that would pass quickly and give rise to the morning. As silence fell over the house, so did a sinister shadow. The shadow crept along the long, narrow hall, almost silently as it slithered among the shadows on the wall. It slithered past her brother's room and settled in front of Hailey's door.

Hailey's door slowly crept open, and the shadow took the place where the door once stood. The slender, snake-like shadow slowly crept along the room as it approached the sleeping Hailey. It was silent and cold as it stretched its claws toward Hailey. Hailey awoke to movement in her room. She knew her hopes had ended, and being eighteen, an adult, would not stop her demon from paying its visit.

She knew what would happen next — she would lie in the bed paralyzed, and it would breathe in her ear, and then the pain would come. All the love that should have been would become absent from her room. The absence of the light gave into hopelessness, and she would become numb, wishing that she were no longer in her own body. This evil creature would come and go, and this would repeat itself in an endless cycle. She counted the days until she graduated and left this house. Maybe it would not follow her; maybe it would remain within the confines of this cold, miserable house.

As the visit continued that night, Hailey closed her eyes, and she prayed. She prayed for the power to stop her demon. She prayed for deliverance; she prayed just as Bea had told her. But this time she did not pray to God; she prayed to any force that would hear her, any force that could give her the power, any force that could give her freedom. She prayed for salvation and did not care who or what answered.

KNOCK, KNOCK, the sound pierced the silence as Terrance read. As someone tapped on the table. Terrance jumped out of his focus in the diary and back to reality as the chief stood in front of him and attempted to get his attention. His heart was beating, and he had to struggle to catch his breath. Terrance was not a skittish man, and it took a lot to scare him. However, tonight he had bats fly at him, he nearly died falling through the ceiling, and someone stole his car. This town was wearing on his nerves.

Terrance was feeling something different about Anderson, and the more he felt, the more he felt as though he was becoming caught in its trap. The secret, whatever it was, spread over decades and time. It caused a town to go from thriving to dying. It had killed and driven people insane. Now that someone had stolen his car, he felt he was in too deep now; however, despite the danger, despite the challenges, he had to see it through.

Terrance looked up and greeted the chief. The chief appeared grumpy and did not return a jovial greeting, instead giving a very brunt response. "You know we haven't had a stolen car in this town in over twenty years, now here you come and kick the beehive and start stirring up the people."

"Look, I'm almost done. Find my car, and I will be out of here tomorrow." Terrance said.

"So, where was the car last seen?" the chief asked.

"I parked around the corner from the old Carmichael House," Terrance responded. Terrance responded.

"Now! I told you not to be nosing around places. The chief paused a moment and took a deep breath before continuing, "Did you see who took it?"

"No, it was gone when I came back."

"Came back?" The chief asked.

"Yes, sir."

"Came back from where?" The chief asked while adjusting his belt.

"I was walking around the house." Terrance said, knowing that he probably just doomed himself.

"What did I tell you would happen if you started breaking the law? You know the house is condemned? It's a deathtrap. You're lucky you didn't die." The chief said in an angry lecturing tone.

Terrance looked down and said, "I know I'm sorry."

"I mean, are you people from Atlanta hard of hearing? Did all the traffic and noise cause some permanent damage to your ears and your brain?" The chief said while nearly yelling at Terrance.

"I'm sorry. I just want my car back, and I will leave."

"Well, I want you out of there, so I will not arrest you. The sooner you leave, the sooner my town will get back to normal." The chief said.

"Thank you," Terrance said with relief.

"For the record, Mr. Greene, I warned you. I was pleasant, and I warned you. I will see what I can do to get your car back, but you just need to be careful." The Chief said to Terrance, looking him directly in the eye.

"Yes, sir," Terrance responded in a quiet tone.

"I've got your tag number from earlier. I will put it into the system. There aren't any cars like yours around here, so I'm sure it will turn up. Did you see anything suspicious before it happened?" The Chief asked.

"I saw a dark pickup truck." Terrance responded.

"Well, that's harder to nail down. Almost everyone has a pickup truck down here." The chief said.

"Do you think you'll find it?" Terrance asked.

"If it means that you'll leave, I will move heaven and earth to find the thing. Most likely, someone was trying to send you a message, so it probably won't be far." The Chief said.

"Thank you." Terrance responded.

"You want a ride back to the hotel?" The chief offered.

"Sure, if you don't mind. My legs are killing me." Terrance responded.

"Alright, come on," the chief offered, motioning for Terrance to follow him.

Terrance collected his belongings and reluctantly walked out with the chief. He didn't really trust the chief, but after the fall, his legs were begging him for a break. After everything that he had been through today, he didn't think that things could get much worse.

Chapter 9

Dark Memories

The chief dropped Terrance off right in front of his hotel room. "Now, stay out of trouble, will you?" The chief said as Terrance got out of the car and began walking towards his room. "Thanks for the ride." Terrance said as he walked away. Without giving a second glance towards him, the chief pulled away as soon as the door closed.

The familiar moldy smell greeted Terrance when he entered his hotel room again. It reminded him of the house, and he wished that somewhere in this town smelled fresh like back home. He was growing tired of the stagnant air that seemed to always assault his senses. He noticed someone had made his bed and had hung the picture that had fallen back on the wall. Terrance was eager to read more of the diary, but it had been a long night, and he still could not get the smell of the old house out of his nose. Sadly, Terrance knew he would never be fully free of the smell while he was in Anderson, but he looked forward to getting a nice hot shower and feeling more like himself again

Terrance opened his suitcase and began preparing for his shower. He sat the diary down on his bed and looked forward to reading more once he got out. Terrance got everything prepared and allowed the water to run for a while. He hoped that the water would be much warmer than it had been this morning. Once he saw some steam finally rise, he got into the shower. As the water hit him, his mind circled back to the events of the day and how close he had come to being seriously injured or dead. His legs still hurt from the fall, but that was so much better than what could have been.

He thought back to his family that was gathering; *perhaps he had made the wrong turn. If I had turned right, I could have enjoyed the smell of some good food. It would've been a lot better than this smell that won't leave.* In the south, death seemed to equal food, and he knew the food would be good. He was growing tired of the food in the cafe. He was also beginning to miss his mother and family. Even though he had cast them aside for most of his adult life, they were still part of who he became. His mother loved him, and he loved her. Though he hadn't seen her in years, he would talk to her over the phone about twice a month. The reality set in, and he grew sad as the realization that those phone calls would forever be absent from his life.

What was he doing? He thought to himself as he bathed. This entire investigation was becoming more complicated and challenging than he would have ever imagined. For the first time in a long time, he felt danger, that his very safety might be at risk. His mind wandered to many things, and he thought of the diary again. He was tired, but he could not wait to open the book again and see what strange things it had to reveal. As he focused on cleaning every pore of his body, he got an uneasy feeling again. He felt as though he were being watched, but he knew there was no one else in the room with him. He tried his best to get his mind off these thoughts, but a loud crash broke the silence once again. Nearly slipping in the shower, he jumped as his entire body then clenched. Turning off the water, he quickly grabbed his towel to wrap himself. He left the confines of the warm shower only to be greeted by frigid air. Turning the corner, something startled him. Once again, the same picture that had fallen earlier was once again on the ground.

This time he inspected it, and everything seemed as it should be. The nail was secure on the wall, and the mounting brackets were secured on the back of the picture. It made little sense why this picture once again fell. Terrance left the picture on the ground and just braced it against the wall. He then decided to once again shrug off the strange events and get dressed for bed. The coldness of the room slowly dissipated. Terrance thought to himself, *No matter what, no more cheap hotels. In the future, I will drive no matter how far to get a better room.*

Warmth returned to the room once more, and Terrance's heart rate returned to normal along with the temperature. As he sat up and began looking around, the diary once again struck his gaze. He began reading the diary to satisfy his craving for more answers. He thumbed through the pages to find where he had left off, and he began reading.

Peace, I finally have peace. This book has given me answers and answered my prayers when no one else would. I feel one with the power that it holds. It warms me and provides the security in my life that I desperately need. I am a new woman, 18 and born anew. The voices inside provide me with a warm blanket. No one will hurt me ever again; my power grows. My name is in the book, and I am free!

<u>The Book of Shadows</u>

Hailey bounded down the stairs with her ponytail swaying. As she descended the kitchen staircase, the smell of morning in the Carmichael House greeted her. Bacon, sausage, pancakes, and coffee all filled the air. Bea was an excellent cook, and her breakfasts were the stuff of legend. They were the perfect start to the morning. Hailey was much chipper than normal. She was not a morning person by nature, so this was a tremendous change for her. It did not go unnoticed as Bea smiled and said, "Good morning child, you sure are in a good mood."

"Yes, ma'am, and the food smells delicious! It feels like it has been ages since I've eaten!" Hailey said with a smile.

"Ms. Hailey, what are you talking about? You got your fill at dinner last night." Bea said with a smile.

"It all tastes so good! You're an amazing cook!" Hailey said as she bounded towards the breakfast table.

She walked around behind her brother and roughly rubbed his head. "Morning, Squirt", she said as she sat beside him.

"Ouch, too rough" her brother exclaimed.

"Oh, quit being a wimp!" Hailey said as she rolled her eyes.

Hailey quickly grabbed her fill of the breakfast items. Bea looked at her and smiled as she asked, "You weren't kidding, child. Are you sure that you're going to eat all that?"

"Yes, ma'am!" Hailey responded as she devoured the items that she had collected on her plate.

The stairs creaked as her mother slowly descended with much less enthusiasm than Hailey had previously. Her mother entered the kitchen stoically. She didn't smile; she did not greet anyone with morning salutations. She simply grabbed her coffee cup and walked with it towards Bea and waited.

"Morning, ma'am!" Bea said as she grabbed the pot of coffee and quickly filled Mrs. Carmichael's cup. Without saying things or acknowledging her, Mrs. Carmichael turned around and walked to join her kids at the breakfast table.

Mrs. Carmichael sat at the head of the breakfast table and looked over at her children. When she looked at Hailey's plate and the way she was gulping her food, she finally broke her silence. "Isn't that a little much for a young lady?" she asked.

"I'm hungry!"

"Well, if you're insisting on becoming a cow, at least do it like a lady." Mrs. Carmichael scolded.

"Good morning to you too, Mother."

"Watch your tone!" Mrs. Carmichael said.

Hailey ignored her as she rolled her eyes and continued eating. "Did you just roll your eyes at me!" Mrs. Carmichael said abruptly.

Hailey continued to ignore her mother's words and ate her food quickly.

"Excuse me! I'm talking to you! Did you just roll your eyes at me?" Mrs. Carmichael asked.

Hailey slammed her fork on the table. "I can't even eat in peace!" she said as she stared back at her mother.

"You will not take that tone towards me, young lady!" Mrs. Carmichael said.

"Why? What are you going to do, beat me? Spank me again? Why don't you do it right here, Mother?" Hailey said, glaring at her mother.

"How dare you!" Mrs. Carmichael said.

"What? Scared to show your true colors, Mother?" Hailey said.

There was a silence that fell over the entire kitchen. Hailey and her mother stared at each other as though they were in a standoff. Mr. Carmichael broke the silence when he walked down the stairs and entered the kitchen, greeting his children and walking over to his wife, planting a kiss upon her cheek.

Hailey continued to eat until her plate was clean. She then jumped up and said, "Time to get ready for school," as she pushed her chair in and walked up the stairs. Mrs. Carmichael spoke up and told Hailey, "We will continue our conversation tonight!"

Hailey responded, "I'm sure we will," as she nonchalantly bounced back up the stairs.

The day went by uneventfully at school. Hailey went about her day talking to friends and flirting with the boys. It was her senior year, and she was one of the most popular girls at school. She was a Carmichael after all, from the richest family in the entire county. She was careful to avoid Mary throughout the day. It seems as of late there had become a rift in their friendship. She had grown to possess a great deal of animosity toward her former friend.

As Hailey became more confident and more aware of the world around her, some things became clearer to her, and she did not like everything that being more aware brought. Today was going to be the day of retribution, though. The stage was being set, and Mary and the others who had wronged her were going to deal with the consequences.

When Hailey came home from school, her mother was absent at a community function, as was common in the Carmichael House. The only adult, Bea, greeted the children and was sure to give them a snack and get them set to do their homework before dinner. Before Hailey dismissed herself to her room, Bea motioned for her to come over to the counter in the kitchen.

"Have you lost your mind, child? Talking to your mom like that," Bea stated.

"I'm over her!" Hailey responded.

"You know how she is; she will not let it slide." Bea said.

"A monster, yes I know what she is, but maybe she isn't the only one." Hailey said.

"What has gotten into you? Is it that book? I told you to stop messing with that stuff!?" Bea said with a stern look on her face.

"That book has set me free."

"Only one book does that!" Bea said.

"What? Your Book of Fairytales?"

"Hailey, please don't talk like that," Bea said in a concerned and soft tone.

"I'm sorry, I am glad that you are concerned about me. You know you have always been the only one who cares in this house."

"And I really worry about you. That book, your momma, baby, you're going to get into a whole lot of trouble." Bea said with tears forming in her eyes.

"She no longer scares me."

"Well, you should be! She is a very vindictive woman." Bea said.

"Things are going to be different."

"I'm really worried about you. You've changed," Bea said.

"I've grown into a woman." Hailey said.

"Ms. Hailey, please, I beg you, stay away from this stuff." Bea said, looking at Hailey with a worried expression.

Hailey turned around and walked up the stairs to her bedroom. Once she got inside, she cast down her schoolbooks and grabbed the black book that was hidden under her mattress. She began reading from its pages and chanting something under her breath. The lights in the house seemed to flicker as a breeze seemed to flow through the room. Hailey continued reciting the words on the pages, then abruptly stopped, as did the breeze and flickering lights. She looked up from the book and muttered under her breath, "We are one."

For the rest of the afternoon, Hailey brushed her hair and sat at her vanity looking at herself in the mirror as though she were in some sort of daze. She then lay down on her bed, staring at the ceiling. The afternoon gave way to evening, and voices began echoing downstairs. Bea rang a bell signaling that dinner was ready. Hailey slowly got out of her bed and walked down the stairs. She was much slower in her descent than she had been at breakfast. She said little to anyone as she took her seat at the table. Her mother was already there, as was her brother. Her father was absent, which was not uncommon. He often worked late nights at the factory or doing whatever he did.

The dinner was silent. Neither Hailey nor her mother said a word to one another. There was a storm brewing, and this was just the calm before the storm. Bea watched like a concerned meteorologist waiting for an approaching hurricane. After dinner, the children began excusing themselves from the table to work on unfinished homework and start the nighttime routine. As Hailey pushed her chair in, Mrs. Carmichael cleared her throat and finally broke the silence. "We have a conversation to finish later." Hailey turned around and looked at her mother and said, "I look forward to it, Mother."

You could see the hate in Mrs. Carmichael's eyes. Typically, no one challenged her, much less her own daughter in her own house. She didn't react in that moment, but kept her seat and kept calm for now.

Much of the night was uneventful. Mr. Carmichael still had not returned from the factory. Hailey knew what he was doing, and further hatred filled her heart the more she thought about it. She still had other, more pressing things to deal with as she got ready for bed and the lights slowly extinguished from the house. Her mother still had not had the conversation, but that was normal. Mrs. Carmichael had her way of discreetly handling those conversations, and they normally waited until the house was quiet and asleep.

Hailey got comfortable in her bed and turned off her light and waited. The house grew silent until discrete steps approaching down the hall broke the silence. Like many other times, the footsteps passed by her brother's room and closed in on her own door. Hailey had once feared these noises, but now she lay there almost eager for the door to open. She had a smile on her face as she stared out of the window.

Hailey's doorknob turned, and the door silently and quietly opened. Footsteps then entered the room and got closer to her bed. She could also hear metal clinging as it got closer to her bed. Then, suddenly, Hailey felt her sheet being ripped back as they had many other times, but this time things were different. When Mrs. Carmichael raised the belt with the metal buckle intent on striking her daughter, Hailey reacted. With the speed of a cheetah, Hailey spun around in the bed and stood up, grabbing her mother's arm, preventing the belt from swinging. She then shoved her mother into the wall.

"I'm going to kill you, little slut!" Mrs. Carmichael muttered as her back struck the wall.

Hailey had the strength of a man as she disarmed the belt from her mother's hand. "Do you know how many days I've gone to school with bruises, barely able to move after some nights?" Hailey said.

"You will be lucky to walk when I get through with you!" Mrs. Carmichael said.

"Not today, mother," Hailey said.

Hailey then took the belt and with full force swung it buckle side towards her mother, striking her left cheek, which parted some flesh with the impact of the blow. Her mother screamed out with the sudden impact and struggled to break free from her daughter's grasp.

"You will hurt us, mother," Hailey said as she glared into her mother's eyes. Her mother called out for help, but Hailey cut off her voice when she grasped her hands around her mother's neck.

"Today it ends!" Hailey said as she stared into her mother's eyes. Mrs. Carmichael attempted to kick, scratch, do anything she could to break free, but she just couldn't break free from Hailey. Mrs. Carmichael was losing the ability to struggle much more as the lack of air was affecting her abilities.

Hailey remained quiet as she just stared into her mother's eyes until life slowly drained. She smiled as the last spark dimmed and her mother's body became lifeless. Hailey then let go, and her mother's lifeless body dropped to the floor. Just then, Bea rushed into the room, hearing the noises and screams. She looked at Mrs. Carmichael on the floor and Hailey standing over her.

"What have you done, Ms. Hailey?" Bea asked.

"We ended it." Hailey said.

"I've got to call the police. I love you, but this isn't right. This isn't you!" Bea said, screaming at Hailey.

With a blank stare towards Bea, Hailey said in a deep, raspy voice. "If you aren't an ally, then you are an enemy." Hailey walked towards Bea and, before she could react, Hailey struck her on the side of her face and head with so much force that it knocked her back where she lost consciousness. "I still have work to do," Hailey said.

Hailey then walked into her brother's room, where he was cowering on the floor by his bed.

"What's going on, Hailey? I'm scared!" he said.

"It's okay; Mother had an accident."

Her brother rushed over to her, and Hailey welcomed the embrace. "You know how many beatings I've gotten over the years because of you? You would torture me to the point I lost it, and then I would get beaten by mother. I know you heard it. I know you lay in this room and laughed." Hailey said as she tightened her embrace of him.

"I didn't mean it. I didn't laugh, I promise!" her brother said.

"Liar, liar, pants on fire," Hailey said with a childlike whisper.

When she was content, Hailey left his room and his now lifeless body. As she walked past her room, Bea had regained some consciousness. "This isn't you, this isn't you, Ms. Hailey!" Bea yelled towards Hailey.

"You're right!" Hailey said in a whisper. "We are one."

"Please, Ms. Hailey," Bea said.

Hailey then leaned down, looking at the woman who had listened to her and cared for her since she was a child. Bea had been the mother that Hailey did not otherwise have, but Hailey was now numb to compassion. The only emotion she felt was anger. Hailey's expression did not change as she reached down and silenced her onetime confidante. Bea's body fell like the others, lifeless upon the floor.

Hailey then stood straight and walked down the hall towards the stairs. The house was quiet now; no noise except the sound of Hailey's steps existed. All life had perished, and only death and darkness now filled the once bustling halls of Carmichael House. Walking through the kitchen, once home to her daily talks with Bea, she found it silent. She walked out of the kitchen and out of the house, her steps intently directed to her waiting Mustang. She calmly entered the car, cranked it, and left the house that she had called home all her life, never to return.

As Hailey's car entered the parking lot of her father's factory, only two vehicles remained. One belonging to her father and the other that she knew all too well. She exited the vehicle and lit a cigarette, and she casually walked towards the side door of the factory. Looking up at the second floor, she could see the lights on in her father's office. She exhaled the smoke from her mouth and extinguished the cigarette on the ground as she quietly entered the building.

With the quietness of a ninja, she scaled the metal staircase leading towards the landing where her father's office was located. She could hear sounds coming from her father's office, but the occupants could not hear her approach. She silently crept upwards, emotionless and without making a noise. As she approached her father's office, she listened and heard the sounds that she was expecting. With a quick jerk, she swung the door open, and it clashed. There she stood, peering downward at her father, who was in a passionate embrace with Mary.

Hailey feigned emotion and yelled out, "How could you! I hate you both!". She then ran out of the office towards the catwalk, leaving her father and Mary both shocked. Mary got up from the floor and gathered some of her scattered clothes. She then ran after Hailey screaming, "Hailey, please wait! It's not what you think!"

Hailey stood faking tears with her back towards the office overlooking the factory floor. Mary was crying too as she approached

Hailey. "Please, it's not what you think. He loves me; we are in love!" she said.

Hailey, still with her back towards Mary, raised her head from her hands and said, "You're an idiot! You are just another conquest to him. He doesn't know how to love anyone but himself."

"I promise it's not like that. I didn't mean to hurt you!" Mary said.

Hailey slowly turned around with a dry face and devoid of any emotion. "Well, you did. You were like a sister to me, and you betrayed me. And for what? Some old, wrinkled man."

"I'm sorry, I love you, Hailey," Mary said in tears. Mary closed her distance between her and Hailey as though to offer some comfort.

"You lie, Mary! You have been jealous of me and my family for years. Let me tell you a secret: we are all monsters! The life that you've yearned for is a fraud. We are all monsters." Hailey said.

"No, I love you. I never meant for you to get hurt!" Mary said.

Hailey took a step towards Mary. "Well, I mean for you to get hurt!" she said as she grabbed Mary from under her arms and lifted her.

"Stop! What are you doing?" Mary screamed.

"Goodbye, Mary", Hailey said as she raised Mary higher until she had just enough clearance for the railing, then she gave that push from under Mary's arms that caused her to go over the railing, falling to the factory floor.

Mary screamed as she felt the force push her over, then she went lifeless as she landed on the factory floor. Mr. Carmichael stood at his office door in shock at what he witnessed. Hailey then looked over towards him with eyes as lifeless as an attacking shark. She then began her deliberate, yet seemingly emotionless walk towards her dad. Her face was as blank as her eyes, and she kept her steady footsteps in his direction.

Mr. Carmichael did not know what to think, but he had just watched his daughter murder his lover. Now she headed in his direction, so he backed away from the door frame. He turned and ran to his desk, where he retrieved a silver revolver. He checked the gun to ensure it was loaded, then aimed it at the door. Hailey approached the door and stopped just before entering.

"Love you too, Father", Hailey said as she stared at her father, who was now just about trembling.

"What have you done, Hailey?" he said to her.

"We took care of business, Father."

"Took care of business, you killed that girl!". He yelled.

"No, Father."

"I saw you! You killed her!" He said.

"No, you killed her father."

"You're crazy!" He yelled.

"Mother found out."

"Mother found out and was going to divorce you. Can you imagine the scandal of Mr. Carmichael cheating on his wife with a high school senior? You would lose everything."

"She..." he said before Hailey interrupted him.

"You couldn't have that, Father. So, you killed them all, Mother, Mary, Tom, Bea, and me. Pull the trigger, Father. Finish it!" Hailey said.

"Them all?" Her father said in disbelief.

"Yes, all dead."

"You monster! You monster!" her father said as he walked closer to her with the gun remaining pointed at her.

"Yes, pull the trigger! Finish it! Make the story complete; Carmichael Kills his Family and Lover."

"You're crazy! You did it! How could you?" Her father said as he continued to close.

"Who will believe that? Especially with my lifeless body lying here. Pull the trigger, Father."

"You...you..." Mr. Carmichael said now within pointblank range.

"It's easy to pull it; just do it! It's easy to stare into their eyes as they take their last breath."

Mr. Carmichael was now shaking between fear and anger. He wanted to kill her, but he still saw his daughter standing in front of him. Not some killer, but the girl that has been part of his life since she was born. So, instead of pulling the trigger, he took the butt of the gun and struck Hailey in the side of her head.

Hailey fell to the ground immediately after being struck. She landed on all fours and began laughing in a maniacal, fierce tone. "There is no way out for you, Father. You killed them all, what you did to that poor girl, and you killed your own daughter when she walked in on you." She said as she continued to laugh.

"You're going to the nuthouse! You crazy bit.." her father said, before Hailey interrupted him.

"No, I'm walking out of here the only survivor." Hailey said as she regained her feet and stood up, staring at her father and stopped laughing.

"The hell you are." He said before Hailey once again broke in.

"You're going to kill yourself. That's the only way out. There is no other way. If you walk out of here, you're a dead man anyway. Everything will come to light! Hailey said as she turned her back on her father.

"Who are you?" he said in confusion.

Hailey stopped and turned around. "We are many. Many names I have. Now, finish this. It is the only way this ends," Hailey said as she walked away.

Her father shook with the gun in his hand. He turned it towards Hailey as she descended the steps. *No, she's right. No one will believe she could kill everyone. If I kill her, they will all point back to me.* He thought to himself.

"Sin equals death, Father. Go ahead and pay your dues," Hailey said as she slowly disappeared in the shadows on the factory floor.

He stood there with the gun in his hand. No matter what she said, he could not bring himself to shoot his daughter. He kept seeing images of the child he once held. He turned the gun toward himself. *She is right. I'm already a dead man. Everything I built, my reputation, everything will be nothing.* He thought to himself.

Hailey stopped just in the shadows and waited. Then it happened. One single gunshot was fired, followed by the sound of metal hitting the floor, followed by a louder organic thud. Hailey smiled and walked out of the factory to her car.

Hailey arrived back at her house. She walked into her bedroom, passing the lifeless bodies on the floor. Under her bed, she grabbed a large black book with a worn cover and stowed it in her arms. She then walked out of the bedroom and back outside.

Free! We are finally free. Now, this world will burn.

Those last words: they struck Terrance as he finished reading the diary in disbelief over what he had just read. Abruptly closing the diary, he sat it down beside him. He leaned down, still shaking his head. He had investigated things in the past, but this disturbed him. This wasn't even the case he was investigating, but it haunted him more than the murdered students that had beckoned him to Anderson. *How did the police not find this diary?* He thought to himself.

Chapter 10

Darkness Returns

The night was growing late, and Terrance's body ached from nearly falling to his death. His lower back and legs burned from the experience. Terrance felt tired from the lack of sleep the previous night. Reading the diary left him mentally drained. His brain bounced around and desperately tried to make sense of the words he read. The diary challenged his thoughts as it challenged his boundaries of the natural world and the nonexistent supernatural.

He tried to rationalize the diary as the words written by a crazed teenage girl, but the text of the diary had taken him down an unexpected road. As his body and brain ached, he found himself too tired to endure his sense of reality being further tested. Now, he struggled to keep his eyes open or to find a comfortable position to sit.

Terrance knew he had a busy day ahead of him. Time was running out for him to get the information he needed for his work. His car was missing. *I hate this place. These incompetent cops will never find it.* He thought to himself. He found comfort only in thoughts centered on the rewards of his findings. *Maybe they will make this into a movie. That would make it all worth it,* he thought to himself. Most of his work had been articles that were sold to local media outlets, but perhaps this would be his chance to own all the work. Right now, those positive thoughts were all that brought him comfort.

Terrance began to stand and walk around the room, turning off some lamps until only one remained by his bedside. To dull the pain of his aching body, he walked over to his overnight bag and retrieved a bottle of ibuprofen. He needed a good night's sleep, and he did not want pain to distract him from it. Once he had taken the medicine, brushed his teeth, and gazed in the mirror, he was finally ready.

He walked over to the creaky bed and tried to find a comfortable position before he turned off the final lamp and began his path to slumber. At first, he lay on his back and stared through the darkness at the popcorn ceiling in the room. He still focused his mind on the mansion, the diary, and Hailey. Slowly though, his thoughts slowed, and the pain in his back and legs numbed just enough to provide some comfort. His breathing slowed to calm, deep breaths, and he was on the threshold of sleep.

The room was silent. There were no sounds of passing traffic, footsteps, or even the nightly cadence of the nocturnal insects. It was silent and restful. A peace fell into the room, and the peace of the night took Terrance to the last steps into his deep sleep. The sound of Terrance snoring slowly replaced the silence.

THE SILENCE AND PEACE that had filled Terrance's room were absent in Frank's trailer. He was once again in his spot on the chair, watching the local news and adding more used beer cans to the collection that was piled on the floor. Frank was tired too; he was ready to leave this town. He was ready to experience a freedom that he had not in quite some time. Yet, something still held him here in Anderson. Perhaps the ties to the past, the few good memories that still lingered against a backdrop of shadows.

Frank looked around the darkened living room and into the kitchen. Trash, food boxes, beer cans, and everything else one could imagine littered nearly every corner. He had a path that led him to key rooms like the kitchen and bathroom. He didn't use the bedroom much anymore; his chair was his bed most nights. So, once you passed the bathroom, the trail got dodgy and more difficult to navigate to the unused rooms.

He remembered his wife; *she would be disappointed in me,* he thought to himself. *I had such a future; now I'm just the town drunk,* he continued to think silently to himself. He didn't know how she did it, but she kept everything in order. She worked as much as he did and spent so much time with his daughter, but somehow, she kept the house in such good shape.

Frank continued to reminisce. *The house would always smell fresh with a lemon scent in the air. There would be no trash littering the floor.* He took a deep breath. The smell and stench that flowed throughout the trailer differed from the fresh lemon odor when she was alive. Frank looked down at himself, his clothes, and the mess that surrounded him. *I hate who I've become;* he thought silently to himself.

Not that Frank was a lazy man. He was once a hardworking man with many skills. Aside from being a great police officer and detective, Frank was also quite a good carpenter. At his old house, he had an old barn that was like his workshop. His wife would give him a list of things she needed fixed, and he would make it a mission to get it done on his days off. It was like a challenge for him to complete. She kept a clean house for sure, but Frank kept the yard, cars, and the structure of the house equally immaculate.

He remembered the playhouse that had once sat in his backyard. His daughter wanted one so that she could play house and host tea parties. So, for her birthday one year, he spent three weeks working in his barn assembling it piece by piece until it all came together to resemble their own house. Though much smaller, he even built it with a gable and small porch to look more like their house. He kept a tarp on it as he put the final touches on it until it was time for his daughter to see the completed work.

Frank thought back to that birthday when he revealed the gift. The eyes of his daughter lit up, and a smile stretched across her face as she jumped for joy, barely able to contain her excitement. She played in that house all day, and that was not the end. Frank was invited over many times to join his daughter for tea parties and even help her with her family of dolls. *Just to have that time back,* Frank thought. On days he was in the backyard cutting the grass, she would stay in the playhouse. She would even meet him as he passed by on the lawnmower with imaginary lemonade on a hot summer day.

Not only were the old house and old life so much cleaner, but they were also full of life, full of joy. Now, this life was devoid of those things. Now, his life was only pain and darkness. Frank continued to drink his beer and chain-smoke cigarettes, hoping to numb his own pain. Unlike Terrance, he could not find the peace to fall asleep regardless of how tired his body and mind had become. He continued to remember the highlights of his old life as the television continued to play in the background.

TERRANCE'S SLEEP SLOWLY came alive with dreams. He dreamed of his homecoming. The excitement of his whole family celebrating his return. He was the one who finally made it! After generations had lived in the same area since the days of slavery and sharecropping. His family was still bound to a generational cycle of poverty, and most never finished school. They would become pregnant early and enter the workplace in menial jobs. Others would get involved in a life of crime and spend their lives as part of a system that instituted its own form of slavery. Despite everything, Terrance had made it! He had defied the odds, and he had broken the cycle of poverty for at least himself.

Dreaming of his welcoming, he was a hero; he was a success! His life was a beacon proving that someone could break the chains. He had never stopped working hard, and even now he was further pushing himself to become more of a success. Even though he had no intention of making deep connections with his family again, he welcomed their celebration and perhaps even envy.

Throughout his childhood, he was not a strong or athletic child. He was tall and skinny and lacked the skills for sports or pretty much anything with his hands. He was smart, though. Where others struggled, he could conquer the most difficult math and literature with ease. People never celebrated him much as a child, but now they celebrate him as a man.

When he walked into the kitchen, everyone smiled and greeted him as if he were a celebrity. Outside, the kids stared in awe at his Mercedes parked among old cars and beat-up pickup trucks. In the kitchen, the sweet tea of his childhood and some of the best fried foods one could ever eat greeted him.

His cousins stood around him, hanging on every word about his life, his conquests, and his condo in Midtown Atlanta. They were envious of his life. He was relishing his celebrity treatment, but the kitchen began to change and take on a life of its own. It slowly changed from the humble kitchen of his mother's house, and before he knew it, he was back in the mansion of the Carmichael House. This time, though it was not in a state of decay and rot. He was in the kitchen, which was full of life. The smells were not much different from those of his mother's. Bea was working feverishly over the fried chicken in the skillet.

A young boy sat at the table reading comics with an action figure in his hand as he attempted to play out the events that he was reading. A girl walked down the stairs and quickly joined him at the table after she gave Bea a hug and complimented her cooking. Terrance was there like a ghost, invisible, yet the environment interacted with him. The smells, the sounds, all filled his senses. As Bea finished cooking, the girl, Hailey, talked with her about all the drama of the school day. Terrance looked at Hailey; she was just like the pictures he had seen. She seemed so full of life and happy. This was in stark contrast to the girl he had met in the diary. Bea explained both parents would be out tonight for various reasons, so it was just them tonight.

They talked at the table. Hailey gave her brother a hard time, as any older sibling would, with Bea reminding her to be kind. Though the crowd was smaller than at the previous kitchen, it was still full of life. As Terrance watched as a silent observer, the night grew darker, and the kitchen became quieter as Hailey and her brother departed on separate paths, leaving Bea to clean up the remaining mess.

Once everyone had left, Terrance watched Bea sit down in the chair previously occupied by Hailey. She bowed her head and began praying. At first, he could not hear her words, but slowly the words became louder.

"Oh sweet Jesus, keep my girl safe. Protect her from evil. God, please keep my baby safe. Keep the devil out of this house and protect us from evil. God, please keep her soul clean and pure and protect us, sweet Jesus."

Terrance was transported from the peaceful kitchen to Hailey's room. The same room that had nearly claimed his life. Now though, the floors were secure, and the room was fresh with pink paint and floral wallpaper covering the walls, with a bed covered by a nearly matching spread. At a vanity, Hailey sat staring at the mirror. The smile that existed downstairs was no longer there. She had taken her ponytail down and now brushed her hair. After she finished brushing her hair, she walked over to grab something from under her bed.

After she bent down and fumbled, she brought out two candles and a black book. She went back to the vanity and cleared the top so that the candles and book would be at the center. Walking over to the door, she ensured it was locked. She grabbed her purse on the way back to her vanity and sat back down. From her purse, she pulled out a lighter and a pack of cigarettes. She then took out a cigarette and lit it.

Hailey continued to stare at herself until she looked down at a picture stuck to the mirror. It was a picture of her and a young woman Terrance assumed was Mary. The more she looked at Mary, the more her eyes filled with tears. "Mary must think me so stupid not to know." She said out loud to herself.

Extinguishing her cigarette, she opened the black book. She then took out her lighter again and lit the candles. Opening the book, she read. She closed her eyes and began chanting something under her breath. It was inaudible to Terrance at first, and what he could hear sounded like another language. Slowly, things changed in the room. Terrance could not explain it, but it felt as though someone else had entered the room. Yet, there was no visible presence — just him and Hailey.

He heard her words break out of an unrecognizable whisper. "Come, my darkness, take my pain, take me from the light and fill me. I am your servant to make this world pay. Use me as your vessel and write my name in the Book of Shadows, fill me with your energy and take away my pain," Hailey said while gazing into the mirror.

Just then the candles flickered, and an icy breeze moved through the room. Hailey's eyes moved to fear temporarily as she felt an energy strike her, but calmness soon replaced the fear. Terrance couldn't take his eyes off of her. He stared at her through the mirror, into her eyes. They slowly changed to pitch black, and she smiled.

Suddenly, she turned, now facing where Terrance stood. She stared directly at him as if she were actually seeing him. "Join me, Terrance!" she said as she stood and grabbed onto Terrance's arm. "Join the darkness and let your hate and pain go!" She said.

Terrance tried to back away and said, "No, get away from me!"

Hailey would not break her hold. "You belong with us. The darkness calls to you, and you know it. You can feel it stirring. You will finally be at peace, able to rest." She said in a calm, unchanging voice.

"No, get away."

"I know you are in much pain. It can all go away," Hailey said.

"Who are you?" Terrance asked.

"I am many. I am you," Hailey said as she grabbed Terrance's head and pulled him onto her lips and began kissing him.

As she began kissing Terrance, he tried to pull away, but he couldn't resist her grip. Those lips felt so familiar; he knew them, and he realized they were the same lips from last night. Terrance continued to fight against Hailey's strength, but he was just too weak to fight her.

FRANK FELT THE EFFECTS of all the beer that he had consumed. They had finally numbed him and relieved him of some of the pain that beckoned in his heart. As he drifted to sleep with the television still playing, the temperature of the room dropped. It went from comfortable to nearly freezing. The sudden drop in temperature seemed to jolt Frank out of an impending sleep.

As he looked around, something startled him. The smell of burning metal overcame the trailer's smell as the air turned icy. He felt the loneliness depart as he felt something else come into his trailer. He preferred the lonely feeling to this one. This was part of his daily ritual, a fight that came every night. He had long fought this battle against the unseen forces that haunted him, but he was tired of fighting.

Frank was tired, tired of feeling the pain of life, and tired of fighting. He could feel the air get stiffer, and the light beside his chair flicker. Images of his wife and daughter, Christmases, birthdays, the first day of school, his wedding—all these images of his former life - flooded his mind. "Leave me alone!" he shouted through the trailer. But the images wouldn't relent. He could have sworn that in the trailer he saw an image of his daughter physically there, smiling at him.

Then it was all gone — the memories that flooded him and the cool air. Frank sat there in his torment, panting as he woke back up from would have been the needed sleep. The sound of small feet running down the hallway suddenly broke the silence. He also heard the distant sound of a child's laughter.

Then he was back at the playhouse. He was sitting on a small chair at a small table. He had to hunch down to avoid hitting his head. Again, he heard the laughter; she smiled at him carrying a tray filled with cups. She sat across from him and passed him a cup of imaginary tea. "It's been so long since you've played with me, Daddy, I've missed you", she said with a smile.

YOU'RE NOT REAL, YOU'RE *not real*, Terrance said to himself as Hailey's lips locked onto his. He struggled to regain himself and break free from his captor. Though part of him did not want to break free.

Hailey broke her kiss with Terrance. "Not real? Yet, I'm here." She said in a sensual tone.

"I do not believe this! It's a dream," Terrance said.

"Maybe, yet here I am," Hailey said as she stared at him now with normal-looking blue eyes.

"None of this. I don't believe in none of this!" Terrance said, trying to pull away.

"We believe in you, Terrance," Hailey said as her eyes went black and she once again latched her lips onto his.

She broke her lips from his. "Now give yourself to me!" she said as she latched her lips back on his.

"YOU'RE NOT REAL", FRANK said as he looked back toward his daughter.

"Why do you hate me, Daddy?" she replied.

"I don't; I love you." Frank responded.

"Then why did you let me die?" she said without breaking eye contact.

"I...I...didn't..." Frank stammered.

"You could've saved me, but you let me die, Daddy." She interrupted.

"No, I would never..." he responded

"But you did, and now you won't even play with me anymore. You hate me! You hate me!" she said with anger.

"No, I loved you!" he said.

Then he was back to sitting in his old chair in his house. His eyes filled with tears. No matter how much he tried to numb his pain, he could never escape.

"Play with me Daddy, come with me and play." His daughter's voice echoed through the trailer.

Frank wept into his hands with those words echoing through his trailer. He felt defeated. These nightly battles were taking a toll on him. No matter what he tried, the ghosts always came back. He wept at his defeat.

The sound of something metal clanking as it fell onto the floor echoed through the silence. He jumped and raised his tear-filled eyes out of his hands and looked to see what had fallen. There at his feet was his gun. It had somehow fallen to the floor and now sat by his right boot. *Salvation*, he thought to himself.

SHE BROKE HER LIPS from his and looked at him with longing eyes. "Terrance, give yourself to me. Give yourself to us. All the pain will go away. Let us have you." She said as she quickly had her lips rejoin his.

Terrance's mind stirred. *What was happening? This is just a dream,* he thought to himself. Hailey was correct; he felt pain each and every day. He would never show it to the outside world, but he was a broken man. All that he had accomplished in his life has merely a façade to hide behind. Now, he just wanted to let go of it all.

Then the door to Hailey's room burst open and there stood a black woman wearing a hat and a long dark dress. Terrance jolted as he broke from Hailey's lips. He turned to get a better look. At first, he thought it was Bea from downstairs, but as he looked closer, the figure was much more familiar. Her dark hair with gray streaks, her face was that of his mother's. She looked at Terrance and showed a disapproving face he had not seen since he had left home for Atlanta. She then looked up at Hailey and yelled, "Get behind me, Satan! Be gone, Demon in the name of Jesus Christ!"

Hailey backed away from Terrance and stared at him. "We aren't done yet!" she said, and then she was gone. All that remained in the room, which had now turned from the pink-filled room back to the one that nearly claimed his life, was him and his mother.

"Get your mind right, boy! The Devil prowls like a hungry lion." She said. Just then, Terrance awoke, jolted from his sleep by a bright light and loud clash of thunder as the thin curtains and walls couldn't contain the sounds and scene of the storm outside.

Terrance breathed heavily as he sat up in the bed. He felt heavy as he tried to make sense of what had just happened. The thunder continued to clash outside as he tried to get his bearings and wake up from yet another sleepless night.

FRANK LEANED DOWN AND grabbed the gun that had fallen. As he had done many times, he examined the gun, the contours, every single detail. He then wept. He wept for his daughter, his wife, and himself.

"Play with me, Daddy," echoed through the trailer.

Frank continued to cry, with tears falling freely down his cheeks, but now he pulled his head back up from his hands and stared at the gun. He turned it towards himself and studied the barrel of the handgun. Something then caught his eye. In front of him stood his daughter, smiling at him. As he looked at her, then at the gun in his hands, she looked at him and said, "Play with me, Daddy." He looked at the gun again and back at her. She looked at him and nodded with a smile. Frank turned his attention back to the gun and stared at the darkness of the barrel, all the light disappearing in its blackened chamber.

A bright flash, immediately followed by a sound like thunder, echoed through Frank's trailer. Then there was another noise that stirred within the trailer. It was the loud thud as Frank's lifeless body fell onto the living room floor, clashing against the trash and sea of beer cans. Frank's pain was gone for now. Silence filled the trailer as it had many times before. Outside, the storm continued to rage as the wind howled, the lightning flashed, and the thunder roared like a hungry lion ready to devour anyone in its path.

Chapter 11

The Sun will Rise

The storm gave way to the rising sun, which filled the room with beaming rays. Terrance could never fall completely asleep again. He got a few moments of light sleep between the intermittent blasts of thunder, but he never fell asleep deep enough to dream again. Frustrated by the lack of sleep, he finally got out of bed. The ibuprofen had worn off, and the pain in his back and legs had once again returned.

He knew he was running out of time before he needed to go to his mother's funeral. So that he could do the rest from the comfort of his home in Atlanta, he needed to put the last pieces of this story together. He was looking forward to leaving and returning home for peace that had been elusive in Anderson. He looked forward to sleeping without dreams that challenged his belief in reality. Investigating the Carmichael House of the 1960s was not his purpose here; He thought that the Carmichael House could be another story for a later time, but for now he needed to focus more.

He felt heaviness in his stomach and dread in his heart as he walked from the parking lot of the hotel towards downtown. There was a coolness in the air as he strolled along the mostly abandoned streets of Anderson. As he walked by the empty storefronts, he took the time to examine them more intently.

Though most of the town now sat abandoned, there were indications that the life of the town had not been extinguished that long ago. In some of the old storefronts, sales signs still hung, barely plastered in the windows. But once he glanced past the signs, all he saw was emptiness. It was the same feeling that was taking him over. He wondered, *Am I like these abandoned storefronts?* On the outside — the brick, the structure, the signs all showed some signs of life, but on the inside, they were truly empty.

Had he been working so hard to find fame and glory that he was just masking his own emptiness? He was in his thirties; he had no family, no wife or girlfriend. His list of friends was limited to work contacts. His social media pages showed many fans but not friends. He thought to himself, *Do I even have any real friends?*

He had long since buried the reason for this emptiness deep behind the walls of his own creation. People disappoint and fail you, so he did not need them in his life. He had no interest in digging more into his past; he would rather continue his journey into the past of Anderson. The lives of the people who lived here and the lives of the few that remain. Perhaps keeping busy was his own way of keeping away his own demons. Yet, this town had somehow seemed to bring the things that he had long since buried subconsciously to the surface. Now he threatened once again to unearth a deeply troubling time in his own life. He was used to unearthing others' secrets, but he did not like that his grew ever closer to the surface.

Terrance continued to walk towards his target. There it was! A large and dark brick structure. Unlike most of the town, this one showed some life, though by no means was it thriving. He walked ever closer as he did; he looked up at the steeple. It had been years since he had walked through the doors of a church, yet here he was. He was not doing this for peace or any type of spiritual awakening. To learn more about Dylan, he wanted to meet the preacher, perhaps even speak to Reverend Davenport. He knew he would have to navigate this interaction cautiously if he wanted it to be productive. So, in order to further his purpose, he walked up the three steps and through the door of Anderson First Baptist.

Inside, people greeted him with suspicion and unwelcoming looks. The smell that welcomed him was equally unwelcoming; it was a hint of mold mixed with the burnt smell that reminded him of the cafe he had previously visited. As he moved toward a pew in the back, he thought, *why does everything in this town smell like this?* Once he sat down, no one approached him to greet him. After the initial stares, they seemed content to just ignore that he was even there. Congregants did not fill the church. There were maybe fewer than twenty people present; most of them were older as gray and white hair seemed to dot across the pews leading to the altar. There was no choir, just one elderly pianist who was playing vaguely familiar tunes on the piano.

The preacher was an older man, perhaps in his mid-sixties. His hair, what remained was graying just like the rest of the congregation. He wasn't heavy set, but not quite fit either. Wearing a dark gray suit, he sported a light blue tie. He sat on the front pew, perhaps in prayer as the elderly pianist continued to play her introduction.

The service began with the congregation singing old hymns from the hymnal. It was nothing special, nothing moving; it was like it was just expected. Terrance was not one to pretend, so when he held the hymnbook, he did not sing. He did not want to sing songs that gave praise to some fictional entity that he had no use for in his life. That was one thing that bothered him most about religious people. The hypocrisy, they come into a building just like this, but once they leave, they become something so much different. He had no use for show or fakeness, and in his mind the church was one of the worst offenders.

Eventually, the singing gave way to prayers. Again, Terrance did not take part, though he acted respectfully to those who did. After prayers and announcements of supper plans for two weeks away finished, the preacher took his place at the pulpit. He looked tired and worn as he slowly walked up the steps to the pulpit.

As the worn preacher took to the pulpit, he began his sermon:

As most of you know, this will be one of the last sermons I preach here. I have loved serving you and the Lord for the past forty years, but like all good things, it must eventually end. As I get ready to turn the page to a new chapter of my life, I want to share a message about chains.

We all know that the Lord Christ Jesus is a chain breaker. He will break away the bonds of sin that keep us tied to pain and suffering, but we have to let Him. He will not do so on His own, but only if we allow it! Join me as we turn to Revelation chapter three, verse twenty. The Word tells us, 'Behold, I stand at the door and knock; if anyone hears My voice and opens the door, I will come in to him, and will dine with him, and he with Me.'

Nowhere in this scripture do you see He will come in and bulldoze the door, but we must open the door. It is a two-step process; we open the door, and He dines with us! He heals us! But we must open the door. But let me warn you, there is another who knocks at the door. This one seeks to destroy and bind us. Who will you let in?

There are two chains that often bind us! The chain of sin that we created and the chain of sin that others created. The Blood of the Lamb will break the chain of sin. But we must surrender it, repent of it, and He will forgive us. That is the easy chain to break! The second is much harder. Just as He forgives our sin, we must forgive the sins of others. No matter how much they hurt us, we have to forgive each other!

Here is the danger: if we cannot forgive the sins of others, the wrongs that they have created, then their sin becomes our own. For so long, this town has been bound by a chain, we could not forgive. We forgive ourselves, but we cannot forget the other. Failing to forgive our brothers and sisters opens the door for sin and evil. As we know, sin equals death! Folks, we must forgive! We must free ourselves! We must answer the door and allow Jesus to break our chains!

The sermon continued, focusing on letting go and forgiving each other. Regarding the freedom that is possible after breaking free. The sermon included words like abundant life and peace. There were a few hymns sung and an altar call, and at ten minutes before twelve the service ended with the preacher's closing remarks.

I will not stand here and say that I have never been in bondage. I have been a slave to sin like many of you, but I made a choice! I make a choice to forgive, a choice to be free. Part of this choice leads me to other places. It has been an honor serving you! I pray that you all have abundant lives, and I leave you with this. He knocks at the door; will you answer?

The service ended, and people slowly exited the church toward the back. The preacher stood at the door shaking hands and giving hugs to some ladies who were quite emotional. Everyone seemed to ignore Terrance as they left. He stayed in the seat, but not in reflection. His heart was still too hardened to have the preacher's words take any effect. Instead, he waited until the small crowd departed so that he could have a few words with the preacher. He felt bad about ambushing the man, but he needed to talk with him, and this might be the only opportunity he had to speak with him.

As the small crowd finally dispersed, Terrance gathered his belongings and began to stand and walk towards the end of the pew. He looked up and found the preacher standing in the aisle, looking at him, which startled him. The preacher extended his hand and said, "Mr. Greene, I assume?"

"Yes, sir, I'm Terrance Greene," he said as he shook the preacher's hand.

"I was wondering when I might see you. I'm Jack Davenport, a pleasure to meet you," the preacher said.

"I'm sorry to just show up here; I just didn't know when I might catch you."

"I know what you want to talk about, and this isn't the right time. I've got to meet with one of the deacons for lunch. But let me tell you what, if you can meet me here at three, I will talk with you." The preacher said.

"I really appreciate it!"

"Of course, Mr. Greene. I will see you in a couple of hours. Just come meet me here, and we will talk." The Preacher responded.

"Thanks again," Terrance said as he walked out of the church and descended the steps back to the sidewalk. He felt a sense of relief as he left the church, almost as if someone had removed a load of bricks from his chest. As he walked down the sidewalk, his eyes found focus across the street and landed on a familiar figure sitting on a park bench. Terrance smiled and carefully crossed the street.

As Terrance approached, he looked at the book that Lily was reading. It was a book about killer whales. Terrance thought this was an odd choice but shrugged it off.

"Good morning, Lily!"

"Good morning, Mr. Greene. It is nice to see you again," Lily said.

"Why do you keep disappearing on me?"

"I'm sorry, I am a busy woman," Lily said with a smile.

"Interesting read, killer whales? We aren't really close to the ocean."

"I find animals interesting. You know the only thing that separates man from animals is a thread of a conscience. You take that away, and humanity is nothing but a bunch of wild animals." Lily said.

"Maybe," Terrance replied.

"These orcas are quite interesting; you know, they like to play with their food. They will take baby seals and throw them around in the air as though it were for sport. Sometimes, they just kill them and leave them, not even eating them. Others torture them before they finally eat them. Quite cruel, wouldn't you say?" Lily asked.

"I guess."

"Yet, people flock to see these things at marine parks and treat them like celebrities. Not all that different from how people flock towards terrible people, is it? Or even flock to hear some man preach." Lily asked.

"I guess not."

Lily peered over Terrance's shoulder and looked at the church. "I would be careful with him if I were you."

"Who? The preacher?"

"Yes, you know the perfect hiding place for a wolf is to pretend to be a shepherd. That way, the prey grows comfortable and complacent." Lily said not breaking her gaze from the church.

"I take it you don't care for the reverend?"

Lily turned her gaze from the church and towards Terrance. "You could say that."

Terrance could see that Lily seemed agitated when he spoke about the preacher, so he attempted to change the subject. "You disappeared on me last night."

"I'm sorry; I knew you were in good hands." Lily said.

"I just have to know. How did you get your hands on the diary?" Terrance asked.

"The same way that you would have, I've been in the house before, and I found it sandwiched between her mattresses." Lily said.

"How did the police miss it?" Terrance asked.

"You know the thing about a family that owns half of the town is that the police almost work for them. There were a lot of things left in that room. It is almost just like she left it," Lily said.

"I guess you're right. How did you know I would be there?" Terrance asked.

"I think you and I are more alike than you know. You did what I would have done. I saw your car hidden around the corner and guessed where you were," Lily said.

"Well, I'm glad that you came inside."

"I know how weak the floors are. I was hoping you would have better sense, but alas there you were dangling from the ceiling." She said, poking fun at him.

"I still can't thank you enough; you saved my life."

"Did I?" Lily responded

Terrance paused and stared at her again. She was such a mystery. He could not guess her motives or her story. This mystery of Lily still added a since of excitement to him. Most of the women he has had in his life were predictable. Their motives were the same; he was well off and somewhat famous in Atlanta. Women always looked for a strong mate, and usually most saw him as a good catch. He saw women as an adventure. He had no thoughts of settling down; he did not want to be a family man. However, Lily differed from all those women. She was comfortable with herself and in some odd way confident. She helped him but would not share the full motives behind her actions. It also seemed odd that she wanted nothing in return. She was driving him crazy, but in a good way.

"So, how was church today?" Lily asked.

"I mean, I just went there to talk with the preacher." Terrance said with a shrug.

"Any luck?" Lily asked.

"Yeah, meeting him in a few."

"Just be careful; remember the wolf pretending to be the shepherd." Lily said.

"I think he's an old harmless man, plus he's retiring, so I need to talk to him while he's here." Terrance said.

"Retiring?" Lily questioned.

"Yeah, he mentioned it twice."

"That's really interesting." Lily said with a smirk.

"Why?"

"Just the timing of things. He's been there for forty years, hiding in plain sight, and now he is ready to leave." Lily said, looking again at the church.

"Have you met him before?"

"No, not over this. I have family in this town, and he did one of them wrong. He had a chance to do the right thing, but he stayed silent. So, why would he talk to me about this?" Lily said with a hint of anger.

"I'm sorry. I didn't mean to open any old wounds."

"No problem. It was years ago. Just be careful with him." Lily said in a gentler tone.

"I will."

"You know, I will not always be there to save you. So, be careful." Lily said while softly brushing his shoulder.

"I appreciate your concern. I promise I will be careful. No more walking into abandoned houses." Terrance said as he brought his own hand up to hers.

"Good!" she said

"Hey, do you want to go to lunch before I come back here?"

"Thanks, but I had a late breakfast. I'm not quite ready to eat again." Lily said as she released his hand.

"Oh, okay," Terrance said with a disappointed look.

"But tell you what. I will take you up on it soon. I can't stay; I've got some leads that I need to follow on my own." Lily said as she packed her book into her purse.

"Care to share?" Terrance asked.

"In good time, a girl has to keep some secrets, you know," Lily said in a flirtatious manner.

"Oh, can I ask you something before you leave?" Terrance asked.

"Of course." Lily responded.

"What is the book that Hailey mentioned it the diary? Since you study the occult, I thought you might know." Terrance asked.

"It is the Book of Shadows. The Bible mentions the Book of Life; this book is the opposite of that." Lily said.

"Did you find that book in the room?" Terrance asked.

"Yes," Lily said.

"Do you have it?"

"It's around." She said.

"Could I see it?"

"Perhaps in time, that book is not something to be toyed with." She said.

"Okay," Terrance said with another look of disappointment.

"I've got to run." Lily said.

"Will I see you again soon, Lily?" Terrance called out.

"I feel destiny has brought our paths together." Lily said as she walked away.

Lily confounded him. She was so mysterious, so strange, but there was also something so intoxicating. She had some kind of pull with him. He couldn't quite explain it, but it was there from the first time their eyes met at the hotel. *Is she playing me?* He questioned himself.

Chapter 12

The Sentinel

Terrance awoke in a fog. He had gotten something that he had not enjoyed since his arrival — a restful sleep. Though it was short, it was just what he needed. The buzzing of the old alarm clock interrupted what had been his most peaceful sleep in a couple of days. There were no dreams, no strange girls, just peace. Struggling to fully wake up, he hit the snooze button twice before he realized he was about to have to run back to the church.

Still amazed at the events of this morning, he couldn't believe that the preacher was going to meet him. He thought this was going to be the hardest meeting to arrange. After all, the preacher lost two children in the school, and one was the primary suspect. It gave him hope that he was finally making progress and that this would provide him the grounding to connect the dots and put this town and the school behind him.

Terrance began his walk back to the church. He was growing tired of walking so much and still very upset about his car. Though Terrance was in pretty good shape, the speed that a car can travel to a destination was much quicker than walking. As he walked along the sidewalk towards the church, the town seemed more lifeless than this morning. He was used to the hustle of Atlanta and was still having difficulty getting used to the slowness of Anderson. Terrance thought deeply about what to ask and how to get information from the preacher without offending him. He continued to be surprised that this meeting was going to take place, and he did not want to ruin it.

Terrance knew himself and his tendency to be blunt and to the point, sometimes to a fault of offending the people he spoke to. His work life often encouraged this level of aggression when talking with corrupt politicians, but aside from Lily, this is the first member of the town who actually agreed to talk to him freely and not out of obligation. The preacher was also the first person in town aside from Lily that actually seemed somewhat friendly to him. He still guarded himself because of memories from his childhood church and the pastor who abandoned his family.

As his mind wandered, he arrived quicker than expected at the church. The only vehicle parked outside was an older black pickup truck. It was dirty with mud stains and had a shotgun rack mounted on the inside. Terrance looked around for signs of any other vehicles, but this truck was all he saw parked nearby. The truck looked familiar, but he brushed it off as being like one of many trucks that he had seen while in south Georgia.

Terrance could hear the engine cooling off, the ticking and dripping sounds. He knew it must have recently parked. As he walked towards the front of the church, he gave the door a try. As Terrance gave the door a tug, it opened right up. The moldy, burnt smell from this morning greeted him again as he stepped through the door. This time, though it was quiet, almost to the point of its being creepy. Despite its being a supposed house of God, there was still an air of uneasiness.

Terrance walked up the aisle looking around, seeing if the pastor was already there, but so far he was just met with silence. As he walked deeper into the sanctuary, he took his time to get a better look at the sanctuary. There was nothing too unusual from the things he remembered about church. The carpet was reddish-burgundy in color, and the walls were painted a faded white. Along the ceiling there hung frosted glass chandeliers with a crucifix outlined on them.

The walls had rows of stained-glass windows along the sides of the sanctuary.

As Terrance continued to scan the interior of the church, looking at every feature and corner, he heard a door off to the side open. The sudden clicking noise caused Terrance to jump slightly as it interrupted the silence. The pastor stepped out of the door wearing the same suit from earlier this morning. "Afternoon, Terrance!" the preacher said in a friendly tone.

"Good afternoon, Pastor, thanks again for meeting with me."

"My pleasure! Please call me Jack; there's no formality here." Jack said in a calm and steady tone.

Jack walked over to Terrance, and the two shook hands once again. He had a firm but friendly handshake as he shook Terrance's hand with a smile. As Terrance shook the pastor's hand, he noticed a scar on Jack's right hand. The sleeve of Jack's suit mostly hid it, but it was there. The scar appeared to be spread throughout the top of his hand. It looked like a scar one would get from a burn. This was not the first burn scar Terrance had seen during his visit, and part of him questioned the coincidence.

Once they broke away from the handshake, then Jack said. "Let's go back to my office; it's a little more comfortable back there. I'm old, and as much as I love these old pews, they just don't love me." Jack guided Terrance through the side door and along a short hall, directly to his office.

"Come on in and get comfortable," Jack said, motioning for Terrance to enter his office.

Terrance walked into the office. The walls of the office were white, just as the rest of the church. The reddish carpet continued, as did the same burnt, moldy smell. There were a few pictures that hung on the walls, mostly depicting old rural churches. There were two large bookshelves full of books that lined the wall. The preacher's desk was neat and well organized with the traditional office tools.

Terrance noticed that there was no computer at Jack's desk, which he thought was unusual in this day and age. On the desk in the center was a Bible that was open, but Terrance could not see the page or section.

Jack walked around his desk and motioned for Terrance to have a seat in one of the chairs that sat in front. Jack sat in his chair and adjusted to get comfortable. After settling, he looked down at the open Bible, then up at Terrance.

"So how can I help you today?" Jack asked.

"First, thanks again for meeting with me. I also want to say I'm sorry about your sons, and I really don't want to open any wounds. I just have some questions."

"You're welcome, and I'm at peace now. It took some time and healing, but I have found my purpose, and it keeps me going." Jack said.

"Do you mind if I ask you about them?"

"Not at all. What do you want to know?" Jack asked.

"Well, could you tell me a little about them, what they were like?"

"Yeah, I had two boys. One was sweet and a 'real' child of God. The other, God rest his soul wherever it found rest, was a monster." Jack said with a face that told he was holding back emotions.

"You talking about Dylan?"

"Dylan was my angel. No, the other one had troubles." Jack responded.

"Chase? The football star?"

"Yes, he was a star because he was ruthless on the field, much like he was off the field." Jack responded.

"I'm sorry, I didn't know that."

"Have you not read any of the papers?" Jack asked.

"I don't have any internet, and the library is closed until Monday. The clippings that I found mentioned nothing really about Chase."

"Yes, the joys of rural life." Jack responded.

"Yeah, a little different from Atlanta."

"I don't have any articles to share here, but didn't you know what they accused him of?" Jack asked.

"No, just information about Dylan being mentioned in the high school incident."

"About a year before the incident, Chase was accused of assaulting a young girl. An underclassman. It was the talk of the town, but the girl changed her story, so the court dropped all the charges. She and her family moved away after that. You didn't know about that?" Jack asked.

"No, I'm sorry."

"That's usually why people want to talk to me — to figure out how the pastor raised such a kid. I thought you reporter types had all the facts." Jack said with a hint of sarcasm.

"I'm afraid that technology has kept me somewhat limited at the moment."

"Yeah, it just about destroyed our family and half the town with it. Chase's arrest happened; they were setting a trial, but then she changed her story. I almost lost my job. The townsfolk here lost faith in me as a pastor since I raised such a child." Jack said.

"I'm sorry, I did not know."

"Yeah, see, I thought that's what you were here for. I almost told you no and just to leave, but something told me I needed to speak with you." Jack said, looking intently at Terrance.

"I'm glad that you met with me."

"So, I guess I am a little confused. If you aren't here to ask about Chase, what are you here for?" Jack questioned.

"About the school. The disappearances."

Jack gave Terrance a confused look as he looked deep in thought. "Go ahead, ask what you had in mind."

"Well, if you don't mind, since you mentioned the thing with Chase. Do you think he did it?"

"Honestly," the old preacher said with a pause, "Yes." Jack adjusted himself in his chair and leaned forward. "I supported the police and the girl's family the entire time. She was a sweet girl, and I was ashamed of what he did. But when she changed the story, they had no choice but to release him."

"Most of the time, the parent covers their kids' transgressions."

"I made a mistake of not listening years ago. I wasn't going to repeat it again. Especially when I knew who he was." Jack said, adjusting once again in his seat.

"I'm sorry."

"You know, most kids when they get arrested or something like that happens, they learn, they get better. But not Chase; when he was released, he just got much worse. He was so cocky and arrogant. This used to be a football town, and everyone else seemed to just ignore it. Just like it never happened." Jack said.

"I'm very sorry. I know this is hard, but I can't tell you how much I appreciate your openness." Terrance said.

Jack took another deep breath and adjusted in his seat once again. He then leaned forward towards Terrance. "My wife and I tried so hard to have children. For years, we prayed, but with no luck. We drove to Macon and all the way to Atlanta, working with specialists to find a way, but nothing worked. We ended up adopting Chase from Russia. You know they have rooms full of orphans there. As infants, they lay in cribs among countless other infants just getting the basics. What they don't get is human touch or love. We thought we were saving him. We loved that kid so much, supported him, and tried to get him help. Nothing worked; he couldn't love people; he just didn't know how. Then, about a year after we adopted Chase, my wife got pregnant with Dylan." Jack leaned back again and snickered slightly. "You know, we didn't trust God's timing; we were impatient. Boy, did we pay for it!" Jack said.

Rubbing his nose, Jack adjusted in his seat again. Jack did not enjoy talking about Chase negatively, but he felt it was time that people heard the truth. Jack took a deep breath and continued, "We loved both boys with all our hearts. We tried to nurture them, but Chase, even at a young age he was cruel. We couldn't have pets; we even had to keep an eye out for our neighbor's pets. He would do unspeakable things to them, as if it were a science experiment. Heck, until Dylan got old enough to defend himself, and even then, he struggled with Chase, we had to keep the boys separate." Jack said.

"I am very sorry to hear all this. I wish I had known."

"I'm an open book; the whole town knows anyway. So, there's not much sense in hiding anything." Jack said.

"So, may I ask, why were the boys there that night?"

"Chase was there for a good time and anything else he could get into. He was dating a new girl after Ashley broke up with him. Ashley, she was a keeper, but that new girl that he was dating, she was just as off as him." Jack said, and afterwards cleared his throat.

"What about Dylan?"

"Dylan, he was there to look after Ashley. He had a crush on that girl since the third grade, so he felt devastated when she started dating Chase. But when she dumped him, that seemed to bring new life into Dylan." Jack said.

"So, he wasn't there to do a ghost hunt?"

Jack laughed. "Ghost hunt? No, he may have used that as an excuse to be there, but he was there to protect Ashley. He didn't trust Chase and his friends. Dylan was worried about what could happen to her after she broke up with him. I honestly don't know why those kids went there, but I suppose in a small town, there are fewer places to go, so they were just making do." Jack said.

"I'm very sorry to bring all this back up." Terrance said.

Jack's eyes watered, and the emotions that he had been holding inside threatened to burst at any moment. "You know I loved them both. Even with all the evil things Chase did, I still loved him. Dylan, though, was so special. He had a heart of gold and would do anything for anyone who asked. He was one of a kind." Jack said.

Terrance, knowing from times he had spent in other interviews that this one was at risk of ending because of the building emotions, decided for the time being that he needed to change the conversation. "So, you said this morning that you were retiring soon?" Terrance asked.

"Not long after we lost those boys, my wife — her heart just couldn't take the heartache. It gave out on her, and it was just me. There was so much pain and hurt in this town. For over a decade, I have stood as a sentinel guarding my flock and trying to give hope. So many remain stuck in this loop, reliving the past in an endless cycle. I have helped some break the chain, but others just can't let it go. Terrance, I'm tired. This old soldier has done his duty. I have remained faithful to my flock, but I'm tired. And now, I'm almost finished. My work is almost complete. It is time." Jack said, still holding back his tears.

"I'm very sorry."

Jack mustered and composed his emotions for the time being and looked up at Terrance. "Terrance, do you go to church?"

"No, sir, not in a long time."

"If you don't mind my asking, why?" Jack asked, staring intently at Terrence.

"I had an awful experience with a pastor who wasn't the man he presented himself to be. He abandoned my family, who had been going there all my life. My father died, and we lost everything, and he turned his back on us."

"I'm very sorry that happened to you. There are rotten apples even in the pulpit. The sad thing is, they do more damage than just about anyone else. Don't let one rotten apple ruin you on the whole bunch." Jack said.

Terrance was now growing emotional himself. He was always so guarded, but the kindness and concern that Jack was showing caught him off guard. *Can he really be this caring?* Terrance questioned himself.

"I'm about out of time today, but let me offer you this. Why don't you join me at Anderson Pond tomorrow afternoon? I'm going fishing and would love some company." Jack said.

"I appreciate it, but I haven't gone fishing since I was a kid, and I'm really running out of time too."

"Time is short. Look, the pond is just outside of town. Sometimes getting away from all this trauma and darkness really helps clear your head. It let's you see things better." Jack said in a serious, but friendly tone.

"I just don't think I can."

Jack got up and walked over to Terrance and placed his hand on his right shoulder. The burn scars now became clearer on both of the old preacher's hands. "There is nothing for you here, Terrance. Just sadness and death, please join me tomorrow." Jack requested with a caring tone.

"I'll see what I can do." Terrance responded.

"Good", Jack said as he patted Terrance's shoulder.

"My duty is coming to an end. Before I leave, I want to go fishing in that pond one more time. Time is short, Terrance. I really hope you will join me." Jack said, flashing a smile down at Terrance.

Terrance got up, and the two men once again shook hands. Jack escorted Terrance through the church. As they walked, Terrance paused and turned to Jack and asked, "I mean no offense, but what is that old burning smell?"

Jack paused with Terrance and looked directly at him. "Sometimes, no matter how hard you try to hide the past; it just keeps coming to the surface."

The answer confused Terrance, but he didn't want to press what he meant any further. *Perhaps there was a fire somewhere in the church,* he thought as he walked with Jack again to the doors.

"I mean it, please join me tomorrow." Jack said.

"I don't have any fishing poles or equipment."

"I've got you covered, so don't you worry." Jack said.

"I will try. I can't commit, but I will try."

"Take care, young man, and may God protect you." Jack said with a smile.

As Terrance walked down the stairs of the church and back to the sidewalk, he glanced back toward the dirty black pickup truck parked in the front. The more he studied it, the more his thoughts went back to the visit to the house. *Could this be the same truck?* He thought to himself.

As much as part of him wanted to believe Jack and trust him, a pastor had burned him once before. *He's still hiding something from me.* Terrance thought to himself. Terrance turned away from the truck and looked back towards the church. He was looking for Jack, but he had already disappeared back into the building. *"The smell, those burn scars. There is more here."* Terrance continued to think to himself as he began walking on the sidewalk.

Terrance walked back towards his hotel, but as he turned the corner, he saw a familiar face. Lily stood there waiting for him with two cups of lemonade in her hands.

"I figured you might want something to drink." Lily said as she handed Terrance his lemonade in a Styrofoam cup.

"Thanks", Terrance said as he gladly accepted Lily's offer.

"Sorry, there is no alcohol, but this is Anderson, and it's a dry town. Anyway, my friend's mother makes the best lemonade straight from freshly squeezed lemons." Lily said with a smile.

Terrance asked, "Is that where you are staying?"

Lily gave a mischievous grin. "Always so worried about where I'm staying." She said playfully.

"Just trying to figure you out," Terrance said, returning the smile.

"Not much to figure out, I am who I am," Lily said once again, grinning.

"Yeah, okay," Terrance said with sarcasm.

"So, how was your talk with the crazy old preacher?" Lily asked.

"He was fine, seemed harmless."

"Yeah, tell that to his wife." Lily rebutted.

"What about his wife?"

"He didn't mention her?" Lily asked.

"He said she basically died of a broken heart. I thought he meant like a heart attack from the stress."

"No, Terrance. She died in a fire. A fire that everyone believes he set." Lily said with a hint of coldness in her tone.

"Wow, that explains the scars."

"Yeah, I figured you would be safe with him in broad daylight. But see, I stayed close." Lily said with a wink.

Terrance became frustrated. He believed this man, and now his suspicions proved to be correct. "I'm getting so tired of this!" Terrance muttered under his breath.

"Come on, Terrance, don't you do this for a living? Anyway, he's mostly harmless. Just a little crazy with a flock that follows him. He probably believes everything that he told you," Lily said with a smile.

"Such a waste of time."

"Well, you live and you learn," Lily replied.

"So, everything he told me about his kids was incorrect. No wonder it didn't match the reports."

"What did he say about them?" she asked.

"That Dylan was more a victim basically, and that Chase was the monster."

"Yeah, that makes sense." She replied as she looked up and nodded.

"Why?"

"They adopted Chase. Things changed for him when they had their own child. From what I have read and what a few people in this town will say to me, they favored Dylan. Even though Chase was a star on the football team, Reverend Davenport and his wife rarely even came to the games to support him. I think when he faced the reality of how evil Dylan was, he snapped."

"That makes sense."

"I don't think he set the fire at his house on purpose. I think it was an accident, but he could never bring himself to face the reality that he was the reason she died. You know, it's really sad when you think about it." She said.

Terrance shook his head and looked defeated, and Lily continued.

"Now, I still don't trust him. He's done some things that are unforgivable, but now he's just a sad, crazy old man." Lily looked at Terrance's posture and face. "What's the matter with you?"

"Just another waste of time!" Terrance said as he kicked the ground. "My car is still gone. Every time I find something, it turns out to be another dead end!"

Lily walked over to Terrance to offer him comfort. "It's going to be okay; I've got faith in you." She said in an encouraging tone.

"Look, Lily, I really appreciate it. But I am running out of time."

Lily jumped back with excitement and said, "I have an idea!"

"Why do I feel I am going to regret asking?"

"We've been into the house. You spoke with the old pastor. There isn't much more you can do until the library opens, so let's go to the school tonight?" Lily said.

"Man, I am not trying to get into any trouble with the police. The chief was already upset about where my car was stolen from yesterday."

"Don't chicken out on me now. You said that time is running out, so let's go to the source!" Lily said in a flirtatious manner.

Terrance sighed and took a deep breath; he knew he did not want to do this, and he also knew that, so far, Lily had looked after him. She was, in fact, the only person he felt he could trust in this place. He wanted her guidance and her protection, but he felt in the back of his mind that he might regret this decision. Looking back at Lily, and those dark eyes, and the way she looked at him. He drew one more deep breath and said, "Okay, I'll go. "

"Great," Lily said. "I've always wanted to go myself, but did not want to wander in the building alone."

"You're sure we're going to be good?" Terrance questioned as he continued to stare into her eyes and smile.

"I'm sure," she said in a reassuring tone.

"Okay, what time and where do you want to meet?"

"Let's shoot for 8:30 at your hotel, then we can walk together. It will be dark enough then that we shouldn't get spotted." She said with excitement.

"We can't just drive in your car?"

"I prefer to walk," she said. "Plus, a car is a good giveaway that we are there. After all, you didn't want to get caught, right?" She said.

"You're right."

The two continued their walk down the sidewalk, talking casually and flirting with each other. They approached a crossroads; one path led to Terrance's hotel and the other in the direction that Lily needed to travel. As they reached the intersection, Lily gave

Terrance a wink. "I think this will be good; maybe we can get some more answers, plus I'll have a big brave man to keep me safe." She said with a smile. She then gave him a gentle kiss on the cheek.

"I don't know about all that. I think the last time it was you who saved me." He said with a smile. Lily turned away and gave him one last smile before she began walking down the sidewalk.

Terrance gave her a small wave, then thought to himself, *What have I gotten myself into now?*

Terrance walked slowly down the sidewalk and enjoyed the tranquility of the town. The birds sang in the trees, and the wind gently rustled through the leaves of the trees. Through the songs of nature, he heard another sound — the sound of the vehicle cranking; he thought little of this sound that invaded his peaceful surroundings.

The sound that was innocent upon its first discovery quickly transitioned to something more urgent. Tires made a screech as the rubber impacted the road and attempted to gain traction. The new sound startled Terrance, and he turned around and noticed a black pickup truck quickly moving in his direction. Before he had a chance to think, the tires left the pavement, jumped the curb and onto the sidewalk heading directly and intentionally in his direction onto the sidewalk. Terrance stood in disbelief as his eyes focused on the bright blue oval on the grill that was growing ever closer to him.

Chapter 13

Ground Zero

Terrance sat on the creaky bed in his hotel room. He felt battered, like a battle-worn soldier returning from the front lines. Both of his knees bore scrapes, and he had a bruise that he was sure would shortly form on his right hip. A few seconds — just a few seconds — saved his life as he leaped into a ditch to nearly miss getting hit by the approaching truck. As soon as the truck had missed its intended target, it sped away and disappeared in the distance. He thought to himself; *It had to be the preacher. The truck looked just like his. It was probably the same truck that night at the house.* Though he tried to read the tag number to be sure as the truck fled, his eyes could not lock on. In his mind, he thought of calling the police, but knew that it would be a fruitless waste of his time. *They're all out to get me!* He thought to himself.

Things were growing increasingly dangerous for him; he thought about his options. He could leave, but his car was still missing. He might walk further away from the town and try to get a signal to call a member of his family to pick him up. But he was so close to perhaps finding out about this town's secrets. *If people are going to this length to get rid of me, this has to be the biggest story yet!* He thought to himself. Terrance was an often-stubborn man; when things became more difficult or more challenging, his motivation to see things through would grow.

This time was no different for Terrance. The more things grew difficult — police threats, nearly falling through a ceiling, his car stolen, and now an attempt on his life — all added fuel to his fire to see this thing through. Prior to his latest near-death experience, he was contemplating backing out of tonight's adventure with Lily, but now as he slowly dragged up his jeans on scraped up legs, his motivation increased even more. Now, *no matter what*, Terrance was going to see this through. He knew that the endgame was going to prove equally rewarding.

A gentle tap interrupted Terrance's thoughts on his door. He looked at the watch on his wrist. *Right on time*, he thought to himself as he laced up his shoes and went to open the door for Lily. However, it was not Lily at the door. Instead, an older man occupied the doorway; the preacher from earlier stood before him.

Jack stood wearing the same clothes as when they had met before. He was looking more worn and tired than he had during their previous meeting; his eyes appeared sunken and tired, and his face more weathered than before.

As soon as Terrance saw the preacher, anger filled him. He looked over the preacher's shoulders, scanning the parking lot for the black truck, but the parking lot was empty. The preacher in a kind voice said, "Good evening, Terrance. I'm sorry for the intrusion, but I made a batch of these cookies that my wife used to make. At least I tried to make them like her." Jack said as he revealed a plate containing cookies wrapped in Saran wrap. "I always end up making more than I can eat, and it goes to waste. I thought you might want a break from the same food at the cafe," he said as he handed the plate over to Terrance.

Terrance was suspicious, but accepted the plate. Having had enough games for now, he got to the point: "Where's your truck?"

Jack looked confused and stared blankly at Terrance. "What truck?" he asked.

"Your truck — the one parked in front of the church." Taking a breath, "The one you tried to kill me with earlier."

Again, the old preacher looked confused and stared blankly at Terrance. "I just have an old Mercury, and it mainly collects dust." Jack responded.

"So, that wasn't your truck parked at the church?"

"No," he said, still looking confused. "I haven't owned a truck for over twenty years. I just have my old Grand Marquis, but I walk mostly."

"So, you walked over here from your home in a suit?" Terrance questioned, still suspicious of the preacher.

"Yes, why would I lie about that?" Jack questioned.

Terrance looked over Jack, and he appeared to have sweat running down his forehead and covering the front of the dress shirt that was under his suit. "So, whose truck was that parked in front of the church earlier?" Terrance questioned.

"I don't know." Jack replied.

"So, that black truck that was parked out front. You don't know who it belongs to?"

"I'll be honest, I wasn't even paying attention. I always come in through the side entrance. What is going on? Why are you so angry suddenly?" Jack asked.

"Someone in a black truck tried to run me over after I left the church!" Terrance said angrily.

Jack stepped forward with a concerned look on his face. "Are you okay? I'm so sorry that happened to you."

"No, I am not okay!" Terrance rebuffed. "Someone stole my car. Now, someone tried to kill me! I think it's the same person or group of people. And I saw the same truck parked outside your church."

Jack looked genuinely concerned. "Is there anything I can do?"

"Yeah, find out whose truck that is and where my car is!"

"This is a quiet town; things like this just don't happen here." Jack responded.

"Yeah, that's what I keep hearing."

"Could someone have followed you here? From one of your previous stories?" Jack asked.

Terrance thought for a moment, *Did someone follow me?* Terrance had his share of enemies across the state. Corrupt officials who had lost their jobs. "It's possible." Terrance responded, "But, I really think it's someone from this town."

"I truly hope not." Jack said, "I know most of these people. They've been through a lot, but they aren't killers or thieves."

Terrance still didn't trust Jack. He thought back to what Lily had said. That means he had already lied to Terrance once, and he could be lying again. *I can't trust anyone.* Terrance thought to himself.

"Well, I am very sorry that happened to you. Do you need anything? You can even borrow my car if you need it." Jack said.

"I'm fine, thank you."

"Anyway. I just wanted to drop these off. They aren't as good as she used to make, but I try," Jack said.

"Thank you. I'm sure they are fine."

"I've got to run, but I also wanted to remind you of the invitation to join me tomorrow." Jack said.

"I will try." Terrance said.

"I hope so. There isn't anything here for you, Terrance. Some fresh air and perspective will do you some good." Jack said as he looked over his shoulder with a quick glance.

"I'm working on some last-minute things; I should be out of here soon." Terrance said.

"You've got road before you, Terrance. Be careful in the way you choose; one leads to death, and one leads to peace. Just keep your focus and keep your eyes open. That's all I ask," Jack said as he pivoted his steps. "Take care," he said as he walked away.

Terrance closed the door as the preacher walked away and began reflecting on this new awkward interaction. *Two roads? Is he trying to warn me? Does he know something, and he's trying to tell me, or is he just crazy?* Terrance thought to himself. Terrance was usually pretty good at reading people and their motivations. On one hand, he got a sense of genuineness from his encounters with the preacher, but on the other, Lily showed he lied. *Maybe he is just a crazy, old, lonely man.* Terrance thought as he looked at the plate full of cookies and considered the purpose of the fishing invitation.

Another knock on the door interrupted Terrance's thoughts. He shook off his thoughts and once again went to the door where Lily now stood. Lily looked different tonight. Her makeup appeared fresher and more defined on her face, bringing to life her plump lips, and the eyeliner made her eyes pop. In most of their previous encounters, Lily had appeared more natural, but tonight she looked livelier. Even the clothes she was wearing — the tight tan shorts and dark-colored top that fit her contours closely.

Terrance almost felt underdressed. He was wearing dark jeans and dark clothing for their covert operation, and she was wearing clothing more akin to a date. "Are you ready?" Lily asked as she flashed a smile at Terrance.

"We're still going to the school tonight?" Terrance asked as he looked at Lily's clothing.

"Yes, I'm sorry. I had to do a video conference call earlier, and I just didn't feel like changing my clothes." She softly replied.

"You sure? I don't know how dirty this place is going to be. If it's anything like the house, I don't want to see you ruin anything."

"I'm fine, but thank you. I think the floors are all concrete, so we shouldn't be falling through any ceilings tonight." Lily said with a flirtatious smile.

Terrance grabbed his phone, even though he could not get any service during his brief stay in Anderson. He then quickly turned out the lights of his room and joined Lily outside. The two walked, and as much as he tried, he just could not get his eyes off of her swaying hips. She was so much more attractive than he first realized. At first she was a mystery; now she was almost intoxicating.

They walked down the street towards the school. Terrance walked with a slight limp, which gained Lily's attention. "What happened?" she asked.

"Someone tried to run me over after we talked earlier."

Lily paused and grabbed Terrance with a concerned look on her face. "Are you alright?" she asked.

"Yes, I got out of the way fast enough."

"I'm so sorry," she said as placed her hand more gently on his forearm. "Did you get hurt?"

"Yeah, just a little bruised."

"I can't believe it. People are dumb here, but I've seen nothing like that." She said while still holding onto his hand.

"Did anyone treat you like this or is it just a way for these rednecks to welcome a black man?" Terrance asked.

"People don't really like me here, but I've had no one steal my car or try to run me over." She said.

"Story of my life."

"You've just got to be careful who you talk to here." She said.

"I know," Terrance responded.

"Did I see the preacher leaving your room?" Lily asked.

"Yeah, why?"

"Just be careful with that one; he seems to have taken an interest in you." She said.

"You think he had something to do with the truck?" Terrance asked.

"Who knows," she said as she shrugged. "Why did he come visit you?"

"He has been inviting me to go fishing and brought some cookies."

"Interesting," Lily responded. "You nearly died after just meeting him. Then, he brings you cookies. And he wants to get you alone in the woods at some lake. Sounds a little off to me."

"It is an interesting coincidence now that you mention it."

"Maybe don't eat the cookies. I don't trust him, and I don't want to see anything bad happen to you," Lily said out of concern.

"Thanks," Terrance responded with a smile.

"I didn't know about you at first, but you've kind of grown on me," Lily said with a smile. "Look, we are here," she said as she pointed to the school ahead of them.

In the darkness, the school stood in the shadows. Its brick silhouette stretched along the background of a line of tall oaks. The streetlights illuminated the sidewalk, but all light seemed to extinguish as the shadow of the old brick high school seemed to swallow all light and life in the area. There was a tall chain-link fence that separated the old school property from the sidewalk, creating an impenetrable web of metal, which sparkled like the morning dew on a spiderweb at sunrise.

Lily took the lead as they examined their surroundings casually to ensure that they did not draw attention from any of the silent neighbors in the quiet area. "I think we will have our best luck in the back," Lily said as she grabbed Terrance's right wrist and guided him to follow her. "We can't use any flashlights, so just stay close." Terrance seemed to resist at first. With everything that had happened thus far, the consequences of getting caught for trespassing moved to the forefront of his thoughts.

"You trust me?" Lily asked.

"Yeah," he responded.

"I've got you; follow me," she said, flashing him another smile.

Terrance reluctantly followed her as their footsteps left the sidewalk and entered the small patch of vegetation between the sidewalk and the fence line. She guided him through some thicker growth, and before he knew it, they were on the side of the campus in thick woods that divided the fence from the visible world. They were now hidden and given the opportunity to look for a hole in the fence or at least a gap that would be large enough for both of them to fit through.

Lily knew exactly where she was heading. Like she had been there before. Terrance was taking notice of this and growing suspicious of her precision as they navigated around the fence line. She had never given him a reason not to trust her motivations before; she had helped him and saved his life. So, he tried to bury the suspicions and go against his own untrusting nature.

The deeper in the woods and closer to the building they walked, the silence increased. Gone now were the sounds of crickets and other nocturnal creatures. An eerie silence replaced those sounds, and it made each footstep echo like drumbeats rather than casual steps on the forest floor. Things also appeared to get darker the deeper they went. The streetlights had disappeared long ago, and now a canopy of trees hid the moonlight above from Terrance and Lily, shrouding them in darkness.

Despite the darkness, Lily still navigated them both through heavy vegetation around the fence and campus of the school. Terrance whispered, "Are you sure you haven't been here before?"

Lily paused in her steps and turned around. "I said I haven't been in the building before," she replied. "I've been around but just didn't have the nerve to go inside alone."

"Really, after going into the house? You think this is worse?" he asked.

"Yes, the house had three murders. This building had multiple," she said as she paused her forward motion to respond to Terrance.

"I didn't think they ever found any bodies here?" Terrance asked.

"No, and that makes it worse. There might be angry spirits here who can't be at rest. When people don't have a burial or closure, it interrupts the natural cycle." She responded.

"Here we go again with ghosts." Terrance joked.

"I'm for real, this building." She said, pointing at the shadow of the building, "It is tainted with pain, anger, and possibly evil. You really shouldn't joke. We are about to step into a dangerous world. One that, with you being a skeptic, makes it even riskier. Do you understand?" Lily said in a serious tone.

Sensing her passion and not wanting to hurt her feelings, "Yes, I'm sorry," Terrance said as he looked down at the ground almost with a sense of guilt over his statement.

"It's okay, but look, there is an opening in the fence. Let's go before someone sees us!" Lily said as she grabbed onto Terrance and began pulling him in an unseen direction.

As they approached the fence, Terrance could see what Lily was talking about. Whether it was caused by time, animals, or humans, close to the ground there was an opening in the fence. It was not big by any measure, but just big enough for a person or small animal to travel through.

"If you're scared, we can turn back," Lily said as they approached the opening.

Terrance had been through so much over the past few days. Even if for a moment he believed in any of this supernatural stuff Lily had built her life around, he would not admit fear. If he feared anything, it was still getting caught by the police after the chief's clear warning about staying away from the building. Terrance took a deep breath. He also liked Lily at this point more than just an acquaintance. He did not want to appear weak in front of her, so without a word he crouched down and crawled through the opening ahead of Lily. "I'm not scared," he said with a sarcastic smile.

"Well, I gave you an out," Lily said, returning the smile and crawling through the opening to join Terrance.

Once on the other side of the fence, the two walked silently and slowly onto the campus itself. From where they now walked, it was no longer just one enormous building, but a series of buildings at the back of the campus. It was still very dark, but as their eyes had adjusted fully to the darkness, they could make out more of the buildings in the lack of light.

Lily pointed at a lone building that stood out several feet from the remaining structures. The parking lot, which had now become overgrown with brush and trees that broke through the unused asphalt, surrounded it. "See that building," Lily pointed. "That was the gym where the students had attended the Fall Ball that night. It was the annual dance and was even more popular than homecoming. After they left the gym, they hid in the shadows much like we are doing." Lily said.

Lily's fingers then followed their path to what remained of a canopy that once stood to protect students from the elements. "They then walked to that door, where the class president, who had stayed back to count money from the dance, let them inside. We are retracing their steps tonight." She said in a serious tone.

"How do you know so much about this?"

"I've spent years researching this town and the night it all happened. This place has become a cornerstone of my career. I have just had no one to share it with." Lily responded.

Terrance felt kind of special that he could be the one to go on this journey with Lily. "I'm glad I get to share it with you." Terrance said.

Lily got close to Terrance and gave him a kiss on the cheek. "Me too," she said. She then grabbed his hand. "Let's go!" she said with an excitement that he had not seen in her before.

Terrance smiled and quickly joined Lily on her route to retrace the students of that night. They approached the same door that the class president had opened for the group of unfortunate students. "This is it. Maybe it will open for us," Lily said as she reached for the door. Though she was hopeful and expected it to open, the door remained sealed and just gave a little as she pulled on it. Terrance could see her disappointment, so he encouraged her to try another way.

Lily stepped back from the door, more determined than ever to find a way into the school building. The pair then walked along the main building, following its path. Lily then pointed to a small courtyard that opened up to different wings. In the courtyard, there was an old pond that still glistened in the moonlight. Lily pointed in the general direction and said, "This was where they found evidence from the first two victims. No one would ever see again the very class president who opened the door. They found part of her dress that had stuck to a rosebush that was over there and one high-heel shoe at the edge of the pond. Then nothing. It was like she just vanished into the pond and into another world."

"How did you find this out? It wasn't in any of the reports."

"You really think the police are going to put that into the report? That a girl was sucked into a two-foot-deep pond and disappeared?" Lily asked.

"But they put some other strange things," Terrance responded.

"There is so much more. So many more secrets that want to be revealed." Lily said as she continued to point into the courtyard, "There in that clearing someone found a flashlight that had the fingerprints of Samantha's boyfriend Nathan. Samantha was among the girls inside the school that night. Nathan was an all-A student and a linebacker on the football team. Folks said he resisted going inside that night because he feared getting into trouble. No one really knows why he was here, but some folks said that maybe he came to be with her. Some of his friends said he had a bad feeling, but he never even got to make it inside to save his little girlfriend." Lily said in an ominous tone.

"I didn't even know about these people," Terrance said.

"Every town has its secrets; this one has so many. So much darkness. That's why I warned you about this place, why I have stayed away from venturing inside alone. People have just vanished, plus the pain. All little Nathan wanted to do was to be there with his girlfriend and save her. But he was taken away, and he wasn't even able to rescue her from the fate that awaited her." Lily said in a tone that almost seemed to mock Nathan.

"So, what happened to them? People just don't vanish into the air," Terrance said.

"That's the mystery. No one knows. Have you ever read about the hunters and hikers in the woods?" Lily asked.

"What are you talking about?" he asked.

"When you get back to where you can use the internet, search missing people in the national parks or even in dense woods. I'm not talking about some little kid that wanders off into the woods, but experienced and armed hunters. Hikers who know how to navigate the terrain, people who have been through survival courses — they just disappear." Lily said.

"No, I've never really heard about that."

"I told you before; there is an unseen world out there. We don't even know the tip. Armed hunters who know the woods, who are strong men just like you, and they just vanish without a sign. So, people do just vanish. Where they go is a mystery." Lily said.

Terrance was feeling uneasy. Though he was a skeptic, the creepy darkness and Lily's stories made the air feel heavy and uneasy. He was a grown man, and he would not let juvenile fear take over now. "Where do you think they go?" Terrance asked.

"I don't know. Maybe something takes them, something hungry." Lily responded, "There are Native American legends of creatures who devour humans, not just the body, but everything, their life force, their souls."

"You think some ancient Native American monster is out preying on people?"

"Often, legends are based on some sort of truth. I don't really know. We will never know at least on this side of life, but there are things out there that remain unseen in the earthly realms." Lily said.

"You and my grandmother would have gotten along," Terrance said. "She believed in all kinds of legends. She used to tell them to me as a kid and scare the hell out of me."

"Like I said, all legends are based on some truth. Some are explanations for why things are the way they are, things we just couldn't explain early. Modern science debunks a lot of them, but others..." As she was about to say more, the sound of a twig snapping seemed to cause both of them to jump. They both looked around, and there was no one and nothing in the vicinity.

"Okay, enough of this heavy talk. We're going to let ourselves get scared. Let's go find a way in." Lily said as she grabbed onto Terrance's hand again.

"I ain't going to lie, that made me jump a little." Terrance said with a laugh.

"Oh, not such a skeptic after all?" Lily responded.

"Just came out of nowhere; I wasn't expecting it," Terrance rebuffed.

"Okay, brave guy," Lily responded. "There might be more things that you aren't expecting tonight. I hope you can handle it."

"Hey, I saw you. You jumped too!"

The two then began moving away from the courtyard and followed the outline of the building, there another door to a different hallway and building emerged. Lily walked over to give this one a chance to be the portal inside, but like the first door, it remained sealed shut and continued to lock the old high school from the outside world.

Though slightly disappointed, Lily was determined to get inside. She had longed for this — to explore this building — and now she was not alone. She was going to find a way in, even if she had to force it. Though finding an unlocked door was much more of the preference, she was not ruling out using a rock or something to enter through a window.

As they walked and followed the building, another set of doors sealed the school from Lily's grasp. Her frustration was growing, but Terrance broke her out of her silent rage. "So, how does the book and Hailey fit into all of this?" Terrance asked. Lily paused in her walk and turned around.

"That's a good question. Now you are opening your mind?" Lily responded.

"I mean, I'm just curious. I read her diary, so there must have been a reason you gave me this, some sort of connection that you wanted me to find," Terrance said.

"She opened a door. Hailey got into some heavy stuff. She was desperate, and when she saw no other way, she turned to the book," Lily said.

"What do you mean, a door?"

"I told you, there is a whole other world, an unnatural one, that exists with ours. You've heard of Ouija or Spirit Boards?"

"Yeah, a little."

"There are ways to open pathways to this other world. A Ouija board opens a door. It is a way for stupid kids to get scared and play games. But make no mistake, when they do this, they open the way for the others to come into our world," Lily said in a serious tone.

"Uh huh" Terrance said with a hint of sarcasm.

"You asked!" Lily responded sharply.

"So, out of curiosity, what happens when a door is opened?"

"It depends. Sometimes a cool breeze enters a room, and the kids get scared. Other times, something else gets through."

"Like what?"

"Since you don't believe in God, you probably won't believe in this — demons or worse." She said in a very direct tone.

"Like actual demons from the Bible?"

Lily stepped closer to Terrance and looked him directly in the eye. "Yes, there are forces at work in this world who want to ruin you along with all of humanity. They come to you all innocent, like a kind old man, or the spirit of a child. They make false promises to make life better. Then, once you let your guard down." She positioned her hand in his face and snapped her fingers. "Then they get you!"

"I don't know about all that."

"They love non-believers, Terrance. It makes it so much easier to slide into your life. See, a believer has their guard up, but skeptics like you are just too easy." She said while staying very close to him.

Terrance still didn't believe in demons or spiritual forces. Everything had a scientific reason. He wanted to determine more about this book and how it may have had a psychological effect on Hailey. "So, what was this book again?" Terrance asked.

"It was a Book of Shadows. I don't think it had a specific name. From what I've read, it had roots in Voodoo or witchcraft — it has an unholy connection to the other world and within it was the ability to open a door large enough to let something through." Lily said.

"You have it?" Terrance questioned.

"Yes, you know I do." Lily said.

"So, have you found any of this in the book? A way to open doors?"

"Books like this only reveal answers when the time is right. I'm not a witch, so I have tried no spells, but it has some interesting stories in it." She responded.

"Think I can see it sometime?" he questioned.

"Like I said earlier, in time, but we need to get into this building first," Lily said with a hint of frustration. She turned back around and made further progress towards finding an unlocked door.

"Okay," he responded, "but if Hailey and this book did open something, how does that impact this school?"

Lily, growing frustrated with the lack of progress, turned to Terrance and said, "I believe she opened a door, and something entered this world. Something that feeds on the negativity that already existed on this land. I believe it was an agent of chaos, and when the negativity ends, it creates its own. That night, I believe something otherworldly and, yes, from that book, from Hailey herself, was at play."

"Oh, okay," he responded.

"If this is true, there should be some evidence inside. Some way that shows it latched on to someone and here. Spirits or entities like this require a host, someone to possess." She said.

"So, you are looking for some evidence of a ceremony or occult stuff?" he asked.

"Yes, something that the police probably missed because they weren't looking for it, but something I am looking for." Lily said.

"So, if something evil lurks here like you are saying, what prevents it from getting us like it did those kids?" he questioned.

"Faith," Lily answered as she led them to another set of doors. Her frustration was growing as this was the last set of doors in this area, and the remaining doors were more visible, possibly threatening to reveal their presence on the property.

Terrance followed her and posed another question: "I didn't think you were into the whole church thing?"

Lily reached for the last set of doors, and as she gave them a tug almost in desperation, they gave way and finally the gateway into the school opened. "Faith is not just a Christian thing. One can have faith in many things," she said as she stepped forward and motioned for Terrance to follow her. Terrance was nervous not from her stories, but from the realization that they were about to enter the building, and he was now crossing the Rubicon between what was legal and criminal.

In the past he had skirted the line sometimes to understand a story, but now he was crossing a threshold that could lead to an arrest or worse. The possibilities unnerved him, but with the smile on her face and the eagerness with which she beckoned him. He ignored the danger and went inside the old building. He had made it this far, so he might as well go the full length of wherever this course was taking him. In the end, he knew that big risks often had big payoffs, and like Lily, he wanted to see this one through. There was no turning back now. He had already ventured into an abandoned house; now he was going against the chief's warning.

In the night's silence, where no crickets or other nocturnal sounds were heard, the pair disappeared into the darkness of the old school building. As they disappeared through the final set of doors, the only sound to pierce the silent night was the clasping of the set of doors. Now, no trace existed of the pair as they entered the labyrinth of Lake County High School.

Chapter 14

A Walk into Darkness

The smell was offensive as they entered the long hallway. It smelled of mold and some type of metallic odor. Lily stopped just a couple of feet in front of the door and pulled out two candles and a box of matches. "I don't want to use flashlights because they are more visible through the windows; this should not make it so obvious that we are here," she said as she handed Terrance the candles to hold. She then expertly struck the match and lit both candles. "We still need to stay away from the doors and windows in the front halls. There aren't many neighbors, so we should be good most of the way." She said, leaving one candle for Terrance as she took the other.

Lily then pulled out a sheet of paper from her bag. She studied it intently before she looked up at Terrance and said, "We are a little off course from where I want to be, but if we follow this hallway to almost the end, we should be able to turn right onto the next hall."

"My life is in your hands." Terrance joked as Lily turned around, and the two began slowly walking through the dark corridor of the hallway. "What is that stench?" Terrance asked. Lily paused and turned around, facing Terrance. She had a blank expression on her face as she replied, "Sulfur".

"Sulfur?" Terrance questioned. "Why would it smell like sulfur?"

"I don't think you really want to know that answer, just stay close to me," Lily said as she turned around and continued her slow walk down the hallway.

"No, really, why does it smell like sulfur? This whole town stinks, but this is the worst," Terrance inquired.

"In a paranormal investigation, this smell is often associated with a demonic entity," Lily said calmly as they continued to walk.

"Paranormal investigation, demons — I'm not down for all that. I'm just here for evidence," Terrance replied.

Lily paused and turned around with a much sterner look on her face. This was in much greater contrast than how the evening had begun. "You are here for your reasons, and I am here for mine. Let's just work together, and we can both leave here with what we want." She said and spun around to lead their walk.

Dang, she's moody. Terrance thought to himself.

The sound in the hall was quiet. Each footstep that they made, though light on the linoleum floor, sounded like the beating drums of an Atlanta Drumline. Each deep breath they took echoed through the halls like the wind blowing through the leaves. They were isolated; they were alone, and the silence proved even more how remote they were as they continued to walk deeper and deeper into the monster that they had dared to enter.

As Terrance followed, he took notice of how cold the building was on the inside. Not only was it cold with its sterile blank institutional walls and a lifeless demeanor, the inside was equally cold in temperature. It reminded him of the same cold that greeted him in his hotel room after he got out of the shower. His mind raced around the dreams, the picture, and now this school. He was adamant that the human mind creates its own reality and that anything that was presently unnerving him had a natural cause versus a supernatural one. Though he tried to comfort himself with his beliefs and the natural world, he could not shake the uneasy feeling that permeated every inch of his body.

As they walked, their shadows, which were cast by the flickering glow of the candle, danced across the blank wall. It was the only sign of life that revealed itself inside the otherwise dead building. Terrance's eyes kept catching the movement of the shadows, and it caused him distraction and caused his mind to race and challenge his very beliefs. Terrance began regretting his decision to join Lily on this adventure. Taking the supernatural possibilities that Terrance presently fought against out of consideration, there was the genuine concern that at any moment a wild animal or some other trespasser could appear from any corner or doorway. Terrance felt scared, though he would never admit it openly. This entire adventure was twisting into regret. *The things I do for women.* Terrance thought to himself as he followed Lily ever closer to the upcoming intersection.

Lily appeared calm and composed. The darkness, the silence did not appear to rattle her at all as she continued to lead them through the hall. She maintained focus and remained on course, not allowing anything in the darkness to cause a distraction. As Lily pushed on, she kept the thoughts that now haunted Terrance out of her mind. She was where she had long wanted to be, and it was not the first time that she had been in a dark setting under similar circumstances. She was as at home in the night as she was in the day, and the things that would unsettle an average person did not even stir her.

Terrance almost felt ashamed of the tense posture of his body and his head, which was now swiveling from side to side, scanning his surroundings like a soldier just waiting for an ambush. As he looked at Lily, he took notice of the difference. *Maybe it was because she had done this type of thing before*, he thought to himself. He was glad that she was in front of him, so that she could not see him flinching at shadows that caught his eye or even at the sounds of their own footsteps.

As they approached the intersection of the two converging hallways, they both looked indistinguishable from one another. The light-colored walls each disappeared in the darkness with vague outlines of classroom doors along their route. Either Terrance had gotten used to the smell or the smell seemed to improve in this part of the school. Lily stopped and turned to face Terrance. She was silent at first, and Terrance looked upon her face, which was being illuminated by the flickering candle. In other circumstances this would have been romantic, but at the current moment. Terrance simply wanted to get this night over with.

"So, if we turn right down this hall, it should take us to a couple of locations where things happened," Lily said as she then turned her body slightly to point towards the hallway leading straight ahead. "If we continue straight, we will bypass those rooms, but it will bring us to where they met and stayed most of the night. What do you think?" Lily asked.

"Whatever way can get us out of here faster." Terrance said.

"I thought you didn't believe. Why are you so eager to leave?" Lily questioned with a smirk.

"Look, there may not be any demons, but there might be animals or people in this building. We found a way inside, so could they." Terrance said as he looked around, glancing down the abandoned halls.

"Who knew you were such a chicken?" Lily said in a mocking tone.

"Look, I live in the city. I don't do snakes. I don't do mice, raccoons, opossums, or any of that mess. This isn't my thing. I left the country for a reason." Terrance replied.

Lily then turned her gaze towards Terrance's left foot; her eyes widened as she stared. "What the hell are you looking at?" Terrance said with stress stirring in his voice. "Don't move; stay perfectly still." Lily said as she moved slowly towards his foot, looking just behind it. "Oh man, don't be playing. What is it!" he said with increased anxiety. Just then, Lily lurched forward and grabbed the back of his leg, causing him to yip and wince. "Just a leg," Lily said as she laughed.

"That isn't even funny! Don't be playing," he yelled.

"You're fine, big boy; nothing is going to get you, now quit being a chicken." Lily said as she once again turned her attention to the map, which she retrieved from her pocket. "Man, that wasn't even cool," Terrance said as she pouted slightly, feeling embarrassed that Lily had found such amusement in his discomfort. *If she weren't so hot, I would leave her here by herself.* Terrance thought to himself as he silently grumbled.

Lily placed the map back into her pocket and said, "Okay, so that we can see everything, we will go right and circle back around and get out of here before any snakes get you," with a sarcastic tone.

"I'm glad you think this is funny." He scoffed. Lily then turned around, facing Terrance and moving closer to him. She now stared at him and was face to face with him. "Look, be a big boy and I will make it all up to you." She said as she caressed his cheek.

Lily then turned around and began once again to lead them as she turned and headed right down another lifeless dark hall. Terrance continued grumbling under his breath as he thought *Women are just too much trouble*. He then cursed himself for getting into this situation. The house was one thing; he knew it was a bad idea, and he nearly died, but now he was tempting fate again.

As they continued, the silence of the hall echoed the footsteps gently pressing against the linoleum. The sound of small feet scurrying carried through the doorway of an abandoned classroom, causing Terrance to cringe as he tried to imagine more pleasant things. He knew they were not alone in the building, but that there were unseen creatures wandering through the building with them.

He couldn't believe that at one time this building had been alive with the sounds of over a thousand students and staff. Ten years ago, this school was bustling; now, there were two occupants and a multitude of unseen vermin in the building. This school, like much of the town that surrounded it, was a tomb, and the deeper they went, the more of an ominous feeling filled Terrance. Lily looked unfazed as she continued pursuing her mission.

Terrance had watched videos online and in passing of people doing stuff like this, but he looked at what Lily had with her and she lacked any of the equipment that he had seen on those shows and videos. It made him wonder further about her motivation. *What was she going to find with no way to collect the evidence?* Terrance questioned silently to himself.

He wondered if, like many times in the past, about what he was letting guide his decisions. At least when he went into the old house, he was on a mission to find evidence to collect and observe. But the disappearances had happened so many years ago that he knew this was going to be a fruitless endeavor. There was always the possibility that this could improve his writing of the story, but in the grand scheme of things this was mostly pointless as he looked at it. Yet here he was, walking deeper into the belly of the beast with a girl he knew very little about. A girl who, in her own way, was shrouded in some sort of mystery. He continued to analyze the situation, but was cut short when Lily stopped in front of what appeared to be an old Teacher's lounge.

"This is it!" Lily exclaimed. "This is where they found Chris's blood smeared on the door." Terrance almost ran into her as she paused, but he stopped just in time, barely bumping against her. "What?" he asked.

"This is where Chris vanished!" she responded.

"In the teacher's lounge?" Terrance asked as he pointed to the doorway.

"Yes, it looks like at some point the group got separated and went in different directions. They gathered in a classroom, partied, and then wandered off." Lily said.

"I guess they watched no scary movies." Terrance said, "Going out alone is how they always get killed in the movies."

"Yes, a predator always seeks to isolate its prey. Get it away from the rest of the herd; it makes it easier to catch." Lily responded.

"Well, I'm telling you right now, we're staying together. So, don't even get any ideas about us taking two different halls or something." He responded.

"Oh, come on, we could cover more ground that way." She joked with him.

"Not tonight," Terrance rebuffed.

Lily walked into the lounge with Terrance following close behind. She began looking at the door from the inside, placing the candle closer to get a better look. Studying the door, she appeared to be in deep thought. Reaching out, she placed her hand upon the door and slid it up and down near the edge with the doorknob. "Reports said that there were scratches from his fingernails on the door. Look!" she exclaimed as the candlelight did in fact reveal marks that resembled scratches made by human fingernails.

Terrance grew uneasy. He had never been to a scene of a murder or whatever this case was, and now he was facing the location of a young man's last moments alive. "He ran in here to use the phone to call for help. They found that phone over there nearly ripped off the wall." Lily said as she pointed towards a counter where there was a black phone still sitting.

"Somehow he got trapped in this room, and whatever came for him attacked him in this very room." She continued.

Terrance examined the door with his own candle. There was no blood, but the closer he looked, the more he could see the clear impression of fingernails clawing against the door. He shuddered as he imagined the young man's last moments of terror while he was attacked by whomever or whatever was after him.

"You know he was a football player. I think he was on the defensive line, if I remember correctly. Yet, all that strength could not save him." Lily said with an odd smirk on her face. She then walked around the room. She was in deep concentration imagining the events of that night. Closing her eyes as she touched things and taking deep breaths. Terrance moved closer to the center of the room and just watched. He was uncomfortable and was counting down the seconds for Lily to be ready to move on to the next location.

After she made her rounds, she eventually seemed content and looked over at Terrance. "You ready to move on?" she asked. Terrance quickly agreed, and the two departed the teacher's lounge and continued their trek down the lonely hallway. The deeper they walked, the colder the building seemed to become. Terrance was almost ready to shiver. He looked at Lily, and she seemed to be unfazed by the temperature changes. This made Terrance question his own senses.

They walked near an opening where a skylight bathed the area with a little more light that cast down from the moon. Lily paused and studied everything closely. There were banks of unused lockers on either side. They were red, matching the school's colors. She continued to look, then said, "This is it!" she said with an excited tone. "This is where they found Katie's belongings."

"Where?" Terrance asked.

Lily pointed towards what appeared to be the girls' restroom. "At some point she went into this restroom, presumably alone. Come on," she said as she motioned for Terrance to follow her into the restroom. As they crossed into the restroom, Terrance's head scraped against a thick spiderweb, which made him cringe once again. He brushed himself off, but he could still feel those tiny legs all over him. Although he knew there was nothing on him since he quickly and discreetly brushed himself off.

"Right here!" Lily pointed as they turned the corner and revealed two sinks. One had a busted mirror over it, and on the other, the mirror was missing. Lily walked over to the first sink, then bent down to look underneath. "They found a tube of Katie's lipstick right here." She said as she turned around, almost retracing Katie's forgotten last steps. "Then," she said, pointing to an open stall directly behind the sink, "her purse was found strewn all over the floor. It was like something grabbed her and forced her into this very stall."

"Again, how do you know all these details?" Terrance questioned.

"I've been here quite longer than you. I have spoken to and interviewed many folks. Give it time, and you would find out the same information." She replied.

Terrance examined the bathroom. It was his first time in the girls' or ladies' room, so he was curious how it looked without the addition of urinals. Lily studied things as well, but she seemed focused on the stall. She placed her free hand on the wall and closed her eyes, imagining the events of that night. As Terrance continued to study his surroundings, glancing occasionally back at Lily, a sound interrupted the silence. Terrance recoiled back, and Lily slowly opened her eyes as a scream, feminine in its sound, pierced the silence. The sound appeared to come from outside the restroom, but it sent chills down Terrance's spine.

"What the..." Terrance uttered in a shocked tone.

Lily looked agitated and casually turned towards Terrance. "A screech owl," she said.

"I've never heard no owl like that!" Terrance rebuffed.

"It was probably nesting near the skylight! You've never heard a screech owl before?" she asked.

"No owl like that!" Terrance said.

"They have a lot of them around here. I promise it was just an owl. Don't get scared on me now." Lily responded.

Terrance abruptly responded, "Can we just get this over with!"

"I think we're done here. Let's continue down the hall." Lily said as she moved around Terrance and once again took the lead.

"I can't believe I got myself into this," Terrance said quietly under his breath

They once again entered the open area of the hall. Lily looked back at Terrance and quietly giggled. "What's so funny?" he asked.

"I brought you here to keep me safe, and I'm the one who's watching over you." She said, continuing to snicker.

"Look, the cops have threatened me, I've almost fallen through a ceiling, and some dang redneck tried to run me over. I'm just trying to get out of this alive. Now I'm in this old school with mice and owls!" Terrance rebuffed.

"Look, I saved you in the house. I got you," Lily said. "We will loop around and finish soon," as she led them away from the lit area below the skylight again, and they walked into the darkness once more.

Terrance mumbled inaudible words to himself as he regretted more and more his decision to join Lily. The only thing that kept him going now was the promise of a reward. As they continued to walk, Lily began acting strangely. Instead of walking in the center of the hall, she began walking on the right side. She switched the candle she was holding to her left hand, and she began running her hand along the walls. In the darkness, Terrance could not tell what her face was doing, but he could swear she was quietly whispering something. *Why do I always end up with the crazy ones?* He questioned himself.

In the hallway, Lily paused. She looked upward, taking a deep breath before returning her gaze to a blank spot on the wall. "This was it! Payton and Ally!" she exclaimed. Terrance once again ignored her but was cautiously examining his own surroundings. He remained so transfixed in his own world he did not notice that she had completely stopped ahead of him. This time he could not stop in time to avoid colliding with her. He fell onto her back, causing her to fall forward into the wall, dropping her candle on the floor, which then caused it to go out. Although Lily could brace herself,

Terrance was not so fortunate. He fell forward, bouncing off of her and landing nearly face first on the cold floor. His candle also fell, causing it to extinguish as it struck the floor, leaving both of them in near total darkness. The only light visible was down the hall under the skylight, but that did little to help illuminate their location.

Terrance panicked. He was done; he was over all this. He fumbled around to find the candle, then tried to pull himself off the ground to reach in and find his phone in his pocket. Even though it did not have service, he still found comfort in having it close by. However, as he feverishly looked and felt for his phone, it was now absent. *No...no.... it must have fallen out when I fell.* He thought to himself. As he was panicking, he didn't even think to check on Lily. He continued to fumble, looking and feeling for anything as he began crawling around and feeling the ground.

Then he heard a match striking, and some light once again joined the hallway as Lily placed the match to her candle. "Really? Walk much, dude?" Lily said to Terrance as she lit her candle. Terrance, now embarrassed that he was on the ground fumbling, watched as she calmly lit her candle. "I can't find my phone; can you shine that over here?" he asked.

Lily, with an annoyed expression on her face, diverted the light over to where Terrance was crawling. He could find his candle and quickly stood up to light it against the flame. He then quickly returned to the floor with his candle in hand, trying to locate his phone. Lily turned away and went back to studying the wall. "This was where something happened to them. They found two flashlights on the floor, and there were scuff marks nearby. On the same wall that you knocked me into, there was one bloody handprint that matched Ally." She whispered. Terrance was not listening; instead, he was still searching for his phone.

"Find it yet?" she asked

"No, it has to be around here. I know I had it with me. It was in my front pocket." He responded.

Lily, now annoyed that Terrance was delaying her progress, leaned down towards the floor and helped him look for it. Terrance crawled, looking in corners and anywhere else it could have fallen. Lily shone her light and then impatiently asked, "Did you even bring it in here?"

"I know I had it. I always have it." He responded.

"Could it have fallen out of your pocket outside? She asked.

Terrance then began doubting himself. "I'm pretty sure I had it when we entered." He said.

"Well, I heard you fall, but I didn't hear anything clash like metal." She responded.

Terrance was growing frustrated. His car had been stolen, and now his phone is gone. He was feeling more desperate and estranged from the world outside of Anderson. "I know I had it," he repeated.

"Look, it's not here. Maybe it fell out the last time we bumped or even going through the fence. But," she said as she used the candle to illuminate the ground, "it's not here."

Terrance was not happy, but he knew he had searched every part of the ground where he had fallen. He also knew that he had been distracted, and it was possible that Lily was right. So, reluctantly, he slowly climbed up off the ground. Lily extended her hand as he got up. "It's going to be okay. We will find it, even if we have to sneak back in the morning." She said.

"I'm not coming back." Terrance rebuffed. "Well, in the daylight I will look for it alone. I'm a big girl." She said smugly.

There was tension forming in the air between Lily and Terrance. She was growing agitated with his behavior, and he was growing annoyed with her and her continued commitment to exploring a building which really wasn't yielding him much information. It wasn't necessary for him to have seen this all for himself. He could have just as well written from seeing these locations drawn out on a map. He knew he would not remember where each of these places was; he had become so distracted that this was essentially a fruitless journey. On top of the lack of reward, now his phone was gone.

Terrance continued to ignore what Lily said, but as he sulked, he glanced over and she appeared as though she was meditating, closing her eyes as she continued to feel the wall where she said the two young ladies disappeared. His infatuation with Lily was disappearing amid his frustration and general feelings about her strange behavior.

Lily eventually came back to reality and looked at Terrance. "We are right where it all happened. Doesn't that excite you at least a little?" she questioned. "This is where your story lies, not in some library, but right here in the heart of it all. Can't you feel it in the air?" she continued.

Terrance paused and took in what she said. He took in her words. *She's right,* he thought to himself. *This is where it all happened,* he continued to realize. He had let stress and perhaps even fear cloud the fact that these very surroundings that were causing him stress could be the very thing that brings his article or even novel to life. He had given up so much: time mourning with his family, his beloved car, which was still missing, risking safety, and now even his phone. Looking back at Lily from the ground, he took a deep breath. "You're right," he said. "I'm sorry, this isn't for me."

"All I'm trying to do is help you," Lily said. "I want to help you reach your dream. It is no accident that we met. So, let me help you."

Terrance spoke softly, "I'm sorry, I'm just letting things get to my head."

Lily smiled. "It's natural; whether or not you believe it, there is an energy here, and it's not a pleasant one. It sometimes gets in your head. Come on, let's finish this together, and I will help you find your phone, I promise!" she said as she extended her hand to Terrance. "I've got you," she reassured him.

Terrance took hold of her hand and said, "Thanks". The two exchanged a glance and continued their journey through the dark halls. During much of their journey, they walked in silence. They held hands for a little while, but Lily released her hand. Terrance was still not comfortable in the building, but he was beginning at least to tolerate his surroundings. There was just something about Lily that seemed to bring him peace. She was odd for sure, but there was just something about her.

They walked slowly and approached a T-intersection in the hallway. Lily looked down at her map again and talked slightly to herself as she traced her finger down possible routes. She looked up at Terrance and said, "Here's where it gets a little risky. We are going to head towards the front, which as we pass the rooms with open doors on the left our light could be visible. So, I need to ask you. Do you trust me?"

Terrance pondered the question and felt extremely uncomfortable. However, his other option was risking attracting attention and an interaction with the police. After an internal debate, he quietly answered, "Yes".

"Great!" she said. "So, this hall on the right is a straight shot to the end, where we will turn left again. Stay really close to me, and we are going to blow out the candles."

"So, no light at all?" he questioned.

"Correct, it's a straight path. Just put your hand on my shoulder. Our eyes will adjust to the dark even more, and the natural light coming from the windows will help us." She said with a reassuring tone.

"And you're sure about this?" he asked.

"You're the one scared of the cops. If someone drives by or a nosy neighbor sees two lights flickering past the windows, they are going to be called." She said.

"Fine!" Terrance replied with trepidation.

The two then blew out their candles, and Terrance placed his left hand on her shoulder. He seldom trusted another person so much, but he felt his choices were limited in the current situation. He continued to think silently to himself about how all his choices thus far had led him to this, but the one thing that kept him going was the possibility of this becoming his most successful story yet.

The hall was quiet, and the darkness seemed to occupy every corner of his vision. Once again, the sound of their quiet footsteps echoed through the hall. She was right, though; the more they trekked through the building without the candles, the more his eyes accepted the current conditions. He was amazed at how much light actually poured into the hall from the open doors. He still kept a close grip on Lily's shoulder; he was sure that he did not want to get separated and turn into one of those stereotypical horror movie characters.

Lily was silent and intent during the walk. In the darkness, she had lost sight of the map that she kept so closely guarded. She was working from memory, and she knew Terrance was reliant on her to lead them through the darkness. The environment did not seem to bother her; she was remarkably at home in the darkness. This was where some of her best work occurred, in the world of unseen things, which was so often attached to the dark.

She continued to walk until they approached the midpoint. This was the most dangerous intersection where they would encounter the greatest risk of exposure. Another hallway approached from the left; this was a short hallway that seemed to blast light into their path. This was the main entrance to the school, where the offices were located and where students and staff used to begin their day. She paused before crossing and looked back over her shoulder at Terrance. "We are going to move as close to the right as possible. I'm going to look down the hallway over there, and when the time is right, we're going to move fast." She said to him.

"Alright, just tell me when." Terrance responded.

"It's going to be quick, so just be ready." She restated.

Terrance gripped her shoulder more firmly as they edged over to the left side of the hall, almost hugging the wall. Lily used the shadows to cover her presence and looked towards the set of doors that were at the end of the hall. "Now!" she whispered, and the two of them quickly bounded across the light that was cast in the intersection and returned once more to the shadows of darkness.

Once they were safe and secure in the shadows, they walked slowly. Terrance maintained his firm grip, ensuring there was no possibility of separation. The hall once again grew cold as they continued their walk. Terrance was feeling his tension return the further that they moved. Lily paused once again just before the entrance to another classroom. "The principal — or at least his blood — was found here. It started in this hallway, like he fell and struck his head, then a trail of blood followed into this room where it just stopped." Lily said quietly.

"So, someone ambushed the principal and dragged his body in there," Terrance confirmed as he retraced the steps that were described by Lily. "Yes, and he was a former football player. By the pictures I've seen, he was a pretty stacked guy," she replied.

"This all just doesn't make any sense. How can they not find any of these bodies? I mean, it just doesn't add up," Terrance replied.

"That's where the supernatural comes in. There's a world around us that can't be seen. This whole incident, this town, Hailey — none of it can be explained in the natural world." Lily explained.

Terrance pondered her words. He was still skeptical of things that could not be explained by logic and science. Lily broke his silence. "We are almost there. Let's move on." She said in almost a whisper.

"Where are we going again?" Terrance asked.

"The room where they met, the room where this all began that night." Lily responded.

"I like the part where we are almost done." He responded.

Terrance once again placed his hand on her shoulder, and they continued to walk in the darkness. It was silent and cold as they pressed forward. Terrance was feeling relief as he knew this adventure was coming to an end. The hall eventually came to another intersection. Another hallway came into their view, which went to the right. Lily paused. "We will be able to light our candles once we start down this hall. The room we are looking for will be about five to six doors on the left. I will look at the map again when we light the candles again." She said.

"Great!" Terrance responded.

The two then turned right, entering a new and even colder hallway. This one seemed much darker than the previous, and Terrance was glad when Lily stopped and said they could once again light the candles. Lily opened her bag and blindly searched for her matches. Terrance nervously looked around, tapping his right foot impatiently.

It seemed like an eternity to Terrance as Lily searched and felt around in her bag. He felt uneasy; it was like an instinctual sense of danger. His heart beat faster, and goosebumps formed up and down his arms. The tension in the air felt thick, and he had the strange feeling that someone else was there with them. As he turned his head slightly, waiting for Lily to find the matches, his eyes caught something in his periphery.

He paused. His head and his thoughts raced. *Don't look, don't look, don't look.* But he could not contain his curiosity any longer, so he cautiously turned his head and saw a girl with long dark hair standing about twenty feet away from them. Terrance screamed in shock, pushing forward, causing Lily to lose her footing. The two once again fell onto the floor in the darkness.

"Have you lost your mind?" Lily shouted at Terrance in anger.

"Someone's here. There was a girl back there! We need to leave!" He said with his words almost coming out in gibberish.

Lily grabbed his hand and said in a calm voice, "Look, we are the only ones here. Your eyes can play tricks in the dark."

"No, I saw her!"

"If you saw someone, then you saw a ghost. Are you ready to admit that?" Lily continued in a calm voice.

Terrance took a deep breath. He knew he could not admit that there were ghosts. As much as his body wanted to panic, he began rationalizing. *Think logical Terrance; there's no such thing as ghosts. We've been in the dark for so long. You know optical illusions are real.* Terrance was ready to cast away his senses and rely on what he knew was real in order to ignore what wasn't.

The sound of a match being struck interrupted Terrance's thoughts. Light once again illuminated their surroundings as she lit the candles. "You've got to pull yourself together, Terrance. I know this is all new to you, but you're going to get one of us hurt!" Lily said with a sense of tenderness in her voice.

"I'm sorry. This just isn't my thing."

"It's okay, but remember I got you." She said as she brushed his left arm.

"I think this lack of sleep is taking its toll on me too. Letting my mind play tricks on me. I'm just exhausted."

"You'll rest soon. Let's finish what we started, shall we?" she said as she turned around.

Despite the candles being lit, the darkness that lay beyond the flickering light seemed even darker than dark could be, yet they still ventured forward. Lily paused for a moment and once again pulled out her map and confirmed the sixth door on the left was their destination.

As Lily counted the doorways, the sixth door silently approached and eventually it was illuminated by her candle. "Well, this is it," she said to Terrance, who finally broke his firm grip on her shoulder. The classroom entrance looked like any of the others, nothing special and nothing unique. There appeared to be a sense of anticipation surrounding the fact that this was where it all began on that fateful night those kids entered the school. This was ground zero for a series of events that would unfold, rather they be natural or supernatural; this was it.

The door was not closed but slightly cracked. From what light that crept inside to light up the interior, there were no unique appearances. It did not seem any different from the rest of the abandoned classrooms that dotted the hallway. "Well, you ready?" Lily asked.

"Sure, let's get this over with." Terrance responded.

So, without further pause, Terrance and Lily entered the dark coldness of Room 720.

Chapter 15

Dancing in the Darkness

The moonlight crept into the room from the single window that faced the courtyard. Old, abandoned world history books littered a bookshelf filled with cobwebs, and the desks that once held high school students scattered about the room in no order. The room was not unlike any other room in the old high school. The air in the room was stale and thick with a hint of mold. An unnatural coolness filled the room.

Lily walked into the room first with a glimmer of excitement in her eyes. She looked around, analyzing her surroundings. This is where she wanted to be. Terrance, on the other hand, entered the room with trepidation. The only thing that made this room more enjoyable for him was that it was their last stop and soon this adventure would end.

Lily sat her candle down on one of the abandoned desks and removed her bookbag from her back, placing it on one of the abandoned desks. She then quickly began running her hands along the other desks, losing herself in the experience. Terrance stared at her awkwardly, trying to figure out her excitement and enjoyment of this entire experience. He had not really found any tangible evidence, just stories, so he struggled to understand how the risk of entering this building had been worth it. He needed facts, not stories, to build credibility.

To Lily, though, this was something special. Of all the places in the building, this one was unique. This was where it all began on that fateful night. The night the devil walked into the school. This was the night that some power spread its horror to the entire town, affecting nearly every life that dwelt here. Despite the misery that began in this room, Lily seemed to take a certain pleasure.

She turned to Terrance, who continued to stare at her with his awkward gaze. "Do you feel it?" she asked. Terrance, never breaking his focus on her, responded, "Feel what?"

She silently chuckled. "This is ground zero. You can't feel the energy that surges through this room? The energy of pure chaos?" she asked.

Terrance would not admit it, but there was a strange feeling that he could not explain. It was like the feeling one gets just before the body decides on a path, *fight or flight*. There was a sense of impending danger. He ignored his instinct and said, "No, It's just a room."

"Oh, it's so much more, my friend. They opened a doorway that night, one that has opened here many times before. It's never been fully closed." Lily said with a smile.

"A door to what?" Terrance asked.

"To chaos," Lily said through her smile.

He was becoming uneasy. He felt something; it was a feeling like he should not be there. Danger alarms sounded in his head and manifested as goosebumps forming up and down his arms. The skeptic in him resisted and would not allow him to run or express his feelings. He fought his emotions and continued to listen to Lily.

"Young people are so stupid and ignorant. They find something and think that they can contain it, control it. But you cannot control chaos. You know if you dance with it, it takes the lead. The dance becomes its dance, and you lose yourself." Lily said as she walked over to where she sat down her bag.

Terrance had his senses return, and he looked over at Lily and asked, "How?"

"How what?" Lily said as she paused and turned back to him.

"How did they open a doorway?" Terrance clarified.

"Good question." She replied as she continued to walk over to her back. She began opening it and fiddling with the contents. Then she pulled out something dark. He could not make out what she was doing. He could tell it was dark and maybe some sort of book. She then turned and walked towards him with a dark book in her hands. "This," she responded as she showed him what appeared to be a book that had stood through the ages. It appeared worn and old.

"You said you wanted to see it. Now here it is. People give it many names, but the proper translation is The Book of Death." She said as she sat it down on the desk in front of him. Terrance felt the return of the feelings that he had been fighting. Lily opened the pages. "It is actually a book of life; it gives the reader, the practitioner, a new life." She said as she then looked up at Terrance.

"How did you get it?" Terrance asked while taking a few steps back.

"You do not find this book. This book finds you. It has now found us." She said.

Terrance began feeling more uneasy. He sensed the change in Lily. She had a determined demeanor that was freaking him out. *Why is she acting crazy now?* He thought to himself.

"Look, I told you I'm not into all this," Terrance said while taking further steps backward.

"Do you think it's a coincidence that we are together? That we met?" Lily asked.

"I was just looking into a story, that's it." Terrance said.

"Everything is by design. We now have all the tools to solve the mystery. Don't you want to know the answers? The truth? I brought you here to help you and for you to help me." She said.

Terrance's heart was now pounding as he was just about ready to run out of the room and take his chances in the halls. Just as he was about to turn around, a sudden sound echoed through the room. Terrance turned around, and the door to the classroom had suddenly slammed shut with an unseen force. Terrance looked now as though he was about to panic. "Do you still doubt this stuff?" Lily asked with a giggle.

"No man, this ain't happening. We got to go!" he said.

Lily then grabbed his arm and said, "I told you I would protect you! Nothing will harm you."

"How are you going to protect me or us? "This isn't right," Terrance said, trying to pull away.

"Stop, look at me and calm down." Lily said.

Terrance paused. There was something about Lily that seemed to give him security. "I will not let anything bad happen to you. You're special to me. Just like I had you at the house, I have you now."

Terrance's breathing slowed, and he looked into her eyes. Her eyes were peaceful and calm. They brought him comfort. "We are going to be okay." She said as she looked at him to give a reassuring smile.

The quiet was once again interrupted, but this time by a whisper or at least that's how Terrance took the sound. In the quiet, the whisper sounded like it said, "Run". It said it with urgency, and he responded by jerking away from Lily and looking around the room to find the source.

Everything he knew was now being challenged. The scream, the figure in the hallway, the door, and now voices. Terrance was in a panic, but not just because of the things happening around him. But now everything he held on to as truth was being challenged by his senses.

"They don't want you to know," Lily said

Terrance could no longer explain the things that were happening with logic and science. "They who? Who's in here other than us?" Terrance said in a panicked voice.

Lily walked closer. "They don't want you to see. They don't want you to know the truth of what they have done." Lily said in a stern voice.

"What?" he responded.

"They are like shadows of the past, stuck in an endless loop. They can cause you no harm." She said.

"This is crazy! We need to leave!" Terrance said with urgency.

"Not yet," Lily said. Lily stated, "We have not finished yet," she said.

"Screw this, we need to leave! I've done what you asked; now we need to leave!" he said, almost screaming.

"Haven't you had a career where you've fought to find the truth? You've let no one bully or scare you away from the truth. You don't even believe in this stuff, but you are so willing to give up when we are so close?" Lily asked.

"This is too much!" Terrance said.

"This could be your biggest story, your life's work complete, and the same with mine. Imagine never having to live from check-to-check, hoping the next story will pay the bills for the month. I don't know about you, but I grow tired of going from town to town looking for answers and evidence. It's all here! It's all here before us!" Lily said.

"This is different," he said.

"Why, because some unseen brats close doors? How many doors have the living tried to close on you before?" she asked.

Terrance took a deep breath and said, "A lot".

"And you've just let them?" Lily asked.

"No,"

"Of course not, you've torn the doors apart! Tear them apart with me now!" Lily said with authority.

"This, I don't even know anymore."

"Is no different. They can't harm you. I've got you. They aren't even on the same plane of existence to touch you." Lily said firmly.

Terrance again felt a sort of ease fill his body. Lily could silence the alarm bells in his mind. Ever since they first met, she had some kind of pull over him. Something that just felt comfortable. Lily walked close again and gently grabbed both of his wrists, pulling him closer to her.

"Nothing is going to harm you. Trust me, you're mine tonight and forever." She said as she leaned in and planted her lips on his. This caught him off guard initially, and at first he tried to pull back, but he gave in to her pillowy lips and returned the kiss. They felt warm, comfortable, and familiar. She then pulled her lips away. "Come sit with me," she said as she pulled him once again towards her.

Terrance could not explain his feelings. One moment ago he was filled with terror; now he was entranced by Lily. He was like a bug caught in a spider's web; he could not pull himself from her. He did not have the energy or even the will to resist her as he followed her towards the ground where she sat and pulled him down.

"I've got you, remember you said that you trust me." She said as she reached up on the desk and grabbed the book.

She set the book down in front of them, then leaned in and gave him another passionate kiss. "Trust me now; tonight we both will have the answers," she said as she opened the book and began searching for a page.

Terrance could not take his eyes off her lips. They were almost magical, just like her touch. He wanted more of them and more of her. He was not paying attention as she flipped through the old, worn pages of the book. Only when she stopped did he look down to realize that she had once again opened the book. He started to get back up once he saw the book sitting before him.

Lily placed her warm hand on his cheek and said, "We are too close now." She then gave him another kiss and returned her focus to the book. She again mesmerized him. "The answers are here." She said. Terrance looked down at the page. It was full of writing and words that he could not understand mixed with symbols that were as much of a mystery to his eyes.

"Tonight, you will have all the answers. You'll never have to worry about money or stories again." She said as she placed her hands on the book, feeling the pages. The room grew electric, as though lightning was about to strike. Terrance felt uneasy again, but she touched his knee to reassure him and comfort him. That seemed to take away the feeling once again. She then looked upward toward the ceiling.

He felt warmth take over his body in the cold room. The warmth gave way to an intoxicating feeling. Things felt as though they weren't real, but they were very much real. He tried to focus on her. She took her hands away from the book and then grabbed both of his hands gently.

He felt powerful energy surging into his body. Something was happening, but he could not explain it. He could not explain his feelings. He was losing himself in that moment. As he sat, he battled his desire to focus and his desire to let go. She was saying something, but he could no longer hear her. She smiled at him briefly to reassure him, but then she continued saying the unheard words. He caught glimpses of her eyes, and they seemed to have changed. They seemed different, darker maybe. His mind tried to question, but he lacked the focus or clarity to even grasp anything.

Then he saw something out of the corner of his eye. It was like a light, a glimmer, something coming from the hallway. He tried to look at it, but his eyes could not investigate or move much like the rest of his body. The door slammed open, and the light flooded inside. There stood a male figure in the shadows. He tried to focus, but it was difficult. His senses were now slowly coming back to him. Then, with a sudden burst of other energy, he heard the figure yelling something that he couldn't quite make out.

Lily turned around abruptly, yelling something inaudible to the shadow. She looked angry, with an anger that he hadn't seen in her eyes before. Then Terrance heard words for the first time since this experience began. "They know you're here; they are coming. We've got to go, Terrance!". He recognized the words; it was the old preacher. "We've got to go! They are coming!" the preacher said.

"Wait, we're not done!" Lily yelled and grabbed onto Terrance's knee.

Fear took over, though. The fight-or-flight response that had been battling inside Terrance finally let loose, and Terrance jumped up and ran towards the door. "Come on," Terrance yelled at Lily.

"This isn't finished," Lily said as she turned back to look at the book once again.

Terrance couldn't fight his need to run, and he quickly joined the preacher at the door. "This way!" The preacher directed. They rushed through the halls, leaving Lily alone in the room. Terrance was so full of the need to escape that he did not even look back; instead, he ran with the preacher through the halls and out an exit door into the courtyard.

Once he had left the school and entered the courtyard, things slowed down for Terrance. He then realized that he had abandoned Lily in the room. He tried to turn around, but the preacher grabbed his arm and said, "She will be fine; they aren't after her." Terrance turned back towards the preacher to question him, but then he heard it. Tires screech and engines rev. "You're almost out of time, son, now run to the hotel. I will hold them back." He said in a tone that sounded like it came from a father figure.

"What about you?" Terrance asked.

"They won't touch me; I'm the preacher," he said, reassuring Terrance. "Now run! Go to the room! I will stop by later and check on you." Terrance turned and ran towards the hole in the fence. He then slipped into the bushes, glancing back briefly to see a dark-colored pickup truck pull into the rear parking lot of the school. He also saw the flicker of blue lights flashing not far behind. Terrance looked back no further. He felt bad about Lily and the preacher, but he took the old man's advice and ran. Blending into the shadows of darkness and the overgrowth, Terrance ran all the way back to his room, quickly locking it and falling onto his bed in exhaustion.

His heart pounded, and he struggled to catch his breath. He felt scared; he felt remorse, but he also understood how trapped he was now. Without a car or phone, he may have lost his two town allies. He was feeling genuine fear for the first time in a long time. He thought about everything. The danger that lurked for him. The weird experiences that science could no longer explain came from the school. He just couldn't process everything that had just happened to him. *Who was after him? How did they find him? What happened to him and Lily? Where did the preacher come from?* These thoughts echoed through his brain. He didn't have any answers. Every time he got close to an answer, three new questions formed. He yearned so much to be with his family now. He regretted his decision to turn to this town. Everything was falling apart around him. Now, he was trapped inside his hotel room.

Dread and fear filled him. *What did he get himself into?* He questioned himself. If he had his car, he would leave and never return. For the first time in his life, he was willing to quit and let the story win. A knock at the door interrupted the silence of the room and the thoughts that danced in his head. His heart nearly stopped as he thought, they found me!

Chapter 16

Darkness and Light

Terrance lay still, sprawled across the hotel bed. He was breathing deeply, and his heart was pounding as once again there was a knock at the door. Terrance cursed himself for having left the lights on in the room. If they had followed him back to the hotel room, he was sure that they knew he was there. He looked around for anything with which to defend himself, but there was nothing of any use in the room. He stood up and started searching for something to defend himself. Opening the drawers quietly, he found a thick Bible that might be useful. There was a knock again, this time more urgent. He decided the Bible was thick enough that it could at least leave its mark if nothing else.

Terrance grabbed the thick book and walked towards the door and whoever was on the other side. He placed the book in his right and reared back, ready to strike any potential threat. He reached for the door with his left hand and took a deep breath while swinging the door open. The preacher stood on the other side of the door. Jack gasped as he saw Terrance rear back his arm to swing his hand and book at him, but Terrance stopped when he realized it was just Jack.

Jack looked at the Bible in Terrance's hand and smiled. "I like your choice of books."

"I'm so sorry, Pastor; I thought you might have been one of those guys after me," Terrance replied. "No, you are safe for now, but time is running out and we have to get you out of here." Terrance invited Jack inside and offered him a seat at a small table that sat just beside the window in front of the old couch.

"I'm sorry, I can't stay long. I mainly wanted to check on you and make sure you made it back all right." Jack said.

"Thank you for your help tonight. Why are they after me?" Terrance asked.

"Maybe they don't like where you're heading with things." Jack replied.

"I'm just trying to find answers." Terrance said.

"I think you already have the answers. Now you just have to make a choice." Jack paused for a moment. He looked tired and more worn than Terrance had previously seen him. He was already an older man, but tonight he looked exhausted. "You know, I think I will take your offer," Jack said as he took a seat at the table. "My time is running out here, Terrance. I'm afraid I just have very little left in me." Jack said as he coughed.

"I really can't thank you enough; I thought we were so careful." Terrance said as he joined Jack at the table.

"Careful, not quite. I know you are looking for answers, but they are staring you right in the face." Jack said as he coughed again.

"Where?"

"First, right there in your hand," Jack replied.

Terrance looked down at his hand and realized that he was still holding the Bible in his hand. He gently placed it down on the table and looked at it. "I told you; I'm not really into that religious stuff." Terrance replied, still staring at the book on the table.

"You saw some stuff that you couldn't explain tonight? Felt something too, I imagine?" Jack questioned.

"You could say that," Terrance said as he thought about some of the strange things that occurred in the old school building.

"All the answers are right there, son," Jack replied while looking at his pocket watch.

"Did Lily make it out?"

"Who?" Jack responded.

"Lily, the girl who was with me," Terrance replied.

"Oh, don't worry about her. She isn't happy right now, but she is going to be just fine." Jack reassured him.

"They didn't hurt her, did they?"

"Who?" Jack asked, looking slightly confused.

"The men in the truck. They didn't hurt her, did they?" Terrance asked with a look of concern on his face.

"No, nobody is going to harm that young woman. They couldn't, even if they wanted." Jack chuckled to himself.

Terrance looked confused. "It is nice that you are concerned about her, but let me be honest with you. You really have to be careful about who you are hanging out with in this town." Jack said.

"What do you mean?"

"When you came to me that day at the church, you asked me about something that you had read. It was a warning. First Peter, chapter five, verse eight: *Be sober-minded; be watchful. Your adversary, the devil, prowls around like a roaring lion, seeking someone to devour.* It's a good warning. You told me you're not a religious man, that you have no faith, but somehow you knew this verse." Jack said to him with a look of concern.

"It was in the police report. It was the words that Dylan, your son, kept uttering." Terrance said.

"No, it wasn't," Jack responded.

"Yes, it was in the police report."

"I buried my son Terrance. I buried both of them and my wife shortly after. He was in bad shape when they found him, and he didn't last long. He said nothing like that. He couldn't even say a word when they found him." Jack said calmly, but with emotion drifting into his voice.

"That's not possible; I read it in the report."

"Son, all you have been seeing is what you want to see. You need to wake up!" Jack replied.

"What are you talking about?"

"Men, we are all just alike. We live in the world, we see the world, but all we really see is what we desire. My eldest son killed everyone there that night. He got mixed up in some stuff. He got mixed up in some really dark stuff. He was looking for answers in all the wrong places. I told you before, he was a troubled boy. I should have seen the signs; heck, I'm a preacher, but like you, I only saw what I wanted to see. By the time I realized it, I had lost two sons and a wife." Jack said as a tear ran down his face.

"This can't be true. Dylan is in an asylum." Terrance said.

"I did something no parent should ever have to do; I buried two sons and even did both funerals. If you don't believe me, go to the cemetery yourself. The one at the back of my church. There you will find both of their graves." Jack said.

Terrance got up and walked over to the couch to look over the papers, the police reports. Jack got up too. "Son, you need to wake up and look around you! Time is running out. Get some rest tonight and meet me at the pond at noon. I will get you out of here," he said as he grunted and held onto his lower back, getting up from his seat to head towards the door.

As Terrance began looking for the file, he struggled to see clearly. Things got fuzzy, and the room around him changed. He was no longer seeing the room that he had called home the past few days, but one that reminded him of the school. The light of the lamps had disappeared, and the room was dark, lit only by the moonlight that was filtering in from broken curtains. From what he could see in the darkness, everything appeared much older and worn. The overwhelming smell that struck his nose was the same odor that assaulted him at the house. The room looked abandoned.

Terrance breathed deeply as he tried to look around and process what he was seeing before his eyes. Just then he turned around to see the old preacher, but there was no one standing behind him. The door was wide open and allowed more natural light to flow inside. *Did he leave?* Terrance thought to himself as he continued scanning the room. His eyes hadn't adjusted to the darkness yet, so everything seemed like a dark blur.

Terrance walked towards the door and peeked out into the parking lot. He was startled to see that everything had changed. The parking lot was empty, and the sign that was once lit was barely still standing on the post. Terrance could not process what he was seeing. *This can't be possible, he thought to himself.* He then wondered if Lily had slipped him something. *That must be it*, he thought as he remembered the intoxicating feeling he had at the school. As he continued to step out into the parking lot, he felt dizzy and lightheaded. The limited light around him faded, and in an instant, he lost consciousness.

Terrance awoke, startled. He was lying on top of the comforter. He was right where he fell into the bed before he heard a knock on the door. *It must have been a dream,* he thought to himself as he slowly got out of bed. He felt weak in the knees as he stood up. He smelled himself; he just couldn't get the smell of that building out of his nostrils, and it seemed to be stuck in his clothes as well. His mind was racing too much to go to sleep. He was struggling to determine if the preacher's visit was a dream, if the things at the school were an illusion, and then about the room changing before his very eyes. He knew he could not fall asleep with so much on his mind. Reaching into his pocket, he thought to grab his phone, but he realized it was gone. He then walked over to the table beside his bed and read the time of two o'clock on the old alarm clock.

He knew it was late, but the smell was really bothering him. A shower, he figured, would solve two problems. It would give him a chance to process things and at least hopefully remove that awful metallic smell from his body and out of his nose. Terrance felt the strength returning to his legs as he walked over to his suitcase and retrieved some clean clothes. As he looked into his suitcase, he realized that his supply of clean clothes was quickly dwindling. He decided he would use the phone in the room to call his family tomorrow. Though his car was still missing, he could get someone to come pick him up.

Though he was not a quitter by nature, this time things were just too much. He could handle some of the physical risks, but now his mind was faltering, and he decided things had gone too far. The time was now to go home. There he would do the rest of his investigating from safety. He believed he could retrieve any information held in the library online as well.

Terrance selected his clothes, and then eagerly went into the shower to feel like himself again. He turned the water on and waited for it to get hot. Terrance looked forward to returning to his shower at home. Not only was it much nicer and cleaner with its modern looks and white tile, but the water would heat almost immediately, saving him this unpleasant time just waiting to see steam rise. He was once again reminded of his childhood home and just how much of a luxury hot showers used to be as a child. With so many brothers and sisters in the house, it was like winning the lottery to get to go first. That was just about the only way to ensure you could leave the shower without freezing to death.

While Terrance reminisced about his childhood shower, the water slowly began to warm and steam slowly rose. Terrance took notice of this sign and transitioned the water from running through the bath faucet to the shower head. It hissed as it ran towards the shower, then finally poured down into the shower. Terrance did the touch test, and once he was confident of the correct water temperature, he entered the shower.

Terrance scrubbed his body and tried to erase the smell. He wished some memories could be washed away as well. Though his body was tired, his mind was racing. *What happened in the room?*

What was Lily doing? Is Lily okay? These thoughts mixed with the guilt of leaving her behind. "Did the preacher actually come to his room, or was he dreaming that?" Terrance then pondered what was a dream and what was reality. The two seemed to mix in his memories, and he was having difficulty processing it all.

His thoughts turned to Lily and those familiar lips. *Did I dream that too?* He wondered. In his life, things had always been black or white. Things were true or false. Now he thought about his experiences, and he could no longer tell. The longer he stayed in this town, the more complicated things became. His mind then went to the black truck that seemed determined to terrorize him. His heart sank as he wondered if the truck now was even watching him with occupants who wanted to destroy him. *Who were they?* He wandered.

The more and more time went on, Terrance regretted his decision. Through all the things that he had experienced, he had no answers. He had nothing he could write about. There had been no mystery solved. It seemed like everything had just been a waste. The more he dug, the more questions rather than answers appeared. Even when he gets back to Atlanta, he wonders if he even has a story to work with.

He thought back on the preacher's warning that he needed to leave, *but did the preacher even speak those words or if it some subliminal message that his mind was sending him in a dream?* He knew he needed to leave this town, but it seemed to make everything that had happened to him — his stolen car, the lost cell phone, the near-death experiences — all were meaningless if his work was not complete.

Terrance then thought about the value of his life. *Was the risk to his own safety worth continued digging, or should he trust his judgement and call the house tomorrow?* Nothing here seemed to make sense. It all started like a typical investigation into a story, but each day made it seem so much more. For the first time in many years, he was now even thinking about religion and the unseen world.

His mind then went back to Lily and the book. *Something seemed to change in her with that book and in that room. She didn't even seem to be the same woman.* He then thought back to himself. He felt intoxicated and powerless. *Was there something supernatural, something in that book?* He thought as he quickly dismissed those thoughts, seeking a more logical answer. His mind then went back to Lily and her face. Right before Jack came into the room, her eyes looked different. It was almost as if she were no longer in control of herself either.

He was so mad at himself. He allowed himself to run out and leave her. Now he had no way to find her or to check on her. She had saved him at the house. Aside from Jack, she was the only one in this town who was truly nice to him or even seemed to want to help him. He felt remorse as he thought about how he had betrayed her. He no longer thought about the events in that classroom, but about his own actions. Running away like a scared child caused him to second-guess himself and his own mental strength. Since adulthood, he has never failed. For the first time in years, he thought of himself as a failure.

Terrance lost himself in thought as he scrubbed his scalp and body. He just couldn't process everything. Never in his life had he been at such a loss as now. He was a college graduate, the first in his family to go to school. An independent researcher, journalist, he had a successful freelance career. He was unaccustomed to not knowing, understanding, or processing things. He always researched and found answers. Even in graduate school, with the stress of trying to work and make it on his own, he could find answers. But now, he felt stifled and blocked. He was confused and lacked clarity. He felt he needed guidance, but there was no one who would understand.

Alone in this town, he did not know who to trust. He grew suspicious of Lily. Even though he felt guilty about how he left things, he still couldn't understand what had happened between them. He felt, in a sense, betrayed and manipulated by her. However, he couldn't quite understand why he felt that way. He still had difficulty even processing what had happened in Room 720 or what had caused him to feel the way he did during their interaction. He still had some strange feelings towards her that he had difficulty processing as well. It was a mixture of intrigue, lust, and maybe something else that continued to draw him to her.

There was the old preacher who seemed keen on helping him. But the more Terrance thought about Jack, the more he grew suspicious of him as well. *Somehow the preacher knew I was in that school. Was he following me?* Terrance thought to himself. *And if so, why was the preacher following me? Was the goal to keep me safe, or was it to interfere with finding answers? What the preacher said in person or even in the dream was contradictory to the evidence that he had and even parts that Lily had told him.* Terrance still did not know if the conversation had occurred in the hotel room or if that had been a dream too.

These thoughts brought him back to the dream itself. *Even if I knew for a fact, it was a dream. The hotel room and everything around me changed. What did that mean?* He thought silently as the warm water rushed down his body.

Terrance was not the type of person who believed dreams had any more significance that things of the subconscious, but that meant that there was some type of meaning or significance that his brain was trying to process. This endless loop and cycle of thoughts continued to play in his mind. The more he cycled through everything, the more distant the solution or truth became. He had now finished showering, but he still just stood under the running water trying to make sense of everything. He knew tomorrow would be his last day here, but he still wanted some type of answers, anything logical to bring back with him before he departed.

As Terrance stood still under the running water, there was a loud clash that came from the bedroom. Terrance jumped at first, his nerves still weary from the school. Then he froze as he became concerned that the occupants of the black truck might have broken in. He stood trying to listen for any sound outside, but there was none. Nothing but silence since that first clash. He eventually got enough confidence to shut off the water and listen more intently for sounds in the silence.

There were still no other sounds, so he wrapped a towel around his body and exited the shower. He knew he was vulnerable and had not even a Bible in his hand to act as a weapon, but he also knew he could not stay in the bathroom forever. So, he took a deep breath, ready for whatever was going to come next. He then opened the door to the bathroom and took that heroic step out into the room.

There was nothing — no sounds, no one in the room — to threaten him. Then he realized the picture. He had not checked to see if anyone had rehung the picture, but that same sound had scared him more than once. So, Terrance turned the corner and, sure enough, the picture was on the ground as it had been so many times before. He lifted it off the ground and just sat it beside the wall. He would not bother hanging it again; he thought it would be much safer for his heart and nerves to keep it on the ground where it could not fall again.

Terrance looked at the bed. He knew he needed to get some more rest. He knew it would be a struggle with all the thoughts still dancing in his head to fall asleep, but he began his routine of getting ready for bed. This was going to be his last night here, and that thought could at least hopefully bring him just enough comfort to fall asleep. He needed at least some sleep for the day ahead.

Chapter 17

The Final Night

Terrance tossed and turned for over an hour with thoughts passing through his mind like two passing semi-trucks. The thoughts were loud, and still he could not put them to rest. Eventually, as the minutes continued to move closer to the rising sun, Terrance fell asleep. The room was quiet, with the sound of the fan giving a slight hum of white noise only to be interrupted by the occasional drip from a faucet in the bathroom.

He fell asleep hard once sleep came. His mind was finally at rest. That rest eventually gave way to vivid dreams. He dreamed of his childhood home and the pleasant memories he had long forgotten. Afternoons on the front porch, wearing down his hands, helping his grandmother with the zipper peas or helping his father and grandfather work on the tractor. They were good memories from his childhood. Filled with nights of chasing lightning bugs through the front yard. Not everything was bad in his childhood home. There was love above all else. There were times of conflict as in any home, especially with as many siblings that crowded the old farmhouse. However, love seemed to permeate the home.

As his dreams progressed through his childhood, his teenage years were a little less peaceful. Especially with his father becoming ill and passing. He relived the old preacher who had tarnished his faith. Then came the moment that he left. He and his mother rarely ever argued or fought, but the day he left to attend Georgia State in Atlanta was one of those times. His mother felt betrayed by his sudden departure on the eve of a great trial for his family. They were struggling to make it and struggling to keep his childhood home, but he was determined to start a new life for himself. He relived the argument, the tears, and the words that kept him from ever returning.

Terrance stood in the living room trying to tell his mom why going away to college would be good. It would change not only his life, but hers. "None of us ever needed to go away for schooling; we need you here." His mother spoke in desperation.

"I'm not built for this life, Momma. This is not my life!" Terrance told his mother passionately.

"This is your life; this is where you belong, Terrance!" his mother said as she raised her voice with tears beginning to collect in her eyes.

"No, Momma, I belong in Atlanta! I belong in the city!" Terrance said as he raised his voice to match hers.

"Boy, you're being selfish, and I didn't raise any selfish children." She said in a loud, authoritative tone.

"I'm sorry that you feel that way! I'm gone!" Terrance said in a loud matching tone. He then reached for the door, opening it just enough to walk through before he slammed the door shut so hard that there was a loud clash upon the ground. On the front porch, he paused just on the other side of the door. He heard his mother screaming his name and crying, but he did not turn back. He walked off the porch and got in the waiting car, where his friend was waiting to drive him to Atlanta.

Terrance's dream did not leave with him; rather, his dream took him to the other side of the door. That was always a regret; he could have at least gone inside and comforted his mother and at least helped her to understand. Inside the house, his mother was crying on her knees as she slowly got up and leaned over the picture that had fallen from the wall. It was a picture of a similar old country church, much like the one that his family attended. The fall had broken the glass, and his mother wept as she collected the pieces of the glass and cried out her son's name.

His dream went back with him on the car ride on the way to Atlanta. He was sad, but excited about his new life in the city. He and his friend made small talk, and Terrance looked at the old familiar views as though to say a last goodbye. As he looked out the side window at passing farms, lakes, and woods, the image of a black pickup truck kept appearing closer and closer in the side-view mirror. It got closer until it was eventually tailgating them. His friend continued to drive and talk about the days of childhood, seemingly oblivious to the threat behind them.

The car halted, and Terrance looked forward to see Lake County High School. He looked over to ask his friend why they had stopped in front of the school, but the driver's seat was now empty. He looked back out the side mirror for the threatening truck, but like the driver's seat, there was nothing. Terrance sat alone in the car before he eventually got out.

He walked to the front of the school. Things were different now; the school was no longer abandoned, but full of life. There were students walking past him who seemed to ignore his presence. They seemed to pass right through him as though he were a ghost. He eventually went inside, and instead of the cold, abandoned halls he had visited when awake, these were alive. The halls were alive with color and banners advertising the upcoming Fall Ball.

The light of the school quickly faded to darkness, and the students who once filled the hall had all disappeared. Terrance continued to walk around the same halls that he had previously visited, but at least now they were lit with security lights. The smell and everything were so different. He heard a door close, and then he heard voices approaching. He ducked around a bank of lockers, unsure if those who approached would see him.

The footsteps and the voices got closer to his position. They seemed young, like teenagers. His heart beat faster as they got closer and closer. They were right on top of him. He closed his eyes, waiting to be discovered, but they continued right past him without taking even a pause. Terrance stepped forward and watched the group continue down the hall. Following them from a distance at first, he grew comfortable that they could not see him, so he moved closer.

He listened to them and heard the familiar names of Chase, Dylan, Ashley, and Peyton. He knew this must be the group of students that had disappeared. Somehow, he was dreaming of the night they disappeared. He counted them; there were ten. *That's not possible,* he thought to himself. *There were only nine, and only Dylan made it out alive. Including the principal, there was one extra person!* Terrance continued to follow them and listen to them talk about football games and other names that he could only assume were classmates. *Wait, what about the other two Lily had mentioned disappearing outside? Why weren't they included in the police reports?*

He was trying to listen to the words that they said as followed them through empty halls, but his mind still raced with questions. They stopped in front of a classroom. Terrance glanced up and saw Room 720. They entered the room with blankets and beer. Dylan watched them joke around, but he seemed to sit separately from most of the group. They passed around beer and began drinking while Dylan continued to sit isolated.

While the teens drank and became intoxicated, Terrance tried to place the different people. There was one that stood out. No matter where he stood, he couldn't get a glimpse of her face. Every time he would turn to face her or try to get a closer look, there was interference, either she moved, or someone got in the way. She was a dark-haired girl, and so far no one had called her by her name.

As they continued to get drunk, their conversations shifted from normal teenage discussions to trying to understand the reality of the universe and the world. That was when, for the first time, he heard the unknown girl speak. The voice sounded oddly familiar, but he could not place it. Unlike everyone else, who seemed under the influence and slurred their words, her voice sounded sober. "The reality is simple; there is no reality. We live in a world separated by only a thin veil," she said. Chase spoke up. "They just don't understand, baby."

Chase's use of the word baby caused an instant reaction from his ex-girlfriend, who gave a scowl towards Chase and this unknown girl. The girl spoke up again, directed towards Chase. "Did you bring the book?" she asked. Chase stood up with a wobble and walked over to a bookbag sitting at an adjacent desk. "Yes! It's right here," he said as he pulled out the book, showing it to the group.

One teen asked about the book, and Chase responded, "This is the book that reveals the unseen. This book reveals the true reality."

"What are you doing?" Ashley asked.

"Opening a door to the other side," Chase said with a smile.

"We are just here for a good time, not crazy witchcraft stuff!" Ashley said as she turned to Peyton and another girl to make a comment.

"Gather around; let's see if this works," Chase said.

There was inaudible banter between the teens as they argued, but one by one they caved to what Chase wanted. The teens gathered in a circle, and Chase held the book out on the floor in front of him. He began uttering phrases and words that Terrance could not understand. Then, out of nowhere, there was a gust of wind that blew through the room with so much force that the door slammed shut. It scared everyone in the room except Chase and the unknown girl. Many of the teens got up, and Ashley complained, "This isn't funny."

Terrance looked at Chase's face; it was different. It was as if he were in a trance. His eyes were closed, and he did not respond to the outside commotion. Then, his eyes opened. They had a black appearance, and everyone reacted with a scream. "What did you do!" Ashley screamed. The unknown girl stood up and moved behind Chase, placing her hands on his shoulders.

"What did you do to him!" Ashley screamed.

"He's mine now," the girl responded with a deep and more mature voice.

Chase just stared with his eyes totally black like the night sky, the mysterious girl standing behind him with her hands firmly planted. The rest of the group stumbled around trying to figure out what was going on.

One teen shouted, "We've got to get out of here!". The unknown girl laughed. Then in a calm voice she said, "You can't leave! We aren't finished yet."

Peyton then screamed in pain, grabbing her left leg, where a series of three scratches appeared seemingly on their own. Ashley tried to comfort her, but Peyton jumped up and followed by another girl. They abruptly ran towards the door, which they quickly opened and ran through the door and disappearing in the darkened hallway.

The girl continued to laugh as she said, "Good luck!" The rest of the teens just stood in shock, sobering quickly as they tried to understand the events that were occurring. Ashley stood up never breaking her gaze at Chase and the girl. "Hailey, what have you done?" she said as she looked at them both.

Terrance could now make out the girl behind Chase. She was a young brunette girl with a ponytail. Her eyes appeared to be as black as Chase's. *No way, this is the same girl,* Terrance thought to himself. Hailey tilted her head towards Ashley. "You wanted to know where I was from; I'm giving you your glimpse," she said in a steady tone.

"Who are you?" Ashley asked.

"I am many things to different people. You do not like what you see?" Hailey responded.

Ashley jumped up. "Screw this!" she said as she turned away, leaving Chase and Hailey to go find her other two friends, who had already fled the classroom.

Chase remained still, as did everyone in the room, who still appeared in shock. Dylan did eventually walk over and kneel in front of Chase. "Chase, come on, man, break out of it!" he said to his brother. "Hailey, please stop all of this! This is too much!" Hailey glared down at Dylan with her pitch-black eyes. "I wanted you to share in this, but I had to settle for him. I told you that you were special to me," she said as she tapped Chase with her hands, saying, "It's time" as she removed both hands.

In a sudden movement, Chase grabbed Dylan, lifting him with unnatural force, and threw him across the classroom. Dylan struck his head on the wall on the other side and lay dazed on the classroom floor with blood slightly running down his face. Terrance was in shock. He wanted to leave, but somehow his dreams trapped him in the room, unable to move.

Chase, moving faster than any human that he had ever seen, then moved to attack the rest of the occupants. He quickly dispatched the other teens effortlessly. One boy escaped the assault. Terrance followed behind him as he made a sprint through the halls. Everything seemed so cold and different now. The teen went for a set of doors, but the exterior doors wouldn't budge. He tried with every bit of force in his body to break through the door, but it wouldn't budge. Then the security lights fluttered, and the teen saw his former friend standing at the opposite end of the hall. Knowing that he could not escape, the teen reached out and pulled a fire alarm as a last-ditch effort for salvation.

The alarm sounded, and the strobe lights flashed. Salvation would not come for the boy though as Chase sprinted in his direction and with the same force he had used on the others he slammed his friend's face first into the wall. Now Terrance stood alone with Chase in the hall. Terrance was now terrified that somehow Chase could see him as he stared directly through him. Chase stood with his face so close to Terrance that he could feel his breath and smell the alcohol on his breath. Just as Terrance was sure that Chase was going to attack him, he simply turned around and walked away.

The alarm echoed through the hall as Terrance stood there alone, then there was a feminine voice, "I told you nothing would hurt you." He twisted his head to see Hailey standing a few feet away from him. She looked directly at him with her black eyes. "We aren't finished yet," she said. This terrified him, and just like the teens earlier, Terrance took off running. As he ran through the halls, he heard another voice. It appeared to be masculine and authoritative. "Who's in here?" the man called out. Thinking of safety, Terrance ran towards the voice.

As Terrance came to the front of the school, he saw the man. He was a grown man, older with gray hair. Terrance called out, "Help!", but the man ignored him. Instead, the man heard a noise in the other direction and turned to investigate. "Don't go!" Terrance called. Suddenly, an unseen force threw the man against a wall. It didn't kill him or knock him out, but he landed on his stomach. The man attempted to get up, but something grabbed him. He screamed and disappeared into another room.

"You're safe with me, Terrance," a voice sounded directly beside his right ear.

Terrance took off running once again with the sound of feminine laughter behind him.

Terrance looked for places to go or any sounds of other life. As he ran through the halls, he was all alone, trapped in the school building once again. As Terrance ran towards an opening with a skylight, he heard crying. He was hoping for someone other than Hailey, and he went into the bathroom where the crying sound was coming from.

As he entered the bathroom, he saw Ashley staring at the mirror above the sink, crying. Terrance remembered the story Lily had told him about this room. Before he could try to interact with Ashley, an unseen force threw her backwards. She screamed an ear-piercing cry as she vanished into the stall behind the sink. Terrance immediately recognized her scream as the same he had heard that night. *It was no owl.* He thought to himself.

Before he could leave the bathroom, a familiar voice greeted him. "You wanted to know the truth; now you have it." Hailey now stood in the doorway, blocking him from escaping. Terrance wanted to cry; he was now trapped by something he could not even understand. He shook with fear as she got closer. "Why?" is all that he could get to escape his lips.

"You wanted your story, now you have it." She replied.

"Who are you?" he asked, with a shake in his voice.

"This is just a dream, just a bad dream." Terrance repeated to himself.

"A dream? Reality? What really is the difference? Most people can't tell anyway." She said in a mocking tone.

"I just need to wake up! Come on, Terrance, wake up!" he continued to say to himself.

"Why? You got your answers, and I told you nothing would harm you." She reassured him.

"Why me? Why am I here?" he asked with a timid voice.

"I like you, Terrance. Just like I liked Dylan. This is our destiny. The choices you've made have intertwined us," she said with a smile. She stepped closer to him.

"We just met; you don't know me! Please, just let me go!" he said.

She stopped her approach to him and said, "We've been friends for a long time, Terrance. I've known you since you were a child stealing money from your mother's purse. You knew the old woman barely had any money, yet you still stole it. Oh, and the day that you broke your mother's heart by abandoning her. You know we've shared so many moments together. I especially liked all those drunken nights at the clubs when you would just use a woman, then throw her away in the morning. You know, I think you really have commitment issues. Fortunate for you with all your faults, I've really grown fond of you, and I've been waiting for today."

Terrance gulped as he stared at her and processed her words. "Just a dream, just a dream," he muttered to himself. Then he looked up at her with a question in his eyes.

"Ask it, go ahead even though you know the answer." She said with a smile.

"Who?" he stammered. "What are you?"

"Like I said, you know the answer to your own question. Why don't you just say it?" she said in an icy voice.

"This is not possible," he whispered to himself.

"Of course it is! After all, what was it your grandmother used to warn you? Oh, yes." Her voice changed and perfectly mimicked his grandmother's. *Keep acting like that, boy, and the devil's gonna take you away.* She then switched to her deeper tone. "Now we're going to finish what we started!" She grabbed him and pulled him close to her. He could only stare into the darkness in her eyes as everything went black, and he lost all senses.

Chapter 18

The Dark

In the dark, he heard the muttering from loud voices that sounded like a chorus of chaos. He could not make out a single familiar voice. It was so loud, then the light returned, and he was standing in a crowd. There beside him was a figure that he was familiar with. It was Robert Sterns, a tall middle-aged man with salt and pepper hair and blue eyes. He was the chief editor of a magazine that he had tried to get his stories published in before. Sterns had a reputation as a beast and was well known for his cruel rejections, but now he stood right beside him.

Sterns then struck his wineglass with a utensil to get everyone's attention to make an announcement. With Terrance beside him, Sterns sat down the utensil and placed his free hand on Terrance's shoulder. "Let me tell you about this man," he said as he looked over at Terrance and then back out to the crowd that had now become completely silent. "This man lets nothing stand in his way to find the truth. Nothing will get in his way, and we need more bulldogs like that here. So, I want to introduce you all to our newest team member, Terrance Greene," he said as the crowd erupted in applause.

Sterns gave Terrance another pat on the shoulder, then disappeared into the crowd. Terrance was now surrounded and met with endless congratulations and welcomes to the team. He had finally made it! He was standing at the forefront of accomplishing all his dreams. Slowly the loud voices of the crowd returned, and Terrance mingled with the others enjoying high-end champagne and hors d'oeuvres. He forgot about the terrifying experiences at the beginning, Lake County High School, and Lily. It was as if those had never happened as he continued to be celebrated.

The girls all looked at him, and the men all shook his hand. This had been Terrance's lifelong goal — to be recognized in such a way. His talent was now seen by all. Everything — all the blood, sweat, and tears — had finally paid off. Terrance was a made man, and the future looked bright.

The more that Terrance reveled in the excitement and consumed endless glasses of champagne, the stranger the room grew. He was feeling like he did that night at the school with Lily. His senses seemed overwhelmed as things spun because of the champagne and stimuli. He was getting lost in a sea of people. Their voices became more like an echo as things spun more and more until he could no longer make out visible figures. Things grew black again as the senses overtook him.

When his senses returned, he was sitting at the kitchen table of his mother's house. It was just how he remembered everything. The same faded tablecloth on the round table and the vintage chairs that were old when he was a child. His siblings were gathered and walking around the kitchen grabbing snacks and drinks, then returning to the living room. He was taking in everything around him. He had not been in the house since he was a teenager, but everything looked exactly as he had remembered it.

His eldest sister came in and leaned down, giving him a big hug. "Hey Stringbean, how's that city life treating you!" she said as she released the hug and then walked away. Then his older brother, a gruff man in his late thirties. He looked so much like their father. Time in the sun had worn his skin. His brother even sported a similar beard that was already showing signs of gray. He leaned in and shook Terrance's hand. His hands were rough and coarse, just like their father's. "See these workingman's hands, city boy." He said as they shook hands. He then stepped back and said, "It's good to see you!"

Terrance was confused, still dazed and trying to figure out what was happening. He realized he was at his mom's house before or after the funeral. The amount of food and family was the giveaway. Even though his family were all on the other side of the kitchen door, he just could not find enough energy to get up from his seat.

People continued to enter the kitchen, acknowledge Terrance, and then leave the room. Terrance remained still, contemplating everything. He wanted to believe this was real and that somehow he was back at his mother's house. Maybe he made that call and had one of his family members come and get him. But he still just couldn't move and free himself.

The noises from the other side of the door soon became a distant echo until all that remained was silence. He now sat alone in his childhood home, in the kitchen at a table where he had received some of the most sage advice from his mother and father. Things were so silent that he heard every drip of the faucet in the kitchen sink. Then, a loud clash from the living room interrupted the silence.

Finally, Terrance could move, and he slowly got up so he would not lose his balance. He still was not feeling himself, and his legs were like rubber as he tried to walk across the floor to the kitchen door. He eventually gathered enough strength to push the door forward and enter the living room.

As he stepped through the door, he looked around. His legs were still weak as he scanned the living room for the offender that had produced that crashing sound. As he scanned the room, he saw family pictures. He walked over to the fireplace to look at a picture that he had not seen there before. As he walked closer, he realized it was a picture of him. It was a picture of his graduating from Georgia State. He did not know any of his family members attended, but there in a dark wooden frame was a picture of him in his graduation apparel walking across a stage.

Terrance felt his eyes begin to tear up. He had long thought that they had abandoned him like he had them, but someone had come to his graduation. Terrance walked over to the bookshelf that stood beside the old brick fireplace, and he saw something else that caught his eye. There was a large envelope that had "Terrance" written on it in dark marker.

He reached over to the envelope and picked it up. It felt heavy with papers, though they were of differing sizes and did not form a neat stack. Terrance carefully opened the envelope and reached his hand inside. There, he felt several papers of varied sizes stacked together. He pulled one of them out, and it was one of his first articles. He pulled out another to find yet another article that he had written. This went on until the envelope was completely empty, each piece of paper another article. *They were still keeping up with me!* Terence thought to himself with surprise. *I may have given up on them, but they never gave up on me.*

Terrance regretted the years that he had wasted without a visit. Though he talked to his mother on the phone, they were always quick conversations. Terrance fretted about the lost time, the lost connections, and now there was nothing he could do to change things.

Terrance sat the envelope back on the shelf and continued to look around at other pictures. They were pictures of married couples and babies. Terrance then realized that many of the faces were foreign to him. He received many invitations to weddings and learned of many new births, but he never went. As he looked over the pictures, he realized just how many new nieces, nephews, and in-laws he had never met. With many of them, this was the first time he had even seen a picture.

Terrance felt convicted about his negligent use of time. He knew he could never get this time back, and he had let it fade away while living in the city. He looked back at his own life and thought of everything he had accomplished. The more he thought about it, the shorter the list of accomplishments became, as the list of regrets quickly overtook it. He had no wife, no kids, nor anyone to really share his life with.

Terrance had colleagues, but not any friends. He had brief relationships with women, but nothing serious. Hailey was right in his earlier dream, so many times he just spent time with a woman, then cast her away. He could not even remember the last serious relationship that he had in his life. The isolation that he felt in Anderson was not much different from that in his daily life.

Terrance stepped back from the pictures, remembering that he had come into the living room to investigate a sound. He scanned for fallen knick-knacks or anything that could have produced the sound, then he saw it. A picture had fallen beside the front door, and the glass covering it shattered across the old wooden floor. Terrance lifted the picture up, and as he did so, a piece of glass stuck into his right index finger.

"Damn!" Terrance said as he pulled his finger back abruptly, revealing fresh blood. He then leaned down more carefully to look at the picture more closely. He examined it and realized its familiarity. It was the same old church from the picture in his hotel room. The same picture that had crashed to the floor every day since his arrival. Terrance remembered he must be dreaming. Terrance sat the picture back down carefully as he did the one in the hotel room. He then stood up and began looking around at the rest of the house.

The silence was once again interrupted, but this time it was the sound of someone moving about the kitchen. It did not sound threatening, but more like someone putting up dishes. He carefully turned around and walked back towards the kitchen. The sounds continued — the clashing and banging. He once again reached for the door and slowly pushed it open.

There at the kitchen sink stood a round, short woman with dark hair. She was wearing a familiar apron that he had seen many times before and a yellow shirt. The woman turned around from the sink and looked directly at Terrance before turning back to continue her work at the sink.

"Momma?" Terrance uttered barely audible under his breath. "It's about time you came home, son! You see what a mess they left me?" she complained as she continued to place dishes in the sink and rinse them off. Terrance could not believe his eyes as he tried to process the sight before him. "Momma", he said again, now more clearly.

She turned around and pointed over to the table where Terrance had sat earlier. "Go sit now and let's talk," she said as she walked over towards the table. Terrance followed his mother's commands and had a seat back at the table. She joined him and started talking. "You've done got yourself in trouble. We have little time. I want you to listen to me carefully." She said in a motherly tone full of concern.

"I'm so sorry, Momma," Terrance said with sincerity in his voice.

"I know, but we haven't got time for that right now." She said abruptly.

"Why? What's going on?" Terrance asked.

"You're in trouble, boy, and I can't save you. This is on you!" she said sternly.

Terrance nodded, but her statement confused him. She continued, "You have to choose. You have to want to be saved! I taught you everything I know. You listening, boy?" She scolded.

"I've just missed you so much, I'm so sorry." Terrance cried.

"Now, enough of that! Now look at me! Look at me!" she commanded.

Terrance looked at her. Once she was content that she had his attention, she continued, "Time is running out! You've got to wake up! Do you hear me! Terrance Eugene Greene, wake up!" Once again, he felt strange, and the room spun around him. His surroundings faded to black.

Terrance now stood on an isolated old country road. It was paved, though potholes and rough pavement made it seem more like an old dirt road. He looked around. Pastures lined both sides of the road. He remembered this road now; this was a road that he had taken many times to his best friend, Moses's house.

Remembering Mo, as he called him, and the days they would spend running around and getting into trouble in some of those pastures brought him a sense of nostalgia. He hadn't seen Mo in over a decade. Hearing that he had gotten several girls pregnant, he now stayed in the county jail. He remembered those simple, carefree days, and part of him yearned for their return.

Continuing his walk down the road, he reminisced about his childhood memories and the good times. He had often forgotten about the good times and allowed only the bad memories to stay on the surface. It always seems that the bad memories jade the past and cover up everything good, and Terrance realized this as he continued reflecting on the past.

He regretted his life choices. When he left, he was mad, and he had allowed anger to keep him from returning, from being part of the lives of his nieces and nephews. It made him sad to think that if he saw them on the street, or they saw him, they would be nothing more than strangers. He wished he had at least come home for the holidays or birthdays. The thoughts of missed opportunities of time that he would never get back filled his mind.

Compared to everything he had experienced until now, this was the most peaceful. He had forgotten what fresh country air smelled like. He had forgotten the sounds of birds and other animals that combined to form the chorus of nature. The sounds of traffic, music, and people covered these sounds up in Atlanta. He had forgotten just how peaceful life could be when one takes a step back and just absorbs the surrounding wonder.

Amidst the peaceful chorus, a familiar sound crept up in the distance. It was the sound of an approaching vehicle. At first, he could just hear the wind and air hitting the car, but he soon heard the engine and the tires roaring down the road. The sound was familiar to him, and he turned to see the approaching vehicle. The vision of a black pickup truck quickly greeted him. It was the same truck that had plagued him so many times.

Terrance had just enough time to react and leap into a ditch before the truck struck him. The safety of his dream was once again violated as his heart raced as the truck raced down the road. He slowly got up from the ditch to see that the truck had stopped not far ahead. Its brake lights looked like two red evil eyes staring back at him.

He remained still as he contemplated his next move and awaited what would happen next. The bright reverse lights replaced the ominous red brake lights as the truck backed up and spun around to face him. Again, his heart raced, and his breathing increased as the truck raced towards him. He ran in the ditch's safety, trying to create as much distance as possible, but the truck left the road and soon joined him in the ditch as it raced towards him, striking up dirt and debris, throwing it many feet behind the truck.

He continued to run as fast as he could as the truck grew closer and closer to him, but his feet just could not carry him the distance that was needed. The sound of the roaring diesel was now merely feet behind him. He could feel the heat of the approaching engine, and he braced for the end. Then once again, there was darkness.

With his eyes shut, he could hear music. The music was so loud he couldn't hear anything but the thumping bass as it vibrated through his body. He looked around and felt himself for damage, but his body was fine and intact. The truck was nowhere to be seen, and the bright sunshine was now replaced with pulsing and flashing lights. He looked around and realized that now he was at a club. It looked like one of his regular Atlanta spots he liked to frequent.

Once again, he tried to understand his surroundings. He was no longer in his childhood past, but back in the present. He was in the middle of the dance floor, and his body was betraying his thoughts as it moved with the rhythm of the music. As he continued to survey his surroundings, he noticed a girl in front of him. Her shape was familiar as it moved with the music and grew closer to him.

He realized he had been here before; it was like the dream that he had on the first night. This girl, whom he couldn't see more than her figure, was now dancing on him. As much as his mind tried to fight his body, the body seemed to win as it joined hers. Now more confused, he continued trying to understand everything that he was seeing and experiencing. Terrance tried to make out the girl's face, but the more he tried to focus, the more it became elusive.

She danced closer to him, and the music seemed to become muffled as the night seemed to center on them. Their bodies became one moving on the dance floor. His mind became intoxicated, and he tried to escape for some clarity, but he could only see her. This unknown figure in the pulsating lights of the club. Everything outside of them became an echo, and his mind became more and more cloudy and reality more obscure.

The club became darker slowly at first, but then the darkness overtook, and the only illumination was that of the pulsating strobe and flashing blue and red lights that were on the ceiling. Terrance looked up and focused on the flashing lights as her body continued to move on the dance floor. The girl's face was now even more obscured by the darkness as he continued trying to get glimpses of it.

Somehow his body position had now changed, and he was on his back. He looked for the girl, but she was no longer visible. The flashing blue and red lights were now replaced by the flickering glow of candles. Just to his right, he saw movement, a motion in the dark shadows. It was the girl again in the same dress as before, but now she was not dancing, but was steady and intentional in her movements.

He tried to make out her face again or at least what she was doing, but his brain continued to be foggy. Again, he was in a daze, much like at school. He felt separated from his senses and the reality of his surroundings. He was a passenger, and his body was no longer his to control. The woman then came closer. He could not move his head or body to gain any further perspective. His heart should be racing, but he could not even feel the beats of his heart or his breath. He was just there, unable to move or control any of the situation. Had it not been for his disoriented thoughts, he would have been terrified.

She moved in the shadows ever closer, in dark clothing. It was like she was part of the shadows that surrounded him. Everything was surreal, then her face peered down at him. The image of her face was once again fuzzy, but coming into focus. He could make out the outlines of her lips, nose, and eyes, but that was about it. Slowly, though, he gained clarity, and through that clarity, the image of her face sharpened. Her dark eyes came into focus, and he realized it was Hailey now standing over him with an ominous smile on her face.

She kneeled to sit beside him, never breaking eye contact. All he saw was her darkness. There was no life in her eyes; they were the lifeless eyes of a shark. She continued to smile as she stared into his eyes. Anxiety started to build, yet the hold remained unbroken. He was stuck as a prisoner on this journey. He was powerless to do anything but wait for what was going to happen next.

She finally broke the silence and said, "I told you, we weren't finished," as she brought the book back into focus. She sat the old black book on his chest and began uttering something that he could not make out as she broke eye contact with him and read from the pages of the book. Terrance could finally feel something again, but he did not like what he felt. It was an unearthly coldness, one that could never be warmed. The cold seemed to travel through his flesh and make its home in his very bones.

She continued saying words he could not understand. Energy filled the room, like electricity. He felt like an insect caught in a web, unable to move as the spider sucked out all life. He felt as though he was going to lose consciousness; things got dark, and the coldness continued to fill every fiber of his being.

Suddenly, the darkness and shadows were illuminated by a bright light. It was a light that he had never seen before. There was warmth in the light, something almost supernatural. He could just move his head enough to see what looked like a shadow or figure just inside the light. Hailey never stopped or paused but seemed to utter words more quickly and desperately.

The figure grew clearer, and Terrance could begin making out certain aspects of who was there in the light. He thought it looked like the old preacher, but unlike the last time he saw the man, this time he was full of authority and life. A voice called out from the light, "Wake up, Terrance!" The look on Hailey's face became full of anger and hatred. She called out words Terrance still could not understand. But over her shouting, he heard the old preacher's voice overtake hers as he called out from the light, "Terrance! Wake up!"

Chapter 19

The Awakening

Terrance breathed heavily. He was wet, covered in sweat. He lay on his back panting and trying to catch his breath. It was morning, and sunlight was creeping into the old hotel room. Terrance tried to sit up, but his body still felt frozen on the bed. He tried to speak, but words would not come out of his mouth. He felt paralyzed, still shocked by the dreams that had haunted him. The more he tried to move, the more his body stubbornly resisted every urge. He could feel his heart pounding and his breath trying to recover to a normal pace, but he still could not move.

As a sudden jolt hit his body, he slowly felt control returning. He moved his arms and legs slowly. His hands and feet slowly joined and had full control over his body. He slowly sat up in the bed, being ever cautious not to try it too quickly at the risk of losing control again. As he sat up, he looked around the room. Everything was as he had left it before he fell asleep. His clothes littered the floor by the bathroom, and the picture remained propped up against the wall. The picture caught his eye, and he looked down at it. He remembered his dream; it was the same picture from his dream that he had knocked down when he slammed the door at his mother's house. *How is this the same picture?* He thought to himself, still dazed from his experience.

Terrance tried to clear his head and process the dream. Not only of the dream, but of the entire night. He felt like he had a hangover, but he had consumed no alcohol. His head pounded, and his brain still had residual fog. The alarm clock beside the bed showed seven o'clock as he looked. He had slept solid for several hours. He pondered everything and its connection to his dreams. *Could the dreams be real, or were they the brain processing the prior night's events?*

He began thinking about Lily again. *Was she okay? How could he have just left her?* He became more agitated the more he thought about it. There was just too much for him to process. The dreams were so vivid, and so connected. *Dreams are merely the brain replaying the events of the day or previous memories.* Terrance worked to make sense of this all, so that he could rest comfortably in his reality. He just could not accept that these things had more of a connection than his brain.

Terrance also considered something he had read years ago about sleep paralysis, which happens when you wake up while your brain remains locked in the REM cycle. He was getting comfortable with the circumstances again, but as his brain and senses came back to what he considered reality, he remembered the black truck and the real tangible threats that existed in this town.

Recalling his plan, he would call his family this morning to see if anyone could pick him up. He had no faith that the police would ever find his vehicle. In fact, he was sure that they had something to do with its missing. He also had no plans to return to the school again to find his phone.

Terrance stood and paced about the room, regaining his strength from a long night both in the awake and sleep phases. He turned on the lamp beside his bed and took a seat. He didn't know how they were going to react to his call, but he knew he had to get out of this town. Despite not getting everything he needed, he still had his life. He really felt in his gut that his life was not secure in this town, and perhaps that's what his brain was trying to relay to him in his dreams.

Terrance leaned over to the old corded phone that still had a rotary dial. Fortunately for him, his grandmother had a similar phone mounted to the wall in her kitchen. He had played with it many times as a kid. What would have confounded most millennials was something that he could actually operate. This was going to be the first time he actually used a phone like this for more than play, but he was confident that he could make it work.

When he picked up the phone and put the receiver to his ear, expecting a dial tone, silence greeted him. He placed the receiver down and tried again. There was still no dial tone. He looked at the back of the phone and followed the cord to the wall. Everything that he could see looked connected. He felt frustrated again. Nothing seemed to work out for him after he arrived in this town. He tried one more time to put the phone down, put it back to his ear, and silence greeted him again.

He felt like throwing the phone across the room, but he resisted the urge. Instead, he took a deep breath and cleaned himself up a bit in order to make the call in the hotel lobby. He needed coffee, and even though it was not very good, any caffeine at this point was better than nothing. Terrance grunted as he got back up and headed to the bathroom. He looked back at his bed and how wet it was from where he had sweated. Shocked, *just how much did I sweat?*. He considered taking another shower, but he didn't want to wait for the shower to warm up.

Looking through his belongings, Terrance finally found something to wear. His most recent adventures were causing most of his clothes to be wearable for only one day. He knew that he would have to wash his clothes somehow when he got to his family. His mind went back to his family. He became worried that they could be mad at him for being so late to his mother's funeral. Terrance thought of his choice to come to Anderson as just another terrible choice among so many he had made in his adult life.

Terrance thought about how he had made material things and status such a central part of his life. Now, he was alone in this small town and estranged from his family. If anything, the dreams he had last night made him think about his family more and the priorities that he had set in life. He was fearful about his sanity, which he felt was growing more confused and distant. Also, his physical safety was at risk, increasingly so each day.

Once dressed, he was ready to leave his room. Before he opened the door, he cautiously approached his window to pull back the curtain and look out into the parking lot. It was emptier than usual, but more importantly, there was no black truck lurking around the lot.

Once he felt safe, Terrance slowly opened the door and walked to the hotel lobby. When he opened the hotel office door, he noticed it seemed eerily quiet and devoid of human presence. The sarcastic clerk was nowhere to be seen, and the pot of hot coffee that he had hoped for was replaced with a dirty empty pot containing little remains of its previous brew.

Terrance walked over to the counter, and it looked as if no one had dusted it in weeks. He tried to remember whether he had noticed the lack of housekeeping before, but he could not recall. However, he noticed it now and just how dirty and unkempt his surroundings were in the lobby. If only he had been this observant upon checking in, then maybe he would have saved himself some trouble by skipping his stay in Anderson. As he thought more about it, he actually was having difficulty remembering the day he checked in. Although it was only a few days ago, there seemed to be a fog in his brain preventing him from remembering everything.

Terrance called out to the clerk and listened for a response, but there was no answer and no sounds from the office. Shrugging it off, thinking she must be in the restroom or handling other hotel duties, he continued to look around and located a phone just on the other side of the counter. He looked around once again for any sign of anyone else around, but he remained the only one present. Cautiously, he reached across the counter and picked up the receiver.

As it had been in his room, the sound of silence once again met his ear. He used his other hand to click the button, hoping to elicit some response, but the phone remained dead.

Terrance pondered his next move. He could wait for the clerk to return and see if there was another phone, or he could head to the library and at least make the best use of his time. Standing still momentarily, he weighed his options and decided to be productive. He hoped he could accomplish two goals: look over some reference materials and perhaps find a working phone so that he could expedite his departure from this town.

Terrance walked back towards the door of the lobby and paused once again, looking outside for the black truck or any other threats. He saw nothing, just an empty parking lot. *Am I the only guest?* He thought for a moment before he pushed open the door and entered the vacant parking lot. As he walked out to the parking lot and towards the sidewalk, he looked back at the hotel and noted the dilapidated state of the hotel. *Have I just not noticed how bad this place really is?*

He shrugged off his observations and walked towards downtown on the sidewalk. His mind raced back to the dream. In the dream where the hotel was abandoned, his room was not in condition for occupancy. But that was not the case; he just slept there, and sure, the bed wasn't in the best condition, but it was livable. He hated that he was even questioning his own senses at this point. This town had taken a physical and emotional toll on him, and he was eager to put it all behind him. Leaving only a memory of this town, which he hoped to forget.

He missed his condo, and he missed Atlanta. He missed the sounds of life; the horns, the sirens, the people, and even the sounds of passing vehicles. The silence here was more noticeable than usual today. He noticed the lack of traffic as he walked closer to town.

It almost seemed abandoned. If he had had his phone, he would have checked the date to confirm that it was Monday. The more he thought about it, the more he decided it had to be Monday. His mother's funeral was Wednesday; he had not lost track of time here. He searched for reasons for the silent nature of his surroundings, and he finally settled on the fact that it was later in the morning, and he must have missed the small-town morning rush hour. *Everyone must be at work by now*, he thought to himself.

He continued his walk towards the town, and his memory went back to Lily and the preacher as he walked past the church. The church seemed empty, then he remembered the preacher had invited him to go fishing today, so his absence made sense. As he passed by the church, he caught a glimpse of the cemetery, and he remembered Jack's words or maybe his words. As Terrance thought about it, he grew frustrated that he was having trouble remembering what came from reality and what had come from his vivid dreams.

Regardless of where the comment came from, he remembered the words, "I buried both of my sons." *If that was true, then the report that Frank had given him along with the newspaper clippings from Lily were false.* The more he thought about it, the more convinced he was that it was just another dream. He wanted to keep walking by and go towards the library, but another set of words echoed in his mind: "Open your eyes!" and "Wake up!"

Terrance paused and made the decision that a quick visit couldn't hurt anything, at least just to check off all possibilities. Once he entered the graveyard, he realized it was much larger than it appeared from the sidewalk. He looked around and saw several graves dating back to the late 1800s and even some belonging to former Confederate soldiers. He looked for the newer graves that had cleaner or more modern-looking headstones.

As he began his search, he considered abandoning it as he realized just how much work this was going to take set in. However, he pressed on systematically, row-to-row, looking for newer graves and those with flowers. Eventually, he found a newer section of graves and walked in that direction.

Grave-by-grave, his search was fruitless. He saw countless headstones bearing various names, but no Davenports. He glanced over his shoulder and realized that he had gone much deeper than expected as the fencing and roadway disappeared from the horizon, being replaced by neatly organized rows of countless headstones. Continuing his walk, he neared the back of the cemetery, where newer graves were visible.

As he searched the upcoming rows of stones that arose from the tall blades of grass, he became more frustrated that this was taking so much time. *Am I wasting time on this fool's errand?* He thought to himself as he still could find nothing. He couldn't find any names familiar to the case, but as he was getting ready to turn around, he finally saw something familiar: the name Carmichael.

It was not the newest grave in the cemetery, but there it stood higher than the others, rising like a small monument from the weeds that otherwise covered the ground. The grave's condition showed a long absence of visitors. The limestone had fallen to time and instead of being a bright gray, mold covered it, making it almost a dark graphite color. "William George Carmichael" and "Hillary Lynette Carmichael" were carved directly under a cross on the timeworn headstone. Under both names, the date of death was March 25, 1968. Just to the right of the grave was another smaller headstone bearing the Carmichael name. This grave belonged to George "Georgie" Stewart Carmichael. Just like the previous one, this one had the date of March 25, 1968. The birthday was January 10, 1958, which placed this young man at about ten years old.

As he studied the names and dates, Terrance realized this was the Carmichael family from the house and factory based on the dates of death. He glanced around looking for Hailey, but there were no other Carmichael graves in the area. The other graves bore different names, and all dated back to earlier in the twentieth century. Terrance stopped in front of the larger headstone and pulled out his backpack and began writing the dates from the headstones into his notebook. As he wrote, he missed his phone and the ability to take pictures.

Terrance looked around for additional graves bearing familiar names, but all the names in the immediate area seemed foreign. He paused and looked over his notes and the old clippings to refresh his memory before proceeding further. After he glanced and felt confident in his memory, he walked once again through the tall grass to the rows that he had not seen. He continued to scan the graves for Hailey's name. As he walked closer to the rear of the cemetery and got deeper into the brush, he felt his shoes bump up against something that offered resistance and seemed to move. He looked down to catch the tail of a snake scurrying away from him and going deeper into the tall grasses. This sudden sight caused Terrance to fall backwards, landing on a rock that struck just to the left of his tailbone. This caused Terrance to feel an abrupt, sharp pain that coursed through his body.

Terrance, though stunned from the fall and the shock of pain, suddenly remembered that he was not alone in the cemetery. He jumped up in a panic to escape the clutches of his slithering foe and, in doing so, lost his balance and lurched forward. To stop his second fall, he reached out and grabbed onto the closest headstone. He paused momentarily to catch his breath and to allow his heart to slow its pounding in his chest. As he looked down at the headstone that had been his saving grace, he noticed another familiar name, Ashley Hartley.

He once again pulled out his bookbag and scribbled down the date of death, October 14th, 2006. Terrance glanced around at the other gravestones and noticed that this was not the only Hartley.

Directly beside Ashley's grave was Warren F. Hartley, with a date of death as February 18, 2007. Based on the age range, Terrance calculated that the young man had to be in his mid-twenties. The odd thing about this grave was the inscription. Not only was there a death date, but it also included the language *End of Watch*.

Terrance looked closer at the headstone and read an additional memorial: *Thank you for your service to the APD. Rest in peace. We have the Watch.* He thought the name sounded familiar. *Had this young man been a police officer?* Terrance thought, *why does this name sound familiar?* Terrance at least knew this was most likely the brother of Ashley or some other relation, so he made notes in his notebook. He sat back up and continued reading the names on the graves, then he came across another familiar name, Dr. Tony Roberts, beloved educator, with a date of death matching the others. Beside Dr. Robert's name was who Terrance assumed was his wife, Miranda Roberts, with a date of death a day after her husband.

As he continued to walk further back in the cemetery, he inspected the dates as he passed more closely. Terrance counted at least three graves with the dates of death being February 18th. The ages of the deceased varied, with some who were elderly and others as young as twenty-five. Terrance stopped at a bench that sat at the crossroads of rows and opened his notebook again. He began looking over the clippings that Hailey had given him. He was looking for anything in them that could have explained February 18, but there was nothing. The clippings contained the same information that he had looked over several times and had almost memorized. The more Terrance thought about it, the more he realized there had to be something significant about that date.

He looked further down the rows and saw a mixture of dates, but there were at least two more that bore the date of death as February 18th, 2007. As Terrance sat resting and thinking about everything he was seeing, he also pondered how much more time he wanted to spend in the cemetery. There were still some graves that he had not seen, namely the Chase Davenport. He continued his trek further into the cemetery to satisfy his quest.

He stretched as he got up. As he stood up, he felt a sharp pain in his side that made him flinch. He looked down and lifted his shirt to check for the cause, and he was shocked to see a large bruise that covered his right side and went up his abdomen. He thought to himself, *Where did this come from?* Feeling around, he analyzed the bruise that somehow he had not seen when he was getting dressed. *There was no way I could have missed it!* He now remembered why he had been so eager to leave this town. Unexplained scratches, dreams, and now a massive bruise. The bruise hurt more, almost linking to his new awareness of it, and it gave him a throbbing pain. He wondered if he had done it when he fell because of the snake, but if anything, his butt should be bruised, not his abdomen. Terrance stood up straight, defiant of the pain. The sooner he finished, the sooner he would use the phone in the library and call home for a ride. He did not have time for any more of this town's mysteries, at least until he got as much as he could about the current one.

He placed his backpack back on and continued walking cautiously in the tall grass, scanning for snakes and also looking closely at the dates on the headstones. The graves of Matthew Ekner and Eric Scarborough had matching death dates: October 14, 2006. Terrance paused again and pulled out his clippings and compared the names of the missing students and confirmed these were two other football players who had joined Chase that night. He wrote the information in his notebook and continued his march forward.

The next familiar grave belonged to Peyton Mullins with the same October date, but she wasn't the only Mullins. The names of who he assumed were her father and mother were on the headstone directly beside hers with the date, February 18th. This was the first time that he had seen two people together with the same date.

However, as he continued his walk. It was not the last. Not only were there husbands and wives who died on the same date, but even a family of four with two children.

Terrance was now convinced that something must have happened on February 18th, something that had to be a major event in Anderson. He wondered why he hadn't heard about this event from anyone, Hailey or Jack. Neither of them so much as mentioned anything on this date, but now by his count there were over thirty people who had died on that date. This date intrigued Terrance because there had to be some significance. He wrote it down in big, bold letters at the top of his paper.

He had just about covered all the grounds of the cemetery, but he was still missing the Davenport grave. There was just one section remaining that he had not explored. He went to the last corner, which was under a large oak, and finished his expedition. As he walked closer to the last section, the noises in the tall grass startled him once again. He stopped and looked around for anything to use for protection, but there was nothing. Terrance wanted desperately to finish this so he could leave the tall grasses behind. He took two slow steps forward, then a burst of motion shattered through the tall grass, causing Terrance to jump back. A rabbit then tore past Terrance, disappearing in the grasses behind him among the headstones.

His breath and heart rate once again increased from yet another jump scare. He was ready to be done, but this last corner under the oak tree beckoned him. As his breathing slowed, he realized that a new pain soon joined the pain in his side and abdomen. As he breathed, he took notice of a sharp pain in his chest and diaphragm. He decided he was too close to stop and continued slowly walking forward. With each step forward to this last corner, the pain in his chest seemed to grow sharper, as if some unseen force was trying to keep him from walking forward. This caused him to grow more defiant and convinced that he had to finish what he started. Though the pain grew in his chest and side, he walked through it, walking closer to the tree.

The increasing pain was not the only thing that Terrance began noticing as he continued his journey. He had been too distracted to notice at first, but the partly cloudy skies had grown covered by clouds, and now a fog seemed to coat not only the cemetery but the surrounding area. It was as if something was trying to keep him from progressing. However, unseen force or not, Terrance was determined that nothing was going to stop him.

As the pain increased slightly with each step, the sounds of nature decreased. The sounds of birds and other wildlife had completely ceased, and the only sounds that remained were his own breathing and footsteps. He approached the old oak tree, which revealed three rows of graves that he had not previously seen. They were much like the rest, unvisited by the townsfolk, with tall grasses and weeds almost hiding them from the world.

He continued to walk forward, and he took notice of a name that seemed familiar, though it was not Davenport; it was David Pierce. He knew he had heard this name before, and he glanced through his notes, but it wasn't until he got to the first page that he saw the name written on his paper. As the words written by his own hand appeared before him, a chill ran down his body — David Pierce–Police Chief.

Terrance stopped dead in his tracks, his heart racing once again as he read the headstone. "Chief David Pierce, beloved public servant. End of Watch March 16, 2007". He was stunned. *This was not possible; this must be some type of mental game. I've met him twice.* He thought to himself as he stood in shock. There was another grave directly beside, Christopher Eugene Peirce, with a birthdate of January 19, 1990, and a date of death March 16, 2007. *His son? On the same day?*

The sound of a twig snapping behind him abruptly cut his shock off. Once again his side and chest were hurting; they were almost on fire, and he quietly stood awaiting another sound. He had the feeling, the instinct, that there was another standing behind him, but there were no other noises. Waiting, he expected the next sound or something to strike, but nothing occurred. He turned around slowly. With the fight-or-flight reaction building in his body ready for the next move, he slowly turned, and there was nothing.

He turned fully around to get a better look, but there was nothing. There were no animals, no people, no snakes, just another row of headstones. That was when his eyes caught just what he was searching for, Davenport. The sight of the name beckoned him, causing him to forget momentarily the chief's grave. He cautiously walked through his pain towards the Davenport graves. As he walked closer, he noticed that there were multiple Davenport graves in this area. The first two names were none that he recognized and had dates that were in the 1970s and 1980s. Then he saw it, Chase Davenport. He scribbled down the location and the date of death, October 14, 2006. Directly beside Chase was another newer grave with the same date; this one bore the name Dylan Davenport.

Terrance once again had cold chills traveling down his spine. The papers in his bookbag conflicted with this. They said Dylan was the only survivor at the high school that night. Even the police report mentioned Dylan's surviving and being transported to the hospital. Terrance was stunned. His eyes were telling him one thing directly in front of him, but everything he had read so far was in direct conflict. As he stood once again in shock, another Davenport grave caught his eye. It was next to Dylan's and had two names written upon it, with the name Davenport. He slowly shook off the revelation about Dylan for a moment and moved closer to the other grave to get a better look at this other grave. The date of death came into focus. The one under the presumed wife read December 7, 2006, but under the other it was the same February date. Margaret Davenport was the first name. He could not fully read the other name because of the moss, but he saw "Stonewall Davenport," and the middle name ended in "SON," although the beginning remained blocked from view.

Terrance began analyzing his memories. *Is this a grandfather or other family member buried beside the boys' mother?* He thought to himself. As he continued looking at the names and dates, he became further confused. He did the math in his head, and the dates would have to be Margaret's spouse, but his date of death were the same as all the others. Jack never mentioned Chase and Dylan were his stepchildren during their conversations. So, he considered this new mystery surrounding the man buried with Jack's wife.

Something began feeling strange as he continued to gaze at the headstone in front of him. Things were not adding up, just as they hadn't added up since he had arrived in Anderson. The throbbing pain in his abdomen interrupted his concentration once again. He winced momentarily, but leaned forward and began dusting off the moss from the middle name on the grave. As he dusted it off, the rest of the name was slowly revealed: "STONEWALL JACKSON DAVENPORT".

He continued to dust off the rest of the headstone and, finally; the tribute revealed itself. The inscription said, "Jack and Marge, devoted servants of the Lord, whose sacrifices will never be forgotten." Terrance's blood ran cold as he read the words to himself, then said out loud, *Who have I been talking to?*

Terrance stood up and became angry as he thought about the deception. He suddenly forgot all his plans to go to the library when he remembered Jack's (or whoever he is) invitation to go fishing. He'd grown weary of the lies and deceit in this town. There was no one to trust, and every time he thought there was an ally, he discovered it to be false. As he stood up, the pain increased, but he was now angry and ready to confront this liar. The anger made him forget his mother's funeral and calling home. He was at his breaking point, and it was time for him to confront this old man and whoever else might get in his way. With determination in his eyes, he packed his bookbag, threw it over his shoulder, and, forgetting the now throbbing pain, to face his foe. As he walked through the tall grasses, he commented to himself, *This ends here!*

Chapter 20

The Encounter

Despite the pain, his walk was brisk as he navigated the empty streets of Anderson's downtown to go towards the pond, which lay on the outskirts of town. It was a long walk of nearly a mile. He knew it passed by Frank's trailer, so despite not having a map for navigation, Terrance felt confident that he could find it. He was so lost in his thoughts and anger that he paid little attention to how quiet the streets of Anderson were on this day. It was as if the whole town had stayed home today. During his walk, he did not encounter a single vehicle. In normal circumstances, he might have taken notice of this and at least thought it strange. However, the combination of anger and fighting the pain kept him distracted just enough not to notice.

It was not just the town's lack of traffic that seemed odd. The downtown almost appeared ghostly, with the dense cloud of fog covering a significant portion of the town and the streets obscuring most things from view. There was a strange energy, but one that Terrance either did not feel or ignored. Despite the oddity of the town this morning, he continued his march to the upcoming battle, a confrontation intent on finally getting the answers that he craved.

His walk took him out of the downtown, and along a quiet and tree-covered state route. He walked further away from the town, disappearing in the fog as he walked up the hill to where Frank's trailer sat. As he walked past the trailer, he glanced over and took notice that it looked in worse shape than when he had visited a few days before. He didn't see Frank's car in the driveway. As he glanced over and took notice of an open front door and lack of a car, he thought to himself; *I guess he finally got out.*

He walked up another gentle hill where the trees gave way to the pond, which lay like a mirror to the right of the roadway. Terrance looked on the shore of the pond to find the old man. Although the fog had become less dense and almost absent as he got closer to the pond, there was no trace of the old man.

The silence from the cemetery was still present, and the pond stood eerily still. There were no sounds of birds, insects, or even aquatic life in the water. As Terrance walked beside the pond, a familiar sound suddenly broke the silence that had followed. The loud revving of an engine and the sound of large truck tires speeding down the road. Startled, Terrance looked back to see the same black truck that had taunted him throughout his visit speeding towards him. Terrance ran towards the safety on the other side of the pond. He knew if he didn't get ahead far enough, his other choice was to attempt jumping over the guardrail and into the pond itself. So, he sprinted like he had many times in track. He ran like a child attempting to run away from the neighbor's dogs. A full sprint, with only the sounds of his feet hitting the pavement and the engine of the truck getting ever closer.

Terrance could see the other side of the pond and the end of the silver barrier. It seemed so close, but at the same time so distant as the sound of the truck got closer. His heart pounded more fiercely than even his feet striking the pavement. The opening crept ever so closer, but so did the sound of the racing truck. He sensed the engine's heat against his back, and as it appeared his fate was sealed, he jumped over the guardrail that had blocked his escape.

He landed not in the pond, but in some brush that broke his fall. While the brush saved him, it also aggravated the injury to Terrance's abdomen and side. The truck sped past, and he gathered himself, lying on his side in the brush. He lay there for a moment, but the sound of the truck's screeching tires as it suddenly applied the brakes forced him to get up. He glanced around to ensure that his bookbag was still on his back. Once he was sure that everything, including himself, was intact, he decided that his next course of action was to find a path deeper into the woods to get further away from the maniac in the truck who seemed bent on his destruction.

With his heart racing, Terrance desperately looked for an opening in the heavy brush to hide deeper in the woods. The pain and panic that he was facing from yet another near-death experience seemed to make things more difficult. Terrance was having trouble forming reasonable thoughts as he tried to find an escape. The roaring sound of the diesel engine still sounded from the roadway, as though it was patiently waiting for him to step back onto the road. To his surprise, he still had heard no one get out. However, this did not cause him to slow as he continued scurrying through the heavy woods.

He finally found an opening, a small footpath that led from the roadway and further into the woods. After everything, the last thing that he wanted was to hike into the woods, but with the truck waiting on the other side of the trail, like some predator stalking its prey, he felt there was no other choice for him to make.

As he walked on the trail, he looked down at his body to inspect for damage from his jump. Besides his bruises, he was now covered with scratches and scrapes. Blood stained his jeans along his right knee, and he noticed rips in his denim. Now that the adrenaline had ceased its flow through his body, he could feel the pain. It was much more intense now. He felt as though someone had beaten him, and his bruises proved his pain. The trail was actually fairly smooth and worn, which made his walk a little easier. Despite the condition of the path, he still limped along the trail, finding it a struggle just to continue.

The trail seemed to follow the pond, and Terrance hoped it circled the entire pond so that he could escape further down, away from the truck. Once his senses returned more from the stress of the truck, he once again noticed the silence. Even further into the woods, things seemed eerily silent. In Atlanta, he would frequent Piedmont Park. It was a popular park and always noisy from the number of visitors. However, even without the sounds of the many human visitors, there were birds chirping and squirrels running up trees. However, here there was nothing, just the sounds of his footsteps.

He regretted not being with his family. Everything seemed to go wrong as soon as he made the choice to come to Anderson. *Why did I make this choice? Why did I turn left?* His mind focused on his choices and where they had led him. Even though he had not looked forward to coming down for his mother's funeral, he would have been secure and safe there. He would have been with family, but now he was all alone. He had no one here to trust, no one here to protect him or have his back. It was just him, and if he disappeared in these woods, no one would ever know or even be able to find him. His car was gone, and his cell phone was lost in some abandoned school. In the past, he had been in some precarious situations, but things were now more dire than they had ever been in his life.

The stillness and quiet bothered him the further he went into the woods and around the pond. Things just seemed to be unnatural, despite the natural facade. He looked upwards at the sky, which had finally given way to allow the sun to shine. The sky was empty. There were not even any birds in flight. The trail bent around the back side of the pond, which further gave him hope the trail would provide that avenue for escape just on the other side.

Terrance continued to take stock of the surroundings. As things seemed to slow, his pain became more noticeable. It was now nearly unbearable, but he knew he had to continue. He was more eager than ever to leave this town somehow. Though he did not have any genuine answers; it seemed the closer he got to satisfying that craving got him closer to death. He was ready to admit defeat for the first time and just let this story slide so that he could at least continue to live.

His mind went to Lily. He was not sure of her intentions or if she was well after the night at the school. He had not seen her since that night; his guilt still filled him for leaving her behind. She had seemed like a friend, but at the same time things did not seem right. Frank, the reason he had come to Anderson, had appeared to have fled the town. Now, even Pastor Jack was some type of imposter. Everything here seemed like a lie, and he was tired of it all. Never in his life had he experienced so much deception.

The trail continued to follow the bank of the pond and headed back towards the roadway. Terrance paused for a moment to listen for the sound of the truck now that he edged his way back closer to the roadway. In the distance, something caught his eye. It looked like a person. His heart raced once again as his mind went to the occupants of the truck. He stopped for a moment and looked around to find something useful as a makeshift weapon. His search was fruitful, and he located a large stick. The stick itself was solid, and he felt it could at least give him a fighting chance.

He got closer to the strange figure fishing on the bank of the pond. The closer he got; he also realized that this was the first living being he had seen today. The oddity of the lack of traffic and people in town had escaped him until now. Just like the lack of animals, there was a lack of people. And even cars, except for that truck that tried to claim his life. *Where is everyone?* He thought to himself.

The figure ahead became clearer. He was an older man with a familiar shape. Terrance realized it was the person he had come here looking for. Anger swelled within him as he remembered the cemetery and the headstone. *Who is this man?* He thought to himself as he got closer. Despite his pain and injuries, his pace increased as he got closer. Everything that had happened in the last fifteen minutes flashed back into his mind. His latest brush with death was now at the forefront. Now he could at least confront someone.

As he got closer, the figure looked up at him and gave him a smile with a friendly wave. This did nothing to soften Terrance's resolve as he angrily moved forward. As he got close to where the old man was fishing, the old man turned around with a smile and said, "Hey there, Terrance, I'm glad that you made it."

"Barely," Terrance said with sarcasm, as he stopped a few feet behind the old man.

The old man sat down his fishing pole and said with concern, "I'm sorry, what happened?"

"Those rednecks in the truck again!" Terrance said, glaring at the old man.

"I'm sorry, but it's time to get you out of here," the old man said, standing up and taking a step towards Terrance.

"Just stop, man!" Terrance said, motioning at the old man with his hand. "I'm not going anywhere with you. I don't even know who you are. You've been playing games with me since we met." Terrance had his stick in his hand, ready to use it if the old man came much closer.

The old man looked at Terrance with a confused stare. "What do you mean?" he asked.

"You're a liar, just like everyone else! You're not Jack Davenport! I saw his grave, Stonewall Jackson Davenport. He died along with all those other people." Terrance said in an angry tone.

The old man looked down at the ground, then back up to Terrance and said, "You know I never liked that name, Stonewall Jackson. Momma named me after a Confederate general. I haven't used that name in decades. It's just Jack."

Terrance looked strangely at the old man. He was trying to make sense of what he had just said and process it. He finally gathered his thoughts enough to say, "So someone else is buried in that grave?"

Jack took a deep breath and looked downward, then back up to Terrance. "No, son, I'm afraid not." he responded in a very calm, but somber tone.

Jack's words again took Terrance back. His mind raced to make sense. *If what Jack was saying is true, then that would mean Jack was dead. Yet here he stood right in front of me.* "You're saying that you're buried in that grave, yet here you are standing and talking to me," Terrance said to Jack.

"Yeah, I suppose that's what I'm saying," Jack replied.

"So you're saying that you are a g...", Terrance said in disbelief.

"Ghost?" Jack said as he finished Terrance's sentence.

"There's no such thing as ghosts. This isn't possible. Who are you?" Terrance said with frustration.

"I've been trying to tell you — open your eyes, Terrance. Ghosts are all you'll find in Anderson." Jack said calmly.

"No, no, this isn't possible." Terrance muttered.

"I'm afraid so," Jack said as he looked straight at Terrance.

"If everyone is a ghost, then how can I see them? How can I interact with them? Are you saying the truck that keeps trying to kill me is a ghost, too? That some ghost stole my car?" Terrance replied angrily, almost snarling at Jack.

"Reality is what we make of it. And you are in between realities, Terrance. Life and death, just open your eyes, son, before it's too late." Jack said with a look of concern.

"This is not real; what you're saying is crazy!" Terrance rebuffed.

"He's been trying to show you since you arrived, but you just won't open your eyes to the truth." Jack said in a calm, reassuring tone.

"What truth?"

"God," Jack said bluntly. "Everyone you've met has a grave in that same cemetery. All of them are trapped. They are stuck, tainted by the past and decisions they made. Forever caught in a loop, doomed to relive their mistakes until the day of judgement. But, Terrance, you don't have to be. The blood, Terrance, the blood protects the lambs." Jack said with a concerned tone.

"I don't believe in God. And I have evidence. I have clippings and reports," Terrance said as he pulled his bookbag off his back and sat it down at his feet and opened it.

"Well, He still believes in you. All you have seen is what you wanted to see. Just like them, they see what they want to see. That's the problem with people. The truth is revealed to them, but they continue living in their own reality," Jack said to Terrance.

"Are you saying that I'm dead?" Terrance asked.

"Not yet. But that's why you have so little time. You are in a fight for your eternity at this very moment. Just as He believes in you, so does the other." Jack replied.

"The other?"

"Yes, and I think you know," Jack responded with a serious tone.

Fear and confusion overwhelmed Terrance. Nothing about his time in Anderson had been normal. Everything was off from the very day he arrived. Overwhelmed, he couldn't process everything. He felt like he was losing his mind, losing himself. Finally, he gathered his thoughts just enough to respond, "So, if everyone is stuck here. You're a preacher. Why are you here?"

"I told you, I'm the old sentinel. I look over my flock and guard those who need it. Right now, I'm guarding you." He responded calmly.

"No, none of this makes sense." Terrance said as he looked through his book bag.

"Open your eyes, Terrance. Open your eyes and wake up. Otherwise, the other awaits you. The blood, Terrance, the blood." Jack responded.

Terrance dug around, but he could not locate the clippings or the police report. He searched, and the only thing he could find was his black notebook. Opening it, he searched for everything he'd written. He found mostly blank pages but came across the one page that had his writing. He recognized it as his own handwriting, but he could not remember writing the words before him:

Anderson — modern ghost town.
Murder at the high school–killed teens and principal.
The fire at the church killed townspeople, with local pastor
Police chief murdered
Police station burned? Arson?
Town abandoned - drive-by? (No residents)

Terrance's blood felt as though it had run cold. This was his own handwriting, but he couldn't remember writing it. In the absence of other writings, he was confused. He remembered a different notebook with different writings. He turned around to say something to Jack, but he was no longer there. Jack and his fishing pole had just vanished, leaving Terrance alone, standing by the pond.

His heart was racing. He was confused and scared. *Is this another dream?* So many weird dreams had haunted him since he got to Anderson. These dreams had gotten into his head. Terrance once again struggled to tell the difference between dreams and reality. His mind told him that there were no such things as ghosts and devils; that this must be another vivid dream like the many before that had haunted him.

His brain was unwilling to accept the things Jack said to him. Terrance thought about what Jack said — "between life and death". He questioned himself about the hidden meaning; *was it a threat, or some coded message?* Then, his mind raced to the interaction. *How did he just vanish? Was he even there?* Terrance wanted safety, security and now, left alone in the woods with troubling thoughts, he had neither. So, did the only thing that he could; he ran. He hobbled along the trail as fast as he could move. He wanted to find others — the lady at the inn, Lily, the chief, anyone. With an urgent sense to make sense of everything, he wanted to prove reality or at least wake up. The things that Jack said could not be possible, and he needed some grounding, so despite his pain, fear, and confusion, he ran.

Chapter 21

Two Paths

Following the trail back around the lake, he got ever closer to the other end. The closer he got to the roadway, the more his mind focused on the black truck. Panic overwhelmed his mind; on one hand, he wanted to get back to civilization, but on the other, he did not want to cross paths with the truck again. The truck would mean a connection to the physical and reality, but it also meant danger. His feet slowed as the path ended on the roadway. He cautiously peeked around the corner of the trees, looking for his foe. However, it was not there. The truck had fled at some point, but in Terrance's mind, the danger remained that it could return at any time. He did not want to be caught unprepared again, so he cautiously entered the roadway and began his walk back to town.

The walk back to town was somber and quiet. Terrance's mind raced. Not just about what Jack had said, but about everything. He seemed more lost now than when he had first entered Anderson. His body felt as beaten as his brain. He desperately wanted to leave, but he needed something grounded in reality before he left.

Choosing to make a quick detour, Terrance paused on the roadway and walked down Frank's overgrown driveway towards his trailer. Terrance was just here a few days ago, but now the overgrown vegetation covered the same driveway that he had driven his car on. The front yard, which was littered with beer cans, was now covered with grass that touched Terrance's knees. The same beer cans were now hidden from view in the tall grass. Terrance once again wrestled with what he thought he knew, and the reality presented before him.

As he walked closer to the trailer, he noticed that the front door was open. He also saw what looked like remnants of used yellow crime-scene tape on the porch and a piece on the silver handle to the right of the door. Concern for Frank's well-being grew in Terrance, yet the remaining tape appeared weathered. This was not new tape, but Terrance could not believe that he had missed observing it on his first visit.

The doorway and a familiar smell soon greeted Terrance. He called out, "Frank! Frank, it's Terrence Greene, are you in there?" and listened for a response. Nervousness filled him, so he would not step further into the trailer without a response. However, there were no sounds from within, just silence. The silence was fleeting, as he once again heard a familiar sound traveling down the road. The truck was back!

Nervousness may have prevented him from stepping further, but fear now drove him through the doorway. He stepped in and to the side to shield himself from the view of the roadway. Placing his body as close as possible to the wall, he stood still and listened. He heard the truck get closer, but it did not stop or slow; it continued on its path. From what Terrance could tell, the truck was driving back towards the pond, perhaps to find him.

He knew eventually they would realize he was no longer at the pond and could come back in this direction. Terrance did not want to remain still for very long. He looked back into the trailer and into the living room. Not much was different, but the chair that Frank sat in was now missing. The beer cans and food containers littering the floor also looked older and worn with time. Now, a mix of old disturbed beer cans and other signs of police and maybe medical personnel littered the floor. Nothing was fresh but seemed to be years old. Used rubber gloves discarded on the floor and a forgotten evidence tag all dotted the landscape of the old trailer's floor.

The visit to the trailer did not offer the comfort that Terrance had hoped. Instead, he was once again questioning everything in his mind. He knew he'd been in this trailer days ago and talked to Frank, but now he saw relics from years past scattered on the floor, and Frank was missing. He wanted seriously to consider that someone was playing tricks on him, but the evidence before his eyes was too obvious and intricate to ignore. His eyes scanned the trailer for more evidence of something that would make sense, but there was nothing.

As he walked around the quiet, old, musty trailer, he meticulously surveyed everything. His eyes fell upon a picture lying face down near Frank's former chair. Terrance kneeled down and picked up the picture and slowly turned it around. The glass was shattered, yet a faded picture remained beneath the broken pieces. As he studied the image, he could make out the image of a much healthier Frank with a little girl at his side as he kneeled down with his arm around her. Directly behind Frank was a woman with both hands resting on his should. He looked at Frank's face; it looked so happy, so full of life. It was a stark contrast to the Frank he had met just days before.

As Terrance continued studying the picture, he heard something. It was a rustling, gentle at first, coming from the kitchen. Initially, he was excited, thinking somehow that Frank was there, but as he turned the corner into the kitchen, there were no signs of a human presence. He pressed forward into the kitchen, trying to hear the sound once again, but there was now just silence. In the kitchen, he once again looked around. The dishes in the sink looked decades old, and the trash in the can had rotted years ago, and what remained looked almost like a pile of dust.

Terrance shook his head in disbelief. He once again could not accept reality and convinced himself this must somehow still be some type of dream. His brain could not accept that the things before him could be real. As he scanned the kitchen, he once again heard the sound. It was coming from the cabinet. He leaned forward curiously, trying to determine the source of the sound. Without thinking, he opened the cabinet door to find the culprit. As he opened the cabinet door, they found him!

Rats! The awful sounds and the opening door frightened them. They rushed towards Terrance and ran past his feet. The feeling of them moving past him and brushing his pants made him squirm. In that moment, he forgot about hiding from the passing truck and could not leave the trailer fast enough. He leaped over-the-counter top and navigated the debris on the floor as though he was running through an obstacle course. Once out of the door of the trailer, he fell as the rotting steps gave way, causing him to fall forward, striking his face in the dirt.

With his face still half buried in the ground, Terrance could not move. The pain that pulsed through his body was almost unbearable. He tried to pick himself up, but he struggled. He coughed into the sandy soil as he tried to catch his breath. In that moment, he felt as though he was going to die right there in the dirt. He felt so defeated, not only by the steps, but with everything that he had seen and heard today. The logic that once dominated his every thought was elusive, and this world no longer made any sense.

Terrance felt safe in the logical world. Safe in a world around him he could control. Now, not even his footing was under his control. He knew he was losing his sanity. Facing death was preferable to the senseless chaos of the world around him. He finally felt as though he had given up. There was no longer any point in continuing. If he lost himself, that was all that he had. Terrance lay still, no longer fighting or desiring to pull himself free. He accepted whatever happened to him now. Either he wakes up from this dream or he will go into the forever slumber.

The air was still and silent. Silence hung in the woods around the trailer; the menacing truck was long gone. The stillness of the surroundings echoed in Terrance's body. There was movement as he breathed in and out, but he was otherwise still. He closed his eyes and just waited for what came next.

In the still silence, something echoed in Terrance's brain. "Wake up, Terrance" broke the silence in a feminine voice. He jolted in response to the sudden words. He couldn't tell if he had really heard those words or if his brain had produced them. "Wake up, Terrance!" now more urgent, echoed once again within him. This time, he knew the voice. It was one he had heard before. It was his mother's voice. A single tear fell from his eye and splattered onto the dust below. Where he was once ready to surrender, there was an energy that surged from within that was ready for at least one more fight.

With what energy remained in his body, he pushed up again the dirt and made progress as his left leg was now set free from the decayed step. His ankle throbbed with intense pain, but he could finally get off the ground. He tried to stand, but the pain echoed from his ankle and traveled through his entire body. Between the pain in his ankle and legs joining his already stinging side, he could barely move. Despite the pain, Terrance decided he had to move forward. He had to get back to town and get help.

The walk was slow and grueling as he hobbled along the roadway towards Anderson. He had a fear at the back of his mind about the truck; he knew he could no longer run if it returned. However, he had no choice but to continue. In his condition, he could not hide along the wood line and try to walk to town hidden from view. He didn't know if he was going to make it back to town or not, but at least he had a fighting chance.

Terrance had never felt such intense pain. It was like his whole body was now joining his brain in defeat, but something still pressed him forward. The final small hill was grueling as he slowly limped forward, knowing the town would appear just beyond the hill. He was tired, thirsty, and in immense pain, but he continued. Step-by-step, he got closer to where the hilltop crested. The town was now in his view. He felt a sense of hope with each step as he got closer to the town.

The closer he walked into downtown Anderson, the quieter things seemed. He had noticed earlier the lack of townspeople, but now it had been hours, and the town still seemed abandoned. Terrance was glad that the black truck had not appeared, but the lack of other vehicles seemed eerie. The closer he limped into town, the stranger the sights before him appeared.

He had noticed abandoned buildings since he first arrived, but now things seemed older and, if possible, more vacant than before. He continued walking and taking notice of there being no one else in the town other than him. As Terrance walked closer to the main intersection, a place that he had been many times before, his blood ran cold.

He had passed the same church hours ago. The same church that he attended a service at and heard Jack preach and later met with in the office. Now in its place was a mostly vacant lot with remnants of the church that bore scars of a fire. He limped at a hastened pace over to the church and wiped his eyes. He then closed them and reopened them, hoping that suddenly his view would change. However, his view did not. He stood dumbfounded, trying to understand what lay before him.

In his current condition, he could not get any closer because of the unstable ground with debris scattered along the surface. He knew he could not risk another fall. His heart raced, and he tried to process everything. Then, he remembered the notes that were in his bookbag. The ones that were changed after he talked to Jack. He slowly undid his backpack and grunted from the pain of twisting his body. Slowly sitting the bookbag on the sidewalk, he opened it and pulled out the notes that he had previously dismissed. Tears formed in his eyes as he read in his own handwriting once again, *Fire at church killed townspeople with local pastor.*

He could no longer dismiss it. There, directly in front of him, it confronted him. Once again, he tried to process everything. *Am I dead?* Terrance thought about himself. *Did I die in one of these near-death encounters? Is this Hell?* These thoughts raced through his mind. He looked over at the cafe that he had eaten at many times to find it closed and abandoned. *How is this possible? Am I going crazy?* He felt cold and scared. He was now truly alone, standing in this town.

Terrance panicked. He did not know where to go. He had no one, and he was lost in his thought once more. Either he was dead, or he was losing his mind, and neither of those options sat very well with him. As he searched for security, the only remaining place that he felt was safe was his room. *"My room still has to be there,"* he thought to himself.

Once again, Terrance felt desperate to find safety, but struggled with his injuries and the pain to continue. He was in a panic. Nothing he was experiencing was possible. He tried as quickly as he could to limp over to his one remaining safe place. As he walked down the sidewalk, he remembered previous conversations at the cafe and church. He knew those were real, but then that thought conflicted with everything he now saw.

Finally, the hotel came into view, but he was once again disappointed to find things not as he remembered. The hotel sign was gone, with just the stand remaining. The entire building looked run down, and there was a hole in the roof over the same office he had visited many times. He looked around at the parking lot, which was dotted with tall grasses that had grown through the cracks in the asphalt. The parking lot looked barely drivable, but he had driven in it and parked right there. His eyes then went over to his room. It looked like the rest of the hotel, but the door was wide open.

Knowing not what to expect, he still felt drawn to the open door. He limped through the tall grass and towards the open door. From what he could see as he got closer, it looked familiar. It was not the familiar room that he had slept in, but the one from the dream that he had where everything changed. From his approach to the doorway, it looked as abandoned as the rest of the hotel. Once again, he questioned what was real. He still lurched forward one slow step at a time. He could smell a strong odor of mold and decay as he got closer to his door. Despair filled his heart as he took the final two steps and entered the room.

The moment he entered, everything changed. As he walked into the room, it was just as he remembered it. Everything was in its place, and his suitcase still sat where he had put it. He breathed a sigh of relief as comfort once again returned to his body. "Where have you been?" he heard in an angry, feminine voice. Terrance quickly turned around and saw Lily standing by the couch.

"I've been worried sick about you!" she said once again, still angry as she was before.

Terrance stood dumbfounded as he stared at her and tried to form something to say in response.

"You aren't well, so you should not be up and moving around." She continued.

"I'm sorry, I don't know what's going on. I'm so glad to see you." He stammered.

"You don't remember?" she asked.

"Remember what?"

"The School," she said.

"I remember being there and running out. I thought I'd left you there." He said. Terrance was weak and confused and trying to grasp at any reality that provided him comfort.

"You fell, Terrance. You hit your head, do you remember?" she asked.

Terrance lifted his hand and felt the front of his head, then the side. He could feel a large goose-egg and even some dry blood. "I don't remember this," he said.

"The chief and I had to carry you back. He wanted to send you to the hospital, but you refused. You only wanted to come back to the room and call home. Does any of this ring a bell?" she asked.

"No, I don't remember any of that," Terrance responded, rubbing his head and still trying to figure everything out.

"Your brother is going to come pick you up this evening and take you back to your mom's. Do you remember talking to him?" Lily said with a concerned look.

"No, the phone...the phone wasn't working." He replied with a sense of confusion.

Lily walked over to Terrance and placed her arm around him. "You don't look good. I'm worried about you; please come lie down," she said.

She placed her hand on his head and quickly pulled it back. "You're burning up, Terrance! We really need to get you to the hospital." She said urgently.

"No, please just give me a minute. Let me lie down for a moment." Terrance said as he tried to walk over to the bed, but almost lost his balance.

Lily walked to his side and offered support as she helped guide him over to his bed.

"I'm so sorry, I don't know what's going on," Terrance said as he balanced himself on Lily and slowly lowered himself onto the bed.

"I thought I'd lost you. I thought I'd lost you at the school." Terrance said as he lay down on the bed.

"You can't get rid of me that easily," she said as she sat directly beside him and caressed his cheek.

Terrance, though confused, felt better than he had all day. He was back with Lily, and everything seemed to make sense. She told him he had struck his head and was even running a fever. This made sense to Terrance and explained his earlier hallucinations. Despite knowing he was injured and probably needed more care, at least he was no longer losing his mind.

For a moment, he just lay still on the bed as Lily caressed his cheek. There was a silence, but this was a peaceful silence, unlike the one he had experienced earlier. He was comfortable, and he even felt the pain in his side and ankle give way. His breathing slowed, and he felt truly relaxed and comfortable. He was happy that Lily was still there, and she was taking care of him.

"You have to be more careful, Terrance. I don't want anything bad to happen to you. You're special to me, and I was worried sick about you!" Lily said as she continued to caress his cheek.

"Thank you, you're special to me too," Terrance responded as he closed his eyes slightly, enjoying the calm in the situation.

"Good, you belong with me, and I'm not letting you get away that easily," Lily said with a smile.

Terrance was relaxed and almost ready to put the day behind him and just rest while Lily caressed him. He felt all was as it should be, and he was happy for the first time in a while. There was something about Lily that always seemed to put him at ease. She was perfect. Her eyes, her hair, and the touch of her soft skin. She always had a way of making him relax. He cracked his eyes to see her leaning towards his face. She kissed his lips, and he felt the comfort of those pillowy lips embracing him.

"I'm so sorry that I took you to that school. I got so scared when you hit your head. You mean the world to me, Terrance." She whispered in his ear.

"Thank you for taking care of me. It's been such a bad day."

"Where did you go?" she asked.

"I thought I was out in town, but nothing made any sense. It was like the town was gone and everything, my work, everything was different. I don't even know anymore. Nothing makes any sense."

"You hit your head really hard. Will you please let me take you to the hospital? I think it would be good to have it checked." Lily said in a soft voice.

"I'm okay, I just need to rest," Terrance said as he adjusted himself on the bed.

Lily caressed his face, tracing the outlines of his features. "I'm worried about you. You don't seem like yourself."

"I'm just exhausted."

She kissed him tenderly on his lips and sat up. "It's going to be okay, Terrance. I'm going to take care of you." She said with a smile.

As soon as her lips parted from his this time, a memory shot through him. *Those lips, those words*. He knew he had felt them before and heard those words before. His memories of the school flooded back into reality, and they differed from the ones she had described, filling his mind. Then, *the dreams, those lips!* He immediately began remembering the dreams that had haunted him. She was always there. Her lips, her touch were there, even if something usually obscured her face. Terrance's eyes shot open, and without a thought, he said loudly, "Hailey!"

She looked at him, and the caring face quickly disappeared. "What did you call me?" she said in a stern voice.

"Hailey!" Terrance said as he tried getting up.

She grabbed his shoulder and clasped it to the bed. Her sudden stern push on his shoulder caused him to wince in pain as all the pain from the day manifested through his body. "You're losing it, Terrance! Just relax and calm down!" she said firmly. Terrance struggled, trying to push past her firm grasp. Everything began coming back into his mind. In his gut, he knew as much as he wanted everything to be real; things were not as they should be.

"Stop fighting me, Terrance. It's your head; you're running a fever! You need to go see a doctor!" she said firmly.

Terrance fought his own mind. What she said made sense, but deep inside, his animalistic instinct told him to run. The thoughts, *Wake up! Wake up Terrance!* kept running through his brain. It was all that seemed to ground him. Then, with every bit of energy he had in his body, he pushed to free himself. He pushed hard and could finally break her grasp. As she lost her grasp, she fell backwards and stumbled towards the wall, knocking down the picture that had fallen many times before. Her face now facing the wall, she laughed quietly.

Terrance got up off the bed and looked over towards Lily, feeling sorry that he had made her fall back in his attempt to break free. As she slowly turned around, all kindness on her face disappeared. The face of Lily was gone, and now as he looked over, the face from his dreams had reappeared.

She stared back at him with pitch-black eyes, the same haunting, soulless eyes that he had seen before. Love, care, and concern were now absent, and only hatred and anger peered down at him. "We aren't finished yet!" she said as she lunged towards him. He tried to move quickly away from her. She lunged forward and barely missed him as he crawled off the foot of the bed. Just as he was about to get off the bed, she grabbed his ankles and began pulling him back. He glanced back at her and stared into the face of evil. She pulled him back with the strength of many men. The struggle had just begun, and he was already losing.

Terrance struggled to hold on and fought desperately to break free. But her hold was too much for him to fight. All the pain in his body, along with the exhaustion that he felt, made him weak and almost helpless against her. He cried out, "Let me go!"

She responded, "Stop fighting, Terrance! You aren't well."

"No!" Terrance yelled as he continued to use the old stained carpet to hold his position, grabbing at it and trying to gain momentum away from her. He then felt her fingernails dig deeply, piercing his leg.

He yelped in pain as she dug her nails deeper into his flesh. She began using her new hold to pull him closer to her. He could feel the blood trickle down his leg around the newly exposed wound. She used her new hold to pull him back, and now climbed on top of him. He felt a coldness as she slithered up his back, each time using her nails to grip him and cause him pain.

Terrance began crying in defeat. He felt like an animal succumbing to a predator. He had no strength to break free, and dread and sorrow filled his heart. "Don't fight Terrance; let us take away all of your pain." She whispered with a hiss in his ear. "This is our destiny," she continued. All Terrance could do was weep as he felt a coldness take over his body. It was not like any cold he had ever felt before. It was a cold that felt like the end, a start of an unending winter. His mind went toward the darkness, things around him losing their solid shapes and becoming a blur. "Just let it all go." She whispered, now grabbing his head while digging her nails into his face to pull his face upward.

As the darkness was taking over, he turned his head slightly towards the door of his room. He could not see outside of the doorway, but what he saw was a bright, nearly blinding light. It seemed to emanate warmth from its glow. *Wake up, Live, Wake up* echoed in his mind as he managed one more burst of strength to push upward against her. She screamed an inhuman screech as she fell off of him. Though all the pain in his body made it difficult, with every bit of strength he had, he crawled towards the light. It was his only hope; it was the only warmth in the room.

Behind him, he heard her snarl like a wild animal, but he dared not look back. He just continued to crawl with every ounce of

strength left in his body. He felt her once again at his legs, pulling
him back with her daggers into his flesh, but he somehow continued
to fight. Terrence's mind grasped whatever memories he could
muster. Then, it came flashing back — what the preacher said. He
couldn't make sense of everything, but in his heart he knew there had
to be hope. The light had to be real! As he got closer to the light, he
screamed out, "God, please help me! Help me wake up!"

ANDERSON STOOD SILENT as it had for many years, wearing
the wounds of many tragic events. The wounds were clear in the
dilapidated hotel, which had not seen a guest in over eight years. The
once welcoming hotel, now filled with mold from the leaking roof.
In the downtown, the square still sat with the charred ruins of the
Baptist Church casting an eerie shadow on much of the downtown
square. Near the church, the Anderson Police Department sat in a
similar state. Once a symbol of law and order, now in ruins. The
roads had seen little traffic in the past years, with weeds and grass
growing through the cracks. In some places, the grass had grown so
tall that the road itself remained barely visible.

The once beautiful tree lined residential roads now resembled
wild forests, where the houses remained hidden away behind tall
brush. Massive mansions now lay open like crypts of their former
owners. Then there was the school. The single-story massive
structure sprawling through neighborhood streets. It lay dormant
and surrounded by overgrowth, like the rest of the town.

There were no signs of human life as it had been for many years.
Anderson had become a ghost town, like so many in South Georgia,
unable to stand the test of time or endure life's tragedies. What
buildings still stood among the ruins were dark and forgotten in
time.

The town sat in silence. No life, but the eerie sound of ghostly whispers in the wind. Anderson was dead, like its inhabitants. Nature itself seemed to stay away from the damned town, as silence and unearthly whispers were all that could be heard. Not even the birds sang, or the crickets chirped. Death was all that remained.

The first signs of life were not visible until about five miles outside of downtown. There were flashing red lights and blue lights with a mix of vehicles. State Troopers, a fire truck, and an ambulance were all sitting blocking the road at the T-intersection.

In the back of the ambulance, the paramedics rushed to stabilize the young man they had been working on for the last fifteen minutes. At first his survival seemed likely, but in that instant, like the town of Anderson itself, all life and hope of saving him disappeared. The paramedics had removed the air pump from his face and given up at last, admitting defeat.

Outside the ambulance, the scene was very different. A black pickup truck sat blocking the road. The front of it was barely visible from the wreckage of a black coupe that had integrated almost seamlessly into the front of the truck. The truck driver sat on the side of the road, with blood on his head, looking down, still in shock at what had occurred so quickly on an otherwise uneventful day.

Just as the paramedic was about to step out of the ambulance and let the trooper know that the young man hadn't made it, there was a gasp. Terrance gasped for breath as he tried to sit up. The paramedics excitedly turned their attention back to Terrance. "He's back!" one of them exclaimed.

Terrence was terrified and looked around, trying to gather his bearings and make sense of his surroundings. The sights, the noises — all overwhelming. He looked around, trying to take in as much as he could see before his vision became obscured by the paramedics providing him aid. Before his view became blocked, he looked out the back of the ambulance and caught sight of the black truck that had been haunting him and the remains of his car, which were embedded in its grill. As the paramedics shut the door of the ambulance, something else caught his eye. Directly beside the wreckage, he could've sworn he saw an old man with a fishing pole waving at him. "Jack!" he said right before the paramedics began placing an oxygen mask on his face, silencing him.

The paramedics glanced at each other, then focused back on Terrance. He was too tired to move, too in pain to think. He simply glanced at the roof of the ambulance, staring upwards at the lights on the ceiling. It was the light that saved him, and it is in the light that he committed himself to live the rest of his life.

www.ingramcontent.com/pod-product-compliance
Lightning Source LLC
Chambersburg PA
CBHW021519240626
47154CB00002B/706